Amelia Edith Huddleston Barr

I, thou and the Other one

A Love Story

Amelia Edith Huddleston Barr

I, thou and the Other one
A Love Story

ISBN/EAN: 9783743400016

Manufactured in Europe, USA, Canada, Australia, Japa

Cover: Foto ©Andreas Hilbeck / pixelio.de

Manufactured and distributed by brebook publishing software (www.brebook.com)

Amelia Edith Huddleston Barr

I, thou and the Other one

I, THOU,
AND THE OTHER ONE

A Love Story

BY

AMELIA E. BARR

NEW YORK
DODD, MEAD AND COMPANY
1899

University Press:

John Wilson and Son, Cambridge, U.S.A.

CONTENTS

I, Thou, and the Other One

CHAPTER FIRST

THE ATHELINGS

*" The Land is a Land of hills and valleys, and drinketh
water of the rain of heaven."*

BEYOND Thirsk and Northallerton, through the
Cleveland Hills to the sea eastward, and by Rose-
berry Topping, northward, there is a lovely, lonely
district, very little known even at the present day.
The winds stream through its hills, as cool and
fresh as living water; and whatever beauty there
is of mountain, valley, or moorland, Farndale and
Westerdale can show it; while no part of England
is so rich in those picturesque manor-houses
which have been the homes of the same families
for twenty generations.

The inhabitants of this region are the incarnation of its health, strength, and beauty, — a tall,
comely race; bold, steadfast, and thrifty, with
very positive opinions on all subjects. There are
no Laodiceans among the men and women of the

North-Riding; they are one thing or another—
Episcopalians or Calvinists; Conservatives or
Radicals; friends or enemies. For friendship
they have a capacity closer than brotherhood.
Once friends, they are friends forever, and can
be relied on in any emergency to "aid, comfort,
and abet," legally or otherwise, with perhaps a
special zest to give assistance, if it just smacks of
the "otherwise."

Of such elements, John Atheling, lord of the
manors of Atheling and Belward, was "kindly
mixed," a man of towering form and great mental
vigour, blunt of speech, single of purpose, leading,
with great natural dignity, a sincere, unsophisti-
cated life.   He began this story one evening in
the May of 1830; though when he left Atheling
manor-house, he had no idea anything out of the
customary order of events would happen.   It is
however just these mysterious conditions of every-
day life that give it such gravity and interest;
for what an hour will bring forth, no man can
say; and when Squire Atheling rode up to the
crowd on the village green, he had no presentiment that he was going to open a new chapter
in his life.

He smiled pleasantly when he saw its occasion.
It was a wrestling match; and the combatants
were his own chief shepherd and a stranger.   In
a few moments the shepherd was handsomely
"thrown" and nobody knew exactly how it had
been done.   But there was hearty applause, led

by the Squire, who, nodding at his big plough-
man, cried out, "Now then, Adam Sedbergh, stand
up for Atheling!" Adam flung off his vest and
stepped confidently forward; but though a famous
wrestler among his fellows, he got as speedy and
as fair a fall as the shepherd had received before
him. The cheers were not quite as hearty at
this result, but the Squire said peremptorily, —

"It is all right. Hold my horse, Jarum. I'll
have to cap this match myself. And stand back
a bit, men, I want room enough to turn in." He
was taking off his fine broadcloth coat and vest as
he spoke, and the lad he was to match, stood looking at him with his hands on his hips, and a smile
on his handsome face. Perhaps the attitude and
the smile nettled the Squire, for he added with
some pride and authority, —

"I would like you to know that I am Squire
Atheling; and I am not going to have a better
wrestler than myself in Atheling Manor, young
man, not if I can help it."

"I know that you are Squire Atheling," answered the stranger. "I have been living with
your son Edgar for a year, why wouldn't I know
you? And if I prove myself the better man, then
you shall stop and listen to me for half-an-hour,
and you may stop a whole hour, if you want to;
and I think you will."

"I know nothing about Edgar Atheling, and I
am not standing here either to talk to thee, or to
listen to thee, but to give thee a fair 'throw' if I

can manage it." He stretched out his left hand
as he spoke, and the young man grasped it with
his right hand. This result was anticipated;
there was a swift twist outward, and a lift upward,
and before anyone realised what would happen,
a pair of shapely young legs were flying over the
Squire's shoulder. Then there rose from twenty
Yorkshire throats a roar of triumph, and the
Squire put his hands on his hips, and looked
complacently at the stranger flicking the Atheling
dust from his trousers. He took his defeat as
cheerily as his triumph. "It was a clever throw,
Squire," he said.

"Try it again, lad."

"Nay, I have had enough."

"I thought so. Now then, don't brag of thy
wrestling till thou understandest a bit of ' In-
play.' But I 'll warrant thou canst talk, so I 'll
give myself a few minutes to listen to thee. I
should say, I am twice as old as thou art, but
I notice that it is the babes and sucklings that
know everything, these days."

As the Squire was speaking, the youth leaped
into an empty cart which someone pushed forward, and he was ready with his answer, —

"Squire," he said, " it will take not babes, but
men like you and these I see around me, for the
wrestling match before us all. What we have to
tackle is the British Government and the two
Houses of Parliament."

The Squire laughed scornfully. "They will

'throw' thee into the strongest jail in England, my lad; they will sink thee four feet under ground, if thou art bound for any of that nonsense."

"They will have enough to do to take care of themselves soon."

"Thou art saying more than thou knowest. Wouldst thou have the horrors of 1792 acted over again, in England? My lad, I was a youngster then, but I saw the red flag, dripping with blood, go round the Champ-de-Mars."

"None of us want to carry the red flag, Squire. It is the tri-colour of Liberty we want; and that flag — in spite of all tyrants can do — will be carried round the world in glory! When I was in America —"

"Wilt thou be quiet about them foreign countries? We have bother enough at home, without going to the world's end for more. And I will have no such talk in my manor. If thou dost not stop it, I shall have to make thee."

"King William, and all his Lords and Commons, cannot stop such talk. It is on every honest tongue, and at every decent table. It is in the air, Squire, and the winds of heaven carry it wherever they go."

"If thou saidst *William Cobbett*, thou mightst happen hit the truth. The winds of heaven have better work to do. What art thou after anyway?"

"Such a Parliamentary Reform as will give every honest man a voice in the Government."

"Just so !   Thou wouldst make the door of the House of Commons big enough for any rubbish to go through."

" The plan has been tried, Squire, in America; and

> As the Liberty Lads over the sea,
> Bought their freedom — and cheaply — with blood ;
>> So we, boys, we
> Will die fighting ; or live free,
> And down with — "

"Stop there !" roared the Squire. "Nonsense in poetry is a bit worse than any other kind of nonsense. Speak in plain words, or be done with it ! Do you know what you want?"

"That we do. We want the big towns, where working men are the many, and rich men, the few, to be represented. We want all sham boroughs thrown out. What do you think of Old Sarum sending a member to Parliament, when there is n't any Old Sarum? There used to be, in the days of King Edward the First, but there is now no more left of it than there is of the Tower of Babel. What do you think of the Member for Ludgershall being not only the Member, but the *whole constituency* of Ludgershall? What do you think of Gatton having just seven voters, and sending *two* members to Parliament?" — then leaning forward, and with burning looks drinking the wind of his own passionate speech — "What do you think of *Leeds ! Man-*

chester ! Birmingham ! Sheffield ! being *without any representation !* "

" My lad," cried the Squire, " have not Leeds, Manchester, Birmingham, Sheffield, done very well without representation ? "

" Squire, a child may grow to a man without love and without care ; but he is a robbed and a wronged child, for all that."

" The Government knows better than thee what to do with big towns full of unruly men and women."

" That is just the question. They are not represented, because they are made up of the working population of England. But the working man has not only his general rights, he has also rights peculiar to his condition ; and it is high time these rights were attended to. Yet these great cities, full of woollen and cotton weavers, and of fine workers in all kinds of metals, have not a man in Parliament to say a word for them."

" What is there to say ? What do they want Parliament to know ? " asked the Squire, scornfully.

" They want Parliament to know that they are being forced to work twelve hours a day, for thirty pennies a week ; and that they have to pay ten pennies for every four-pound loaf of bread. And they expect that when Parliament knows these two facts, something will be done to help them in their poverty and misery. They believe that the people of England will *compel* Parliament to do something."

" There are Members in both Houses that know
these things, why do they not speak? — if it was
reasonable to do so."

" Squire, they dare not.   They have not the
power, even if they had the will.   The Peers and
the great Landlords *own* two-thirds of the House
of Commons.   They *own* their boroughs and
members, just as they own their parks and cattle.   One duke returns eleven members ; another
duke returns nine members ; and such a city as
Manchester cannot return one!   If this state of
things does not need reforming, I do not know
what does."

So far his words had rushed rattling on one
another, like the ring of iron on iron in a day of
old-world battle; but at this point, the Squire
managed again to interrupt them.   From his
saddle he had something of an advantage, as he
called out in an angry voice, —

" And pray now, what are *you* to make by this
business?   Is it a bit of brass — or land — or
power that you look forward to?"

" None of them.   I have set my heart on the
goal, and not on the prize.   Let the men who
come after me reap ; I am glad enough if I may
but plough and sow.   The Americans — "

" *Chaff*, on the Americans!   We are North-
Riding men.   We are Englishmen.   We are
sound-hearted, upstanding fellows who do our
day's work, enjoy our meat and drinking, pay our
debts, and die in our beds; and we want none of

thy Reform talk! It is all scandalous rubbish!
Bouncing, swaggering, new-fashioned trumpery!
We don't hold with Reformers, nor with any of
their ways! I will listen to thee no longer. Thou
mayst talk to my men, if they will be bothered
with thee. I'm not afraid of anything thou canst
say to them."

"I think they will be bothered with me, Squire.
They do not look like fools."

"At any rate, there is n't one Reform fool
among them; but I 'll tell thee something—go to
a looking-glass, and thou mayst shake thy fist in
the face of one of the biggest fools in England,"
— and to the laughter this sally provoked the
Squire galloped away.

For a short distance, horse and rider kept up
the pace of enthusiasm; but when the village was
left behind, the Squire's mood fell below its
level; and a sudden depression assailed him.
He had "thrown" his man; he had "threeped"
him down in argument; but he had denied his
son, and he brought a hungry heart from his
victory. The bright face of his banished boy
haunted the evening shadows; he grew sorrowfully impatient at the memories of the past; and
when he could bear them no longer, he struck
the horse a smart blow, and said angrily, —

"Dal it all! Sons and daughters indeed! A
bitter, bitter pleasure!"

At this exclamation, a turn in the road brought
him in sight of two horsemen. "*Whew!* I am

having a night of it!" he muttered. For he recognised immediately the portly figure of the great
Duke of Richmoor, and he did not doubt that the
slighter man at his side was his son, Lord Exham.
The recognition was mutual; and on the Duke's
side very satisfactory. He quickened his horse's
speed, and cried out as he neared the Squire, —

"Well met, Atheling! You are the very man
I wished to see! Do you remember Exham?"

There was a little complimentary speaking, and
then the Duke said earnestly: "Squire, if there
is one thing above another that at this time the
landed interest ought to do, it is to stand together. The country is going to the devil; it is
on the verge of revolution. We must have a
majority in the next Parliament; and we want
you for the borough of Asketh. Exham has
come back from Italy purposely to take Gaythorne. What do you say?"

It was the great ambition of the Squire to go to
Parliament, and the little dispute he had just had
with the stranger on the green had whetted this
desire to a point which made the Duke's question a very interesting one to him; but he was
too shrewd to make this satisfaction apparent.
"There are younger men, Duke," he answered
slowly; "and they who go to the next Parliament
will have a trying time of it. I hear queer tales,
too, of Parliament men; and the House keeps
late hours; and late hours never did suit my
constitution."

" Come, Atheling, that is poor talk at a crisis like this. There will be a meeting at the Castle on Friday — a very important meeting — and I shall expect you to take the chair. We are in for such a fight as England has not had since the days of Oliver Cromwell; and it would not be like John Atheling to keep out of it."

" It would n't. If there is anything worth fighting for, John Atheling will be thereabouts, I 'll warrant him."

"Then we may depend upon you — Friday, and two in the afternoon, is the day and the hour. You will not fail us? "

" Duke, you may depend upon me." And so the men parted; the Squire, in the unexpected proposal just made him, hardly comprehending the messages of friendly courtesy which Lord Exham charged him to deliver to Mrs. and Miss Atheling.

" My word! My word! " he exclaimed, as soon as the Duke and he were far enough back to back. "Won't Maude be set up? Won't little Kitty plume her wings? " and in this vague, purposeless sense of wonder and elation he reached his home. The gates to the large, sweet garden stood open, but after a moment's thought, he passed them, and went round to the farm court at the back of the house. The stables occupied one side of this court, and he left his horse there, and proceeded to the kitchen. The girls were starting the fires under the coppers for the quarterly brewing; they said " the Missis was in the house-place," and the Squire opened the door between the two rooms, and went into the houseplace. But the large room was empty, though the lattices were open, and a sudden great waft of honey-suckle fragance saluted him as he passed them. He noticed it, and he noticed also the full moon-light on the rows of shining pewter plates and flagons, though he was not conscious at the time that these things had made any impression upon him.

Two or three steps at the west end of this room led to a door which opened into Mrs. Atheling's parlour; and the Squire passed it impatiently. The news of the night had become too much for him; he wanted to tell his wife. But Mrs. Atheling was not in her parlour. A few ash logs were burning brightly on the hearth, and there was a round table spread for supper, and the candles were lit, and showed him the mis-tress's little basket containing her keys and her knitting, but neither wife nor daughter were to be seen.

" It is always the way," he muttered. " It is enough to vex any man. Women are sure to be out of the road when they are wanted; and in the road when nobody cares to see them. Wherever has Maude taken herself? " Then he opened a door and called " Maude! Maude! " in no gentle voice.

In a few minutes the call was answered. Mrs.

Atheling came hurriedly into the room. There was a pleasant smile on her large, handsome face, and she carried in her hands a bowl of cream and a loaf of white bread. "Why, John!" she exclaimed, "whatever is to do? I was getting a bit of supper for you. You are late home to-night, aren't you?"

"I should think I was — all of an hour-and-a-half late."

"But you are not ill, John? There is nothing wrong, I hope?"

"If things go a bit out of the common way, women always ask if they have gone wrong. I should think, they might as well go right."

"So they might. Here is some fresh cream, John. I saw after it myself; and the haver-cake is toasted, and — "

"Nay, but I'll have my drinking to-night, Maude. I have been flustered more than a little, I can tell thee that."

"Then you shall have your drinking. We tapped a fresh barrel of old ale an hour ago. It is that strong and fine as never was; by the time you get to your third pint, you will be ready to make faces at Goliath."

"Well, Maude, if making faces means making fight, there will be enough of that in every county of England soon, — if Dukes and Radical orators are to be believed."

"Have you seen the Duke to-night?"

"I have. He has offered me a seat in the next

Parliament. He thinks there is a big fight before us."

"Parliament! And the Duke of Richmoor to seat you! Why, John, I am astonished!"

"I felt like I was dreaming. Now then, where is Kate? I want to tell the little maid about it. It will be a grand thing for Kate. She will have some chances in London, and I'll warrant she is Yorkshire enough to take the best of them."

"Kate was at Dashwood's all the afternoon; and they were riding races; and she came home tired to death. I tucked her up in her bed an hour ago."

"I am a bit disappointed; but things are mostly ordered that way. There is something else to tell you, Maude. I saw a stranger on the green throw Bill Verity and Adam Sedbergh; and I could not stand such nonsense as that, so I off with my coat and settled him."

"You promised me that you would not 'stand up' any more, John. Some of them youngsters will give you a 'throw' that you won't get easy over. And you out of practice too."

"Out of practice! Nothing of the sort. What do you think I do with myself on wet afternoons? What could I do with myself, but go to the granary and have an hour or two's play with Verity and Sedbergh, or any other of the lads that care to feel my grip? I have something else to tell you, Maude. I had a talk with this strange lad. He began some Reform nonsense; and I settled him very cleverly."

"Poor lad!" She spoke sadly and absently, and it nettled the Squire. "I know what you are thinking, Mistress," he said; "but the time has come when we are bound to stick to our own side."

"The poor are suffering terribly, John. They are starved and driven to the last pinch. There never was anything like it before."

"Women are a soft lot; it would not do to give up to their notions."

"If you mean that women have soft hearts, it is a good thing for men that women are that way made."

"I have not done with my wonders yet. Who do you think was with the Duke?"

"I don't know, and I can't say that I care."

"Yes, but you do. It was Lord Exham. He said this and that about you, but I did not take much notice of his fine words." Then he rose and pushed his chair aside, and as he left the room added, —

"That stranger lad I had the tussle with to-night says he knows your son Edgar — that they have lived and worked together for a year, — a very unlikely thing."

"Stop a minute, Squire. Are you not ashamed of yourself to keep this news for a tag-end? Why it is the best thing I have heard to-night; and I 'll be bound you let it go past you like a waft of wind. What did you ask the stranger about *my* son?"

"Nothing.   Not a word."

"It was like your stubborn heart. *My son* indeed! If ever you had a son, it is Edgar. You were just like him when I married you — not as handsome — but very near; and you are as like as two garden peas in your pride, and self-will, and foolish anger. Don't talk to me of Dukes, and Lords, and Parliaments, and wrestling matches. I want to hear about *my* son. If you have nothing to say about Edgar, I care little for your other news."

"Why, Maude! Whatever is the matter with you? I have lived with you thirty years, and it seems that I have never known you yet."

"But I know you, John Atheling. And I am ashamed of myself for having made nothing better out of you in thirty years. I thought I had you better shaped than you appear to be."

"I shall need nothing but my shroud, when thou, or any other mortal, shapest me."

"Fiddlesticks! Go away with your pride! I have shaped everything for you, — your house, and your eating ; your clothes, and your religion ; and if I had ever thought you would have fallen into Duke Richmoor's hands, I would have shaped your politics before this time of day."

"Now, Maude, thou canst easily go further than thou canst come back, if thou dost not take care. Thou must remember that I am thy lord and husband."

"To be sure, thou hast that name. But thou hast always found it best to do as thy lady and mistress told thee to do; and if ever thou didst take thy own way, sorry enough thou hast been for it. Talk of clay in the hands of the potter! Clay is free and independent to what a man is in the hands of his wife. Now, John, go to bed. I won't speak to thee again till I find out something about *my* son Edgar."

"Very well, Madame."

"I have been thy guardian angel for thirty years" — and Mrs. Atheling put her head in her hands, and began to cry a little. The Squire could not bear that argument; he turned backward a few steps, and said in a more conciliatory voice, —

"Come now, Maude. Thou hast been my master for thirty years; for that is what thou meanest by ' guardian angel.' But there is nothing worth crying about. I thought I had brought news that would set thee up a bit; but women are never satisfied. What dost thou want more?"

"I want thee to go in the morning and find out all about Edgar. I want thee to bring his friend up here. I would like to question him myself."

"I will not do it."

"Then thou oughtest to be ashamed of thyself for as cruel, and stubborn, and ill-conditioned a father as I know of. John, dear John, I am very

unhappy about the lad. He went away without
a rag of his best clothes. There's the twelve
fine linen shirts Kitty made him, backstitched
and everything, lying in his drawers yet, and
his top-coat hanging on the peg in his room,
and his hat and cane so natural like; and he
never was a lad to take care of his health; and
so — "

"Now, Maude, I have humbled a bit to thee
many a time; and I don't mind it at all; for
thou art only a woman — and a woman and a
wife can blackguard a man as no other body
has either the right or the power to do — but I
will not humble to Edgar Atheling. No, I won't!
He is about as bad a prodigal son as any father
could have."

"Well, I never! Putting thy own son down
with harlots and swine, and such like!"

"I do nothing of the sort, Maude. There's
all kinds of prodigals. Has not Edgar left his
home and gone away with Radicals and Reformers, and poor, discontented beggars of all
makes and kinds? Happen, I could have for-
given him easier if it had been a bit of pleasur-
ing, — wine and a bonny lass, or a race-horse or
two. But mechanics' meetings, and pandering to
ranting Radicals — I call it scandalous!"

"Edgar has a good heart."

"A good heart! A cat and a fiddle! And
that friend of his thou wantest me to run after, he
is nothing but a bouncing, swaggering puppy!

Body of me, Maude! I will not have this subject
named again. If thou thinkest I will ever humble
to Edgar Atheling, thou art off thy horse; for I
will not — *never !*"

"Well, John, as none of thy family were ever
out of their senses before, I do hope thou wilt
come round; I do indeed!"

"Make thyself easy on that score. Lord!
What did the Almighty make women of? It
confounds me."

"To be sure it does. Didst thou expect the
Almighty to tell thee? He has so ordered things
that men get wed, and then try and find the
secret out. Thou hadst better go to bed, John
Atheling. I see plainly there is neither sense
nor reason in thee to-night. I fancy thou art a
bit set up with the thought of being sent to
Parliament by Duke Richmoor. I would n't if
I was thee, for thou wilt have to do just what
he tells thee to do."

"What an aggravating woman thou art!" and
with the words he passed through the door,
clashing it after him in a way that made Mistress
Atheling smile and nod her handsome head
understandingly. She stood waiting until she
heard a door clash sympathetically up-stairs, and
then she said softly, —

"He did not manage to 'throw' or 'threep'
me; if he was cock of the walk down on the
green — what fools men are! — I see clear
through him — stubborn though — takes after

his mother — and there never was a woman more stubborn than Dame Joan Atheling."

During this soliloquy she was locking up the cupboards in the parlour and houseplace. Then she opened the kitchen door and sharply gave the two women watching the malt mash her last orders; after which she took off her slippers at the foot of the stairs, and went very quietly up them. She had no light, but without any hesitation she turned towards a certain corridor, and gently pushed open a door. It let her into a large, low room; and the moonlight showed in the centre of it a high canopied bedstead, piled with snowy pillows and drapery, and among them, lying with closed eyes, her daughter Kate.

"Kate! Kitty darling! Are you awake?" she whispered.

"Mother! Yes, dear Mother, I am wide awake."

"Your father has been in one of his tantrums again — fretting and fuming like everything."

"Poor father! What angered him?"

"Well, child, I angered him. Why wouldn't I? He saw a man in the village who has been living with Edgar for a year, and he never asked him whether your poor brother was alive or dead. What do you think of that?"

"It was too bad. Never mind, Mother. I will go to the village in the morning, and I will find the man, and hear all about Edgar. If there is any chance, and you want to see him, I will bring him here."

"I would like him to come here, Kitty; for you know he might take Edgar his best clothes. The poor lad must be in rags by this time."

"Don't fret, Mother. I'll manage it."

"I knew you would. Your father is going to Parliament, Kate. The Duke offers to seat him, and you will get up to London. What do you think of that?"

"I am very glad to hear it. Father ought to be in Parliament. He is such a straight-forward man."

"Well, I don't know whether that kind of man is wanted there, Kate; but he will do right, and speak plain, I have no doubt. I thought I would tell you at once. It is something to look forward to. Now go to sleep and dream of what may come out of it, — for one thing, you shall have plenty of fine new dresses — good-night, my dear child."

"Good-night, Mother. You may go sweetly to sleep, for I will find out all about Edgar. You shall be at rest before dinner-time to-morrow." Then the mother stooped and tucked in the bedclothing, not because it needed it, but because it was a natural and instinctive way to express her care and tenderness. Very softly she stepped to the door, but ere she reached it, turned back to the bed, and laying her hand upon Kitty's head whispered, "Lord Exham is home again. He is coming here to-morrow."

And Kate neither spoke nor moved; but when she knew that she was quite alone, a sweet smile gathered round her lips, and with a gentle sigh she went quickly away to the Land of Happy Dreams.

CHAPTER SECOND

CECIL AND EDGAR

EARLY the next morning the Squire was in the parlour standing at the open lattices, and whistling to a robin on a branch of the cherry-tree above them. The robin sang, and the Squire whistled, scattering crumbs as he did so, and it was this kindly picture which met Kate's eyes as she opened the door of the room. To watch and to listen was natural; and she stood on the threshold doing so until the Squire came to the last bars of his melody. Then in a gay voice she took it up, and sang to his whistling:

" York! York! for my money!" [1]

"Hello, Kate!" he cried in his delight as he turned to her; and as joyously as the birds sing "Spring!" she called, "Good-morning, Father!"

"God bless thee, Kate!" and for a moment he let his eyes rest on the vision of her girlish beauty. For there was none like Kate Atheling

---

[1] "York! York for my monie
Of all the places I ever did see
This is the place for good companie
Except the city of London."

in all the North-Riding; from her sandalled feet
to her shining hair, she was the fairest, sweetest
maid that ever Yorkshire bred, — an adorable
creature of exquisite form and superb colouring;
merry as a bird, with a fine spirit and a most
affectionate heart. As he gazed at her she came
close to him, put her fingers on his big shoulders,
and stood on tiptoes to give him his morning
greeting. He lifted her bodily and kissed her
several times; and she said with a laugh, —

"One kiss for my duty, and one for my pleasure, and all the rest are stolen. Put me down,
Father; and what will you do for me to-day?"

"What wouldst thou like me to do?"

"May I ride with you?"

"Nay; I can't take thee with me to-day. I
am going to Squire Ayton's, and from there to
Rudby's, and very like as far as Ormesby and
Pickering."

"Then you will not be home to dinner?"

"Not I. I shall get my dinner somewhere."

"Can I come and meet you?"

"Thou hadst better not."

At this moment Mrs. Atheling entered, and
Kate, turning to her, said, "Mother, I am not to
ride with father to-day. He is going a visiting,
— going to get his dinner 'somewhere,' and he
thinks I had better not come to meet him."

"Father is right. Father knows he is not to
trust to when he goes 'somewhere' for his
dinner. For he will call for Ayton, and they

two will get Rudby, and then it will be Ormesby, and so by dinner-time they may draw rein at Pickering, and Pickering will start ' Corn Laws' and ' Protection for the Farmers,' and midnight will be talked away. Is not that about right, John?" but she asked the question with a smile that proved Maude Atheling was once more the wise and loving "guardian angel" of her husband.

" Thou knowest all about it, Maude."

" I know enough, any way, to advise thee to stand by thy own heart, and to say and do what it counsels thee. Pickering is made after the meanest model of a Yorkshireman; and when a Yorkshireman turns out to be a failure, he is a ruin, and no mistake."

" What by that? I can't quarrel with Pickering. You may kick up a dust with your neighbour, but, sooner or later, it will settle on your own doorstone. It is years and years since I learned that lesson. And as for Pickering's ideas, many a good squire holds the same."

" I don't doubt it. Whatever the Ass says, the asses believe; thou wilt find that out when thou goest to Parliament."

" Are you really going to Parliament, Father?"

" Wouldst thou like me to go, Kate?"

" Yes, if I may go to London with you."

" It is n't likely I would go without thee. Did thy mother tell thee, Lord Exham has come back from Italy to sit for Gaythorne."

" A long way to come for so little," she answered. " Why, Father! there are only a few
hovels in Gaythorne, and all the men worth anything have gone to Leeds to comb wool. Poor
fellows ! "

" Why dost thou say ' poor fellows '? "

" Because, when a man has been brought up
to do his day's work in fields and barns, among
grass, and wheat, and cattle, it is a big change to
sit twelve hours a day in ' the Devil's Hole,' for
Martha Coates told me that is what the wool-
combing room is called."

" There is no sense in such a name."

" It is a very good name, I think, for rooms so
hot and crowded, and so sickening with the smells
of soap, and wool, and oil, and steam. Martha
says her lads have turned Radicals and Metho-
dists, and she does n't wonder. Neither do I."

" Ay; it is as natural as can be. To do his
duty by the land used to be religion enough for
any Yorkshire lad; but when they go to big
towns, they get into bad company; and there
could n't be worse company than those weaving
chaps of all kinds. No wonder the Government
does n't want to hear from the big towns; they
are full of a ranting crowd of Non-contents."

" Well, Father, if I was in their place, and the
question of Content, or Non-content, was put to
me, I should very quickly say, ' Non-content.'"

" Nobody is going to put the question to thee.
Thy mother has not managed to bring up a

daughter any better than herself, I see that.
Kate, my little maid, Lord Exham will be here
to-day; see that thou art civil enough to him;
it may make a lot of difference both to thee
and me."

"John Atheling!" cried his wife, "what a blun-
derer thou art! Why can't thou let women and
their ways alone?"

When they rose from the breakfast-table, the
Squire called for his horse, and his favourite dogs,
and bustled about until he had Mrs. Atheling and
half-a-dozen men and women waiting upon him.
But there was much good temper in all his
authoritative brusqueness, and he went away in a
little flurry of éclat, his wife and daughter, his men
and maid-servants, all watching him down the avenue with a loving and proud allegiance. He was
so physically the expression of his place and
surroundings that not a soul in Atheling ever
doubted that the Squire was in the exact place
to which God Almighty had called him.

On this morning he was dressed in a riding
suit of dark blue broadcloth trimmed with gilt
buttons; his vest was white, his cravat white, and
his hat of black beaver. As he galloped away,
he swept it from his brow to his stirrups in an
adieu to his wife and daughter; but the men and
women-servants took their share in the courtesy,
and it was easy to feel the cheer of admiration,
only expressed by their broad smiles and sympathetic glances. As soon as "the Master" was

out of sight, they turned away, each to his or her daily task; and Kate looked at her mother inquiringly. There was an instant understanding, and very few words were needed.

"Thou hadst better lose no time. He might get away early."

"He will not leave until he sees us, Mother. That is what he came to Atheling for, — I 'll warrant it, — and if I don't go to the village, he will come here; I know he will."

"Kitty, I can't, I can't trust to that — and you promised."

"I am going to keep my promise, Mother. Have my mare at the door in ten minutes, and I will be ready."

Mrs. Atheling had attended to this necessity before breakfast, and the mare was immediately waiting. She was a creature worthy of the Beauty she had to carry, — dark chestnut in colour, with wide haunches and deep oblique shoulders. Her mane was fine, her ears tremulous, her nostrils thin as parchment, her eyes human in intelligence, her skin like tissue-paper, showing the warm blood pressing against it, and the veins standing clearly out. Waiting fretted her, and she pawed the garden gravel impatiently with her round, dark, shining hoofs until Kate appeared. Then she uttered a low whinny of pleasure, and bent her head for the girl to lay her face against it.

A light leap from the groom's hand put Kate

in her seat, and a lovelier woman never gathered
reins in hand. In those days also, the riding
dress of women did not disfigure them; it was a
garb that gave to Kate Atheling's loveliness
grace and dignity, an air of discreet freedom,
and of sweet supremacy, — a close-fitting habit of
fine cloth, falling far below her feet in graceful
folds, and a low beaver hat, crowned with drooping plumes, shadowing her smiling face. One
word to the mare was sufficient; she needed no
whip, and Kate would not have insulted her
friend and companion by carrying one.

For a little while they went swiftly, then Kate
bent and patted the mare's neck, and she instantly obeyed the signal for a slower pace. For
Kate had seen before them a young man sitting
on a stile, and teaching two dogs to leap over the
whip which he held in his hand. She felt sure
this was the person she had to interview; yet
she passed him without a look, and went forward
towards the village. After riding half-a-mile she
took herself to task for her cowardice, and turned
back again. The stranger was still sitting on the
stile, and as she approached him she heard a
hearty laugh, evoked doubtless by some antic or
mistake of the dogs he was playing with. She
now walked her mare toward him, and the young
man instantly rose, uncovered his head, and, pushing the dogs away, bowed — not ungracefully —
to her. Yet he did not immediately speak, and
Kate felt that she must open the conversation.

"Do you — do you want to find any place?"
she asked. "I think you are a stranger — and I
am at home here."

He smiled brightly and answered, "Thank
you. I want to find Atheling Manor-house. I
have a message for Mrs. and Miss Atheling."

"I am Miss Atheling; and I am now returning
to the house. I suppose that you are the Wrestler and Orator of last night. My father told us
about the contest. Mother wishes to talk with
you — we have heard that you know my brother
Edgar — we are very unhappy about Edgar. Do
you know anything of him? Will you come and
see mother — *now* — she is very anxious?"

These questions and remarks fell stumblingly
from her lips, one after the other; she was excited
and trembling at her own temerity, and yet all the
time conscious she was Squire Atheling's daughter and in her father's Manor, having a kind of
right to assume a little authority and ask questions. The stranger listened gravely till Kate
ceased speaking, then he said, —

"My name is Cecil North. I know Edgar
Atheling very well. I am ready to do now whatever you wish."

"Then, Mr. North, I wish you would come
with me. It is but a short walk to the house;
Candace will take little steps, and I will show you
the way."

"Thank you."

He said only these two words, but they broke

up his face as if there was music in them; for he
smiled with his lips and his eyes at the same
time. Kate glanced down at him as he walked
by her side. She saw that he was tall, finely
formed, and had a handsome face; that he was
well dressed, and had an air of distinction; and
yet she divined in some occult way that this
animal young beauty was only the husk of his
being. After a few moments' silence, he began
that commonplace chat about horses which in
Yorkshire takes the place that weather does in
other localities. He praised the beauty and
docility of Candace, and Kate hoped she was
walking slowly enough; and then Cecil North
admired her feet and her step, and asked if she
ever stumbled or tripped. This question brought
forth an eager denial of any such fault, and an
opinion that the rider was to blame when such
an accident happened.

"In a general way, you are right, Miss Atheling," answered North. "If the rider sits just
and upright, then any sudden jerk forward
throws the shoulders backward; and in that case,
if a horse thinks proper to fall, *he* will be the suf-
ferer. He may cut his forehead, or hurt his nose,
or bark his knees, but he will be a buffer to his
rider."

"Candace has never tripped with me. I have
had her four years. I will never part with her."

"That is right. Don't keep a horse you dislike, and don't part with one that suits you."

"Do you love horses?"

"Yes. A few years ago I was all for horses.
I could sit anything. I could jump everything,
right and left. I had a horse then that was made
to measure, and foaled to order. No one bor-
rowed him twice. He had a way of coming
home without a rider. But I have something
better than horses to care for now; and all I need
is a good roadster."

"My father likes an Irish cob for that
purpose."

"Nothing better. I have one in the village
that beats all. He can trot fourteen miles an
hour, and take a six-foot wall at the end of it."

"Do you ride much?"

"I ride all over England."

She looked curiously at him, but asked no
questions; and North continued the conversation
by pointing out to her the several points which
made Candace so valuable. "In the first place,"
he said, "her colour is good, — that dark chestnut
shaded with black usually denotes speed. She
has all the signs of a thoroughbred; do you
know them?"

"No; but I should like to."

"They are three things long, — long ears, long
neck, and long forelegs. Three things short, —
short dock, short back, and short hindlegs. Three
things broad, — broad forehead, broad chest, and
broad croup. Three things clean, — clean skin,
clean eyes, and clean hoofs. Then the nostrils

must be quite black. If there had been any white in the nostrils of Candace, I would have ranked her only 'middling.'"

Kate laughed pleasantly, and said over several times the long, short, broad, and clean points that went to the making of a thoroughbred; and, by the time the lesson was learned, they were at the door of the Manor-house. Mrs. Atheling stood just within it, and when Kate said, —

"Mother, this is Edgar's friend, Mr. Cecil North," she gave him her hand and answered:

"Come in! Come in! Indeed I am fain and glad to see you!" and all the way through the great hall, and into her parlour, she was beaming and uttering welcomes. "First of all, you must have a bit of eating and drinking," she said, "and then you will tell me about my boy."

"Thank you. I will take a glass of ale, if it will please you."

"It will please me beyond everything. You shall have it from the Squire's special tap: ale smooth as oil, sweet as milk, clear as amber, fourteen years old next twenty-ninth of March. And so you know my son Edgar?"

"I know him, and I love him with all my heart. He is as good as gold, and as true as steel."

"To be sure, he is. I'm his mother, and I ought to know him; and that is what I say. How did you come together?"

"We met first at Cambridge; but we were not in the same college or set, so that I only knew him slightly there. Fortune had appointed a nobler introduction for us. I was in Glasgow nearly a year ago, and I wandered down to the Green, and was soon aware that the crowd was streaming to one point. Edgar was talking to this crowd. Have you ever heard him talk to a crowd?"

The mother shook her head, and Kate said softly: "We have never heard him." She had taken off her hat, and her face was full of interest and happy expectation.

"Well," continued North, " he was standing on a platform of rough boards that had been hastily put together, and I remembered instantly his tall, strong, graceful figure, and his bright, purposeful face. He was tanned to the temples, his cheeks were flushed, the wind was in his hair, the sunlight in his eyes; and, with fiery precipitance of assailing words, he was explaining to men mad with hunger and injustice the source of all their woes and the remedy to be applied. I became a man as I listened to him. That hour I put self behind me and vowed my life, and all I have, to the cause of Reform; because he showed me plainly that Parliamentary Reform included the righting of every social wrong and cruelty."

"Do you really think so?" asked Kate.

"Indeed, I am sure of it. A Parliament that represented the great middle and working classes of England would quickly do away with both

black and white slavery, — would repeal those infamous Corn Laws which have starved the working-
man to make rich the farmer; would open our
ports freely to the trade of all the world; would
educate the poor; give much shorter hours of
labour, and wages that a man could live on. Can
I ever forget that hour? Never! I was born
again in it!"

"That was the kind of talk that he angered
his father with," said Mrs. Atheling, between
tears and smiles. "You see it was all against
the land and the land-owners; and Edgar would
not be quiet, no matter what I said to him."

"He *could not* be quiet. He had *no right* to
be quiet. Why! he sent every man and woman
home that night with hope in their hearts and a
purpose in their wretched lives. Oh, if you
could have seen those sad, cold faces light and
brighten as they listened to him."

"Was there no one there that did n't think as
he did?"

"I heard only one dissenting voice. It came
from a Minister. He called out, 'Lads and lasses,
take no heed of what this fellow says to you. He
is nothing but a Dreamer.' Instantly Edgar took
up the word. 'A Dreamer!' he cried joyfully. 'So
be it! What says the old Hebrew prophet?
Look to your Bible, sir. Let him that hath a
dream tell it. Dreamers have been the creators,
the leaders, the saviours of the world. And we
will go on dreaming until our dream comes true!'

The crowd answered him with a sob and a shout —
and, oh, I wish you had been there!"

Kate uttered involuntarily a low, sympathetic
cry that she could not control, and Mrs. Atheling
wept and smiled; and when North added, in a
lower voice full of feeling, "There is no one like
Edgar, and I love him as Jonathan loved David!"
she went straight to the speaker, took both his
hands in hers, and kissed him.

"Thou art the same as a son to me," she said,
"and thou mayst count on my love as long as
ever thou livest." And in this cry from her heart
she forgot her company pronoun, and fell naturally into the familiar and affectionate "thou."

Fortunately at this point of intense emotion a
servant entered with a flagon of the famous ale,
and some bread and cheese; and the little interruption enabled all to bring themselves to a nor-
mal state of feeling. Then the mother thought
of Edgar's clothing, and asked North if he could
take it to him. North smiled. "He is a little of
a dandy already," he answered. "I saw him last
week at Lady Durham's, and he was the best
dressed man in her saloon."

"Now then!" said Mrs. Atheling, "thou art
joking a bit. Whatever would Edgar be doing at
Lady Durham's?"

"He had every right there, as he is one of
Lord Durham's confidential secretaries."

"Art thou telling me some romance?"

"I am telling you the simple truth."

" Then thou must tell me how such a thing came about."

" Very naturally. I told Lord Grey and his son-in-law, Lord Durham, about Edgar — and I persuaded Edgar to come and speak to the spur and saddle-makers at Ripon Cross; and the two lords heard him with delight, and took him, there and then, to Studley Royal, where they were staying; and it was in those glorious gardens, and among the ruins of Fountains Abbey, they planned together the Reform Campaign for the next Parliament."

" The Squire thinks little of Lord Grey," said Mrs. Atheling.

" That is not to be wondered at," answered North. " Lord Grey is the head and heart of Reform. When he was Mr. Charles Grey, and the pupil of Fox, he presented to Parliament the famous Prayer, from the Society of Friends, for Reform. That was thirty-seven years ago, but he has never since lost sight of his object. By the side of such leaders as Burke, and Fox, and Sheridan, his lofty eloquence has charmed the House until the morning sun shone on its ancient tapestries. He and his son-in-law, Lord Durham, have the confidence of every honest man in England. And he is brave as he is true. More than once he has had the courage to tell the King to his face what it was his duty to do."

" And what of Lord Durham?" asked Kate.

" He is a masterful man, — a bolder Radical than

most Radicals. All over the country he is known as Radical Jack. He has a strong, resolute will, but during the last half-year he has leaned in all executive matters upon ' Mr. Atheling.' Indeed, there was enthusiastic talk last week at Lady Durham's of sending ' Mr. Atheling ' to the next Parliament."

" My word! But that would never do!" exclaimed Mr. Atheling's mother. " His father is going there for the landed interest; and if Edgar goes for the people, there will be trouble between them. They will get to talking back at each other, and the Squire will pontify and lay down the law, even if the King and the Law-makers are all present. He will indeed!"

" It would be an argument worth hearing, for Edgar would neither lose his temper nor his cause. Oh, I tell you there will be great doings in London next winter! The Duke of Wellington and Mr. Peel will have to go out; and Earl Grey will surely form a new Government."

"The Squire says Earl Grey and Reform will bring us into civil war."

" On the contrary, only Reform can prevent civil war. Hitherto, the question has been, ' What will the Lords do?' Now it is, ' What must be done with the Lords?' For once, all England is in dead earnest; and the cry everywhere is, ' The Bill, the whole Bill, and nothing but The Bill ! ' And if we win, as win we must, we shall remember how Edgar Atheling has championed the

cause. George the Fourth is on his death-bed,"
he added in a lower voice. " He will leave his
kingdom in a worse plight than any king before
him. I, who have been through the land, may
declare so much."

" The poor are very poor indeed," said Mrs.
Atheling. " Kate and I do what we can, but the
most is little."

" The whole story of the poor is — slow starvation. The best silk weavers in England are not
able to make more than eight or nine shillings a
week. Thousands of men in the large towns are
working for two-pence half-penny a day; and
thousands have no work at all."

"What do they do? " whispered Kate.

"They die. But I did not come here to talk
on these subjects — only when the heart is full,
the mouth must speak. I have brought a letter
and a remembrance from Edgar," and he took
from his pocket a letter and two gold rings, and
gave the letter and one ring to Mrs. Atheling,
and the other ring to Kate. " He bid me tell
you," said North, " that some day he will set the
gold round with diamonds; but now every penny
goes for Reform."

" And you tell Edgar, sir, that his mother is
prouder of the gold thread than of diamonds.
Tell him, she holds her Reform ring next to
her wedding ring," — and with the words Mrs.
Atheling drew off her " guard " of rubies, and put
the slender thread of gold her son had sent her

next her wedding ring. At the same moment
Kate slipped upon her " heart finger " the golden
token. Her face shone, her voice was like music:
" Tell Edgar, Mr. North," she said, " that my
love for him is like this ring : I do not know its
beginning ; but I do know it can have no end."

Then North rose to go, and would not be detained ; and the women walked with him to the
very gates, and there they said " good-bye." And
all the way through the garden Mrs. Atheling
was sending tender messages to her boy, though
at the last she urged North to warn him against
saying anything " beyond bearing " to his father,
if they should meet on the battle-ground of the
House of Commons. " It is so easy to quarrel
on politics," she said with all the pathos of reminiscent disputes.

" It has always been an easy quarrel, I think,"
answered North. " Don't you remember when
Joseph wanted to pick a quarrel with his breth-
ren, he pretended to think they were a special
commission sent to Egypt to spy out the naked-
ness of the land ? "

" To be sure ! And that is a long time ago.
Good-bye ! and God bless thee ! I shall never
forget thy visit ! "

" And we wish ' The Cause ' success ! " added
Kate.

" Thank you. Success will come. They who
care and *dare* can do anything." With these
words he passed through the gates, and Mrs.

Atheling and Kate went slowly back to the house, both of them turning the new ring on their fingers. It was dinner-time, but little dinner was eaten. Edgar's letter was to read; Mr. North to speculate about; and if either of the women remembered Lord Exham's expected call, no remark was made about it.

Yet Kate was neither forgetful of the visit, nor indifferent to it. A sweet trouble of heart, half-fear and half-hope, flushed her cheeks and sent a tender light into her star-like eyes. In the very depths of her being there existed a feeling she did not understand, and did not investigate. Was it Memory? Was it Hope? Was it Love? She asked none of these questions. But she dressed like a girl in a dream; and just as she was sliding the silver buckle on her belt, a sudden trick of memory brought back to her the rhyme of her childhood. And though she blushed to the remembrance, and would not for anything repeat the words, her heart sang softly to itself, —

> "It may so happen, it may so fall,
> That I shall be Lady of Exham Hall."

CHAPTER THIRD

THE LORD OF EXHAM

ON the very edge of the deep, tumbling becks which feed the Esk stands Exham Hall. It is a stately, irregular building of gray stone; and when the sunshine is on its many windows, and the flag of Richmoor flying from its central tower, it looks gaily down into the hearts of many valleys, where

> "The oak, and the ash, and the bonny ivy-tree,
> Flourish at home in the North Countree."

Otherwise, it has, at a distance, a stern and forbidding aspect. For it is in a great solitude, and the babble of the beck, and the cawing of the rooks, are the only sounds that usually break the silence. The north part was built in A. D. 1320; and the most modern part in the reign of James the First; and yet so well has it stood the wear and tear of elemental and human life in this secluded Yorkshire vale that it does not appear to be above a century old.

It was usually tenanted either by the dowager of the family, or the heir of the dukedom; and it had been opened at this time to receive its young lord on his return from Italy. So it happened that at the very hour when Mrs. and Miss Atheling were talking with Cecil North, Piers Exham was sitting in a parlour of Exham Hall, thinking of Kate, and recalling the events of their acquaintanceship. It had begun when he was seventeen years old, and Kate Atheling exactly twelve. Indeed, because it was her birthday, she was permitted to accompany an old servant going to Exham Hall to visit the housekeeper, who was her cousin.

This event made a powerful impression on Kate's imagination. It was like a visit to some enchanted castle. She felt all its glamour and mystery as soon as her small feet trod the vast entrance hall with its hangings of Arras tapestry, and its flags and weapons from every English battlefield. Her fingers touched lightly standards from Crecy, and Agincourt, and the walls of Jerusalem; and her heart throbbed to the touch. And as she climbed the prodigiously wide staircase of carved and polished oak, she thought of the generations of knights, and lords and ladies, who had gone up and down it, and wondered where they were. And oh, the marvellous old rooms with their shadowy portraits, and their treasures from countries far away! — shells, and carved ivories, and sandalwood boxes; strange perfumes, and old idols, melancholy, fantastic, odd; musky-smelling things from Asia; and ornaments and pottery from Africa, their gloomy,

primitive simplicity, mingling with pretty French
trifles, and Italian bronzes, and costly bits of
china.

It was all like an Arabian Night's adventure,
and hardly needed the touches of romance and
superstition the housekeeper quite incidentally
threw in: thus, as they passed a very, very tall
old clock with a silver dial on a golden face, she
said: "Happen, you would not believe it, but on
every tenth of June, a cold queer light travels all
round that dial. It begins an hour past midnight, and stops at an hour past noon. I've seen
it myself a score of times." And again, in going
through a state bed-room, she pointed out a
cross and a candlestick, and said, "They are
made from bits of a famous ship that was blown
up with an Exham, fighting on the Spanish
Main. I've heard tell that candles were once
lighted in that stick on his birthday; but there's
been no candle-lighting for a century, anyway."
And Kate thought it was a shame, and wished she
knew his birthday, and might light candles again
in honour of the hero.

With such sights and tales, her childish head
and heart were filled; and the mazy gardens,
with their monkish fish-ponds and hedges, their
old sun-dials and terraces, their ripening berries
and gorgeous flower-beds, completed her fascination. She went back to Atheling ravished and
spellbound; too wrapt and charmed to talk
much of what she had seen, and glad when she

could escape into the Atheling garden to think it
all over again.　She went straight to her swing.
It was hung between two large ash-trees, and
there were high laurel hedges on each side.　In
this solitude she sat down to remember, and, as
she did so, began to swing gently to-and-fro, and
to sing to her movement, —

> " It may so happen, it may so fall,
>   That I shall be Lady of Exham Hall."

And as she sung these lines over and over —
being much pleased with their unexpected rhyming — the young Lord of Exham Hall came
through Atheling garden.　He heard his own
name, and stood still to listen; then he softly
parted the laurel bushes, and watched the little
maid, and heard her sing her couplet, and merrily laugh to herself as she did so.　And he saw
how beautiful she was, and there came into his
heart a singular warmth and pleasure; but, without discovering himself to the girl, he delivered
his message to Squire Atheling, and rode away.

The next morning, however, he managed to
carry his fishing-rod to the same beck where
Edgar Atheling was casting his line, and to
so charm the warm-hearted youth that meeting
after meeting grew out of it.　Nor was it long
until the friendship of the youths included that
of the girl; so that it was a very ordinary thing
for Kate to go with her brother and Piers Exham
to the hill-streams for trout.　As the summer

grew they tossed the hay together, and rode after
the harvest wagons, and danced at the Ingather-
ing Feast, and dressed the ancient church at
Christmastide, and so, with ever-increasing kindness and interest, shared each other's joy and
sorrows for nearly two years.

Then there was a break in the happy routine.
Kate put on long dresses; she was going to a
fine ladies' school in York to be " finished," and
Edgar also was entered at Cambridge.   Piers was
to go to Oxford.   He begged to go to Cambridge
with his friend; but the Duke approved the Tory
principles of his own University, and equally
disapproved of those of Cambridge, which he
declared were deeply tainted with Whig and
even Radical ideas.   Perhaps also he was inclined
to break up the close friendship between the
Athelings and his heir.   "No one can be insensible to the beauty of Kate Atheling," he said
to the Duchess; " and Piers' constant association
with such a lovely girl may not be without
danger."   The Duchess smiled at the supposition.   A royal princess, in her estimation, was
not above her son's deserts and expectations;
and the Squire's little home-bred girl was be-
neath either her fears or her suppositions.   This
also was the tone in which she received all her
son's conversation about the Athelings.   "Very
nice people, I dare say, Piers," she would remark;
" and I am glad you have such thoroughly re-
spectable companions; but you will, of course,

forget them when you go to College, and begin
your independent life." And there was such an
air of finality in these assertions that it was only
rarely Piers had the spirit to answer, "Indeed, I
shall never forget them !"

So it happened that the last few weeks of their
friendship missed much of the easy familiarity
and sweet confidence that had hitherto marked
its every change. Kate, with the new consciousness of dawning womanhood, was shy, less frank,
and less intimate. Strangers began to call her
"Miss" Atheling; and there were hours when
the little beauty's airs of maidenly pride and
reserve made Piers feel that any other address
would be impertinent. And this change had
come, no one knew how, only it was there, and
not to be gainsaid; and every day's events
added some trifling look, or word, or act which
widened the space between them, though the
space itself was full of sweet and kindly hours.

Then there came a day in autumn when Kate
was to leave her home for the York school.
Edgar was already in Cambridge. Piers was to
enter Oxford the following week. This chapter
of life was finished; and the three happy souls
that had made it, were to separate. Piers, who
had a poetic nature, and was really in love —
though he suspected it not — was most impressed with the passing away. He could not
keep from Atheling, and though he had bid
Kate "good-bye" in the afternoon, he was not

satisfied with the parting. She had then been
full of business: the Squire was addressing her
trunks; Mrs. Atheling crimping the lace frill of
her muslin tippets; and Kate herself bringing,
one by one, some extra trifle that at the last
moment impressed her with its necessity. It
was in this hurry of household love and care
that he had said " good-bye," and he felt that it
had been a mere form.

Perhaps Kate felt it also; for when he rode
up to Atheling gates in the gloaming, he saw
her sauntering up the avenue. He thought
there was both melancholy and expectation in
her attitude and air. He tied his horse outside,
and joined her. She met him with a smile. He
took her hand, and she permitted him to retain
it. He said, " Kate!" and she answered the
word with a glance that made him joyous,
ardent, hopeful. He was too happy to speak;
he feared to break the heavenly peace between
them by a word. Oh, this is the way of Love!
But neither knew the ways of Love. They were
after all but children, and the sweet thoughts in
their hearts had not come to speech. They
wandered about the garden until the gloaming
became moonlight, and they heard Mrs. Atheling
calling her daughter. Then their eyes met, and,
swift as the firing of a gun, their pupils dilated
and flashed with tender feeling; over their
faces rushed the crimson blood; and Piers said
sorrowfully, " Kate! Sweet Kate! I shall never

forget you!" He raised the hand he held to
his lips, kissed it, and went hurriedly away
from her.

Kate was not able to say a word, but she
felt the kiss on her hand through all her sleep
and dreams that night. Indeed five years of
change and absence had not chilled its warm
remembrance; there were hours when it was
still a real expression, when the hand itself was
conscious of the experience, and willingly cherished it. All through Cecil North's visit, she
had been aware of a sense of expectancy. Interested as she was in Edgar, the thought of
Lord Exham would not be put down. For a
short time it was held in abeyance; but when
the early dinner was over, and she was in the
solitude of her own room, Piers put Edgar out
of consideration. As she sat brushing and
dressing her long brown hair, she recalled little
incidents concerning Piers, — how once in the
harvest-field her hair had tumbled down, and
Piers praised its tangled beauty; how he had
liked this and the other dress; how he had
praised her dancing, and vowed she was the
best rider in the county. He had given her a
little gold brooch for a Christmas present, and
she took it from its box, and said to herself she
would wear it, and see if it evoked its own
memory in Exham's heart.

It had been her intention to put on a white
gown, but the day darkened and chilled; and

4

then she had a certain shyness about betraying,
even to her mother, her anxiety to look beautiful. Perhaps Piers might not now think her
beautiful in any garb. Perhaps he had forgotten
— everything. So, impelled by a kind of perverse indifference, she wore only the gray woollen
gown that was her usual afternoon attire. But
the fashion of the day left her lovely arms uncovered, and only veiled her shoulders in a
shadowing tippet of lace. , She fastened this
tippet with the little gold brooch, just where the
folds crossed the bosom. She had hastened
rather than delayed her dressing; and when
Mrs. Atheling came downstairs in her afternoon
black silk dress, she found Kate already in the
parlour. She had taken from her work-box a
piece of fine cambric, and was stitching it indus-
triously; and Mrs. Atheling lifted her own work,
and began to talk of Edgar, and Edgar's great
fortune, and what his father would say about it.
This subject soon absorbed her; she forgot
everything in it; but Kate heard through all
the radical turmoil of the conversation the
gallop of a strange horse on the gravelled
avenue, and the echo of strange footsteps on
the flagged halls of the house.

In the middle of some grand prophecy for
Edgar's future, the parlour door was opened, and
Lord Exham entered. He came forward with
something of his boyhood's enthusiasm, and
took Mrs. Atheling's hands, and said a few

words of pleasant greeting, indistinctly heard in the fluttering gladness of Mrs. Atheling's reception. Then he turned to Kate. She had risen, but she held her work in her left hand. He took it from her, and laid it on her workbox, and then clasped both her hands in his. The firm, lingering pressure had its own eloquence. In matters of love, they who are to understand, *do* understand; and no interpreter is needed.

The conversation then became general and full of interest; but from Oxford, and France, and Italy, it quickly drifted — as all conversation did in those days — to Reform. And Mrs. Atheling could not keep the news that had come to her that day. She magnified Edgar with a sweet motherly vanity that was delightful, and to which Piers listened with pleasure; for the listening gave him opportunity to watch Kate's eloquent face, and to flash his sympathy into it. He thought her marvellously beautiful. Her shining hair, her rich colouring, and her large gray eyes were admirably emphasised by the homely sweetness of her dress. After the lavish proportions, and gaily attired women of Italy, nothing could have been more enchanting to Piers Exham than Kate's subdued, gray-eyed loveliness, clad in gray garments. The charming background of her picturesque home added to this effect; and this background he saw and realised; but she had also a moral background of purity and absolute sincerity which he did not see, but which he undoubtedly felt.

While Piers was experiencing this revelation of womanhood, it was not likely Kate was without impressions. In his early youth, Exham had a slight resemblance to Lord Byron; and he had been vain of the likeness, and accentuated it by adopting the open collar, loose tie, and other peculiarities of the poetic nobleman. Kate was glad to see this servile imitation had been discarded. Exham was now emphatically individual. He was not above medium height; but his figure was good, and his manner gentle and courteous, as the manner of all superior men is. Grave and high-bred, he had also much of the melancholy, mythical air of an English nobleman, conscious of long antecedents, and dwelling in the seclusion of shaded parks, and great houses steeped in the human aura of centuries. His hair was very black, and worn rather long, and his complexion, a pale bronze; but this lack of red colouring added to the fascination of his dark eyes, which were remarkable for that deep glow always meaning mental or moral power of some kind. They were often half shut — and then — who could tell what was passing behind them? And yet, when all this had been observed by Kate, she was sure that something — perhaps the most essential part — had escaped her.

This latter estimate was the correct one. No one as yet had learned the heart or mind of Piers

Exham. It is doubtful if he understood his own
peculiarities; for he had few traits of distinctive
pre-eminence, his character being very like an
opal, where all colours are fused and veiled in a
radiant dimness. So that, after all, this meeting
was a first meeting; and Kate did not feel that
the past offered her any intelligible solution of
the present man.

The conversation having drifted to Edgar and
Reform, stayed there. Lord Exham spoke with a
polite, but stubborn emphasis in favour of his own
caste, as the governing caste, and thought that
the honour and welfare of England might still
be left " to those great Houses which represented
the collective wisdom of the nation." Nor was
he disturbed when Mrs. Atheling, with some
scorn and temper, said "they represented mostly
the collective folly of the nation." He bowed
and smiled at the dictum, but Kate understood
the smile; it was of that peculiarly sweet kind
which is equivalent to having the last word. He
admitted that some things wanted changing, but
he said, " Changes could not be manufactured;
they must grow." "True," replied Kate, "but
Reform has been growing for sixty years." " That
is as it should be," he continued. " You cannot
write Reforms on human beings, as you write it
on paper. Two or three generations are not
enough." In all that was said — and Mrs. Atheling said some very strong things — he took a
polite interest; but he made no surrender. Even

if his words were conciliatory, Kate saw in his
eyes — languid but obstinately masterful — the
stubborn, headstrong will of a man who had inherited his prejudices, and who had considered
them in the light of his interest, and did not
choose to bring them to the light of reason.

Still the conversation was a satisfactory and
delightful vehicle of human revelation. The two
women paled and flushed, and grew sad or happy
in its possibilities, with a charming frankness.
No social subject could have revealed them so
completely; and Exham enjoyed the disclosures
of feeling which this passionate interest evoked,
— enjoyed it so much that he forgot the lapse of
time, and stayed till tea was ready, and then was
delighted to stay and take it with them. Mrs.
Atheling was usually relieved of the duty of making it by Kate; and Piers could not keep his
glowing eyes off the girl as her hands moved
about the exquisite Derby teacups, and handed
him the sweet, refreshing drink. She remembered
that he loved sugar; that he did not love cream;
that he preferred his toast not buttered; that he
liked apricot jelly; and he was charmed and
astonished at these proofs of remembrance, so
much so indeed that he permitted Mrs. Atheling to
appropriate the whole argument. For this sweet
hour he resigned his heart to be pleased and
happy. Too wise in some things, not wise enough
in others, Piers Exham had at least one great
compensating quality — the courage to be happy.

He let all other feelings and purposes lapse for this one. He gave himself up to charm, and to be charmed; he flattered Mrs. Atheling into absolute complaisance; he persuaded Kate to walk through the garden and orchard with him, and then, with caressing voice and a gentle pressure of the hand, reminded her of days and events they had shared together. Smiles flashed from face to face. Her simple sweetness, her ready sympathy, her ingenuous girlish expressions, carried him back to his boyhood. Kate shone on his heart like sunshine; and he did not know that it had become dark until he had left Atheling behind, and found himself Exham-way, riding rapidly to the joyful whirl and hurry of his thoughts.

Now happiness, as well as sorrow, is selfish. Kate was happy and not disposed to talk about her happiness. Her mother's insistent questions about Lord Exham troubled her. She desired to go into solitude with the new emotions this wonderful day had produced; but the force of those lovely habits of respect and obedience, which had become by constant practice a second nature, kept her at her mother's side, listening with sweet credulousness to all her opinions, and answering her hopes with her own assurances. The reward of such dutiful deference was not long in coming. In a short time Mrs. Atheling said, —

"It has been such a day as never was, Kate;

and you must be tired. Now then, go to bed,
my girl, and sleep; for goodness knows when
your father will get home!"

So Kate kissed her mother — kissed her twice
— as if she was dimly conscious of unfairly keeping back some pleasure, and would thus atone
for her selfishness. And Mrs. Atheling sat down
in the chimney-corner with the gray stocking
she was knitting, and pondered her son's good
fortune for a while. Then she rose and sent the
maids to bed, putting the clock an hour forward
ere she did so, and excusing the act by saying,
" If I don't set it fast, we shall soon be on the
wrong side of everything."

Another hour she sat calmly knitting, while in
the dead silence of the house the clock's regular
"*tick ! tick !*" was like breathing. It seemed to
live, and to watch with her. As the Squire came
noisily into the room it struck eleven. " My
word, Maude ! " he said with great good humour,
" I am sorry to keep you waiting; but there has
been some good work done to-night, so you
won't mind it, I 'll warrant."

"Well now, John, if you and your friends
have been at Pickering's, and have done any
' good ' work there, I will be astonished ! You
may warrant *that* with every guinea you have."

"We were at Rudby's. There were as many
as nine landed men of us together; and for once
there was one mind in nine men."

" That is, you were all for yourselves."

"No! Dal it, we were all for old England and the Constitution! The Constitution, just as it is, and no tinkering with it."

"I wonder which of the nine was the biggest fool among you?"

"Thou shouldst not talk in that way, Maude. The country is in real danger with this Reform nonsense. Every Reformer ought to be hung, and I wish they were hung."

"I would be ashamed to say such words, John. Thou knowest well that thy own son is a Reformer."

"More shame to him, and to me, and to thee! I would have brought up a better lad, or else I would hold my tongue about him. It was thy fault he went to Cambridge. I spent good money then to spoil a fine fellow."

"Now, John Atheling, I won't have one word said against Edgar in this house."

"It is my house."

"Nay, but it isn't. Thou only hast the life rent of it. It is Edgar's as much as thine. He will be here, like enough, when I and thou have gone the way we shall never come back."

"Maybe he will — and maybe he will not. I can break the entail if it suits me."

"Thou canst not. For, with all thy faults, thou art an upright man, and thy conscience would n't let thee do anything as mean and spiteful as that. How could we rest in our graves if there was any one but an Atheling in Atheling?"

" He is a disgrace to the name."

" He is nothing of that kind.   He will bring the old name new honour.   See if he does not! And as for the Constitution of England, it is about as great a ruin as thy constitution was when thou hadst rheumatic fever, and could n't turn thyself, nor help thyself, nor put a morsel of bread into thy mouth.   But thou hadst a good doctor, and he set thee up; and a good House of Commons — Reforming Commons — will happen do as much for the country; 'though when every artisan and every farm labourer is hungry and naked, it will be hard to spread the plaster as far as the sore.   It would make thy heart ache to hear what they suffer."

" Don't bother thy head about weavers, and cutlers, and artisans.   If the Agriculture of the country is taken care of—"

" Now, John, do be quiet.   There is not an idiot in the land who won't talk of Agriculture."

" We have got to stick by the land, Maude."

" The land will take care of itself.   If thou wouldst only send for thy son, and have a little talk with him, he might let some light and wisdom into thee."

" I have nothing to say on such subjects to Edgar Atheling — not a word."

" If thou goest to Parliament, thou mayst have to ' say ' to him, no matter whether thou wantest to or not; that is, unless thou art willing to let Edgar have both sides of the argument."

" What tom-foolery art thou talking? "

" I am only telling thee that Edgar is as like to go to Parliament as thou art."

" To be sure — when beggars are kings."

" Earl Grey will seat him — or Lord Durham; and I would advise thee to study up things a bit. There are new ideas about, John; and thou wouldst look foolish if thy own son had to put any of thy mistakes right for thee."

" I suppose, Maude, thou still hast a bit of faith left in the Bible. And I 'll warrant thou knowest every word it says about children obeying their parents, and honouring their parents, and so on. And I can remember thee telling Edgar, when he was a little lad, about Absalom going against his father, and what came of it; now then, is the Bible, as well as the Constitution, a ruin? Is it good for nothing but to be pitched into limbo, or to be ' reformed '? I 'm astonished at thee ! "

" The Bible has nothing to do with politics, John. I wish it had ! Happen then we would have a few wise-like, honest politicians. The Bible divides men into good men and bad men; but thou dividest all men into Tories and Radicals; and the Bible has nothing to do with either of them. I can tell thee that. Nay, but I 'm wrong; it does say a deal about doing justice, and loving mercy, and treating your neighbour and poor working-folk as you would like to be treated yourself. Radicals can get a good deal out of the New Testament."

"I don't believe a word of what thou art saying."

"I don't wonder at that. Thou readest nothing but the newspapers; if thou didst happen to read a few words out of Christ's own mouth, thou wouldst say, 'Thou never heardest the like,' and thou wouldst think the man who quoted them wrote them out of his own head, and call him a Radical. Get off to thy bed, John. I can always tell when thou hast been drinking Rudby's port-wine. It is too heavy and heady for thee. As soon as thou art thyself again, I will tell thee what a grand son thou art the father of. My word! If the Duke gives thee a seat at his mahogany two or three times a year, thou art as proud as a peacock; now then, thy son Edgar is hob-nobbing with earls and lords every day of his life, and they are proud of his company."

The Squire laughed boisterously. "It is time, Maude," he said, "I went to my bed; and it is high time for thee to wake up and get thy head on a feather pillow; then, perhaps, thou will not dream such raving nonsense."

With these scornful words he left the room, and Mrs. Atheling rose and put away her knitting. She was satisfied with herself. She expected her mysterious words to keep the Squire awake with curiosity; and in such case, she was resolved to make another effort to reconcile her husband to his son. But the Squire gave her no opportunity; he slept with an indifferent continu-

ity that it was useless to interrupt. Perhaps
there was intention in this heavy sleep, for when
he came downstairs in the morning he went at
once to seek Kate. He soon saw her in the herb
garden; for she had on a white dimity gown, and
was standing upright, shading her eyes with her
hands to watch his approach. A good breeze
of wind from the wolds fluttered her snowy
skirts, and tossed the penetrating scents of
thyme and marjoram, mint and pennyroyal upward, and she drew them through her parted
lips and distended nostrils.

"They are so heavenly sweet!" she said with
a smile of sensuous pleasure. "They smell like
Paradise, Father."

"Ay, herbs are good and healthy. The smell
of them makes me hungry. I did n't see thee
last night, Kitty; and I wanted to see thee."

"I was so tired, Father. It was a day to tire
any one. Was it not?"

"I should say it was," he replied with conscious diplomacy. "Now what part of it pleased
thee best?"

"Well, Mr. North's visit was of course wonderful; and Lord Exham's visit was very pleasant.
I enjoyed both; but Mr. North's news was so
very surprising."

"To be sure. What dost thou think of it?"

"Of course, Edgar is on the other side, Father.
In some respects that is a pity."

"It is a shame! It is a great shame!"

" Nay, nay, Father! We won't have 'shame' mixed up with Edgar. He is in dead earnest, and he has taken luck with him. Just think of our Edgar being one of Lord Durham's favourites, of him speaking all over England and Scotland for Reform. Mr. North says there is no one like him in the drawing-rooms of the Reform ladies; and no one like him on the Reform platforms; and he was made a member of the new Reform Club in London by acclamation. And Earl Grey will get him a seat in Parliament next election."

" Who is this Mr. North?"

" Why, Father! You heard him speak, and you 'threw' him down on the Green, you know."

" *Oh! Him!* Dost thou believe all this palaver on the word of a travelling mountebank?"

" He is not a travelling mountebank. I am sure he is a gentleman. You should n't call a man names that you have 'thrown' fairly. You know better than that."

" I know nothing about the lad. And he does not seem to have told thee anything about himself. As for thy mother — " and then he hesitated, and looked at Kate meaningly and inquiringly.

" Mother liked him. She liked him very much indeed. He brought both mother and me a ring from Edgar," and she put out her hand and showed the Squire the little gold circle.

" Trumpery rubbish!" he said scornfully. "It

did n't cost half a crown. Give it to me, and I will get thee a ring worth wearing, — sapphires or rubies."

" I would not part with it for loops and hoops of sapphires and rubies. Edgar sent it as a love-token; he wants his money for nobler things than rubies — but, dear me! you can't buy love for any money. Oh, Father! I do wish you would be friends with Edgar."

" My little lass, I cannot be friends with any one if he goes against the land, and the King, and the Constitution. I am loyal straight through; up and down to-day, and to-morrow, and every day; and I can't bear traitors, — men that would sell their country for a bit of mob power or mob glory. All of Edgar's friends and neighbours are for the King and the Laws; and it shames me and pains me beyond everything to have a rascal and a Radical in my family. The Duke and his son are finger and thumb, buckle and belt; and Edgar and I ought to be the same. And it stands to reason that a father knows more than his own lad of twenty-six years old. What dost thou think of Lord Exham?"

· The question was asked at a venture; but Kate had no suspicion, and she answered frankly, "I think very well of him. He talked mostly of politics; but every one does that. It was pleasant to see him at our tea-table again."

" To be sure. So he stayed to tea?"

" Yes; did not mother tell you?"

" Nay, we were talking of other things.   What does he look like? "

" I think he is much improved."

" Well, he ought to be.   He must have learned a little, and he has seen a lot since we saw him. Come, let us go and find out what kind of a breakfast mother can give us.   I am hungry enough for two."

So Kate lifted the herbs which she had cut into her garden apron, and cruddling close to her father's side, they went in together, with the smell of the thyme and marjoram all about them.   Mrs. Atheling drew it in as they entered the parlour, and then turned to them with a smile.   The Squire went to her side, and promptly kissed her.   It was one of his ways to ignore their little tiffs; and this morning Mrs. Atheling was also agreeable.   She looked into his eyes, and said:

" Why, John! are you really awake.   You lay like the Seven Sleepers when I got up, and I said to myself, ' John will sleep the clock round,' so Kate and I will have our breakfasts."

" Nay, I have too much to look after, Maude." Then he turned the conversation to the farms, and talked of the draining to be done, and the meadows to be left for grass; but he eschewed politics altogether, and, greatly to Mrs. Atheling's wonder, never alluded to the information she had given him about their son Edgar.   Did he really think she had been telling him a made-up story? She could not otherwise understand this self-control in her curious lord. However, sometime during the morning, Kate told her about the conversation in the herb garden; then she was content. She knew just where she had her husband; and the little laugh with which she terminated the conversation was her expression of conscious power over him, and of a retaliation quite within her reach.

CHAPTER FOURTH

THE DAWN OF LOVE

THERE is always in every life some little part which even those dearer than life to us cannot enter. Kate had become conscious of this fact. She hoped her mother would not talk of Lord Exham; for she did not as yet understand anything about the feelings his return had evoked. She would have needed the uncertain, enigmatical language which comes in dreams to explain the "yes" and the "no" of the vague, trembling memories, prepossessions, and hopes which fluttered in her breast.

Fortunately Mrs. Atheling had some dim perception of this condition, and without analysing her reasons, she was aware "it was best not to meddle" between two lives so surrounded by contradictious circumstances as were those of her daughter and Lord Exham. Besides, as she said to her husband, "It was no time for love-making, with the King dying, and the country on the quaking edge of revolution, and starvation and misery all over the land." And the Squire answered: "Exham has not one thought of love-making. He is far too much in with a lot

of men who have the country and their own
estates to save. He won't bother himself with
women-folk now, whatever he may do in idle
times."

They had both forgotten, or their own love
affair had been of such Arcadian straightness and
simplicity that they had never learned Love's
ability to domineer all circumstances that can
stir this mortal frame. Exham had indeed en-
listed himself with passionate earnestness in the
cause of his class, which he called the cause of
his country — but as the drop of

"lucent sirup tinct with cinnamon"

is forever flavoured and perfumed by the spice, so
Exham's life was coloured and prepossessed by
the thought of the sweet girl who had been
blended with so many of his purest and happiest
hours.

It was then of Kate he thought as he wandered about the stately rooms and beautiful gardens of Exham Hall. He was not oblivious of
his engagements with the Duke and the tenants;
but he was considering how best to keep these
engagements, and yet not miss a visit to her.
The dying King, the riotous land, were acciden-
tals of his life and condition; his love for Kate
Atheling was at the root of his existence; it was
a fundamental of the past and of the future.
For five years of constant change and movement,
it had lain in abeyance; but old love is a danger-

ous thing to awaken; and Piers Exham found in doing this thing that every event of the past strengthened the influence of the present, and fixed his heart more passionately on the girl he had first found fair; the

> — "rosebud set with little, wilful thorns,
> And sweet as English airs could make her,"

that had sung and swung herself into his affection when she was only twelve years old.

He was however quite aware that any proposal to marry Kate Atheling would meet with prompt opposition from his family; indeed the Duke had already mentioned a very different alliance; and in that case, he did not doubt but that Squire Atheling would be equally resolved never to allow his daughter to enter a home where she would be regarded by any member of it as an intruder. But he put all such considerations for the present behind him. He said to himself, "The first thing to do, is to win Kate's love; with that sweet consciousness, I shall be ready for all opposition." For his heart kept assuring him that every trouble and obstacle has an hour in which it may be conquered, — an hour when Fate and Will become One, and are then as irresistible as a great force of Nature. He was sure the hour for this conflict had not yet come. It was the day for a different fight. His home, his estate, his title, and all the privileges of his nobility were in danger. When they were placed beyond peril, then he would fight for the wife he wanted, and win her against all opposition. And who could tell in what way the first conflict would bring forth circumstances to insure victory to the last?

He was deeply in love; he was full of hope; he was at Atheling some part of every day. If he came in the afternoon, Kate's pony was saddled, and they rode far and away, to where the shadows and sunshine elbowed one another on the moors. The golden gorse shed its perfume over their heads; the linnets sang to them of love; they talked, and laughed, and rode swiftly until their pace brought them among the mountains that looked like a Titanic staircase going up to the skies. There, they always drew rein, and went slower, and spoke softer, and indeed often became quite silent, and knew such silence to be the sweetest eloquence. Then after a little interval Piers would say one word, "*Kate!*" and Kate only answer with a blush, and a smile, and an upturned face. For Love can put a volume in four letters; and souls say in a glance what a thousand words would only blunder about. Then there was the gallop home, and the merry cup of tea, and the saunter in the garden, and the long tender "good-bye" at the threshold where the damask roses made the air heavy with their sweetness.

So Lord Exham did not find his politics hard to bear with such delicious experiences between whiles.   And Kate?   What were Kate's experiences?   Oh, any woman who has once loved, any pure girl who longs to love, may divine them! For Love is always the same.   The tale he told Kate on the Atheling moors and under the damask roses was the very same tale he told high in Paradise by the four rivers where the first roses blew.

As the summer advanced, startling notes from the outside world forced themselves into this heavenly solitude.   On the twenty-sixth of June, King George died; and this death proved to be the first of a series of great events.   Piers felt it to be a warning bell.   It said to him, "The charming overture of Love, with its restless pleasure, its delicate hopes and fears, is nearly at an end."   He had been with Kate for three divine hours.   They had sat among the brackens at the foot of the mountains, and been twenty times on the very point of saying audibly the word " Love!" and twenty times had felt the delicious uncertainty of non-confession to be too sweet for surrender.   Nay, they did not reason about it; they simply obeyed that wise, natural self-restraint which knew its own hour, and would not hurry it.

With a sigh of rapture, they rose as the sun began to wester, and rode slowly back to Atheling. No one was at the door to receive them, and Kate wondered a little; but when they entered the hall, the omission was at once understood.   There was

a large open fireplace at the northern extremity,
and over it the Atheling arms, with their motto,
"*Feare God! Honour the Kinge! Laus Deo!*"
Squire Atheling was draping this panel with
crape; and Mrs. Atheling stood near him with
some streamers of the gloomy fabric in her
hands. She pointed to the King's picture —
which already wore the emblem of mourning —
and said, "The King is dead."

"The King lives! God save the King!" replied
the Squire, instantly. "God save King William
the Fourth!"

Then all the clocks in the house were stopped,
and draped, and when this ceremony was over,
they had tea together. And as it is a Yorkshire
custom to make funeral feasts, Mrs. Atheling
gave to the meal an air of special entertainment.
The royal Derby china added its splendour to the
fine old silver and delicate damask. There were
delicious cheese-cakes, and Queen's-cakes, and
savoury potted meats, and fresh crumpets; and
the ripe red strawberries filled the room with
their ethereal scent. No one was at all depressed
by the news. If King George was dead, King
William was alive; and the Squire thought,
"Everything might be hoped from 'The Sailor
King.' Why!" he said, "he is that good-
natured he won't say a bad word about the
Reformers; though, God knows, they are a disgrace to themselves, and to all that back them
up."

"There will now be a general election," said Exham positively.

"To be sure," answered the Squire. "And it is to be hoped we may get together a few men that will take the Bull of Reform by the horns, and put a stop to that nonsense forever in England."

"Before they do that," said Mrs. Atheling, "they will have to consider the swarms of people they have brought up in dirt, and rags, and misery. For if they don't, they will bring ruin to the nation that owns them."

"King William is a fighter. He will back the Law with bayonets, if he thinks it right," said the Squire.

Mrs. Atheling looked at him indignantly. Then, putting her cup down with unmistakable emphasis, she exclaimed, "The Lord forgive thee, John Atheling! I'll say one thing, and I'll say it now, and forever, it isn't law backed with bayonets that has saved England so far; it is the bit of religion in every man's heart, and his trust that somehow God will see him righted. If it wasn't for that it would have been all up with our set long ago.

"That is just the way women talk politics," said the Squire, with some contempt. "If there was nothing else in this Reform business to make a man sick, the way they have given in to women, and got them to form clubs and make speeches, is enough to set any sensible person against Reform; and if there is no way of talking people into doing what is right — then they must be *made* to do right; and that's all there is about it."

"Very well, John; but there are two sides to play at making other people do right. I'll tell you one thing, the Government will have to take a lot of things into consideration before they put their trust in backing law with bayonets. It won't work! Let them start doing it, and we shall all find ourselves in a wrong box."

"I think there is much good sense in what Mrs. Atheling believes," said Lord Exham.

"And as for the Reformers getting round the women of the country," she continued, "that is as it should be. Men have done all the governing for six thousand years; and, in the main, they have made a very bad job of it. Happen, a few kind-hearted women would help things forwarder. There is going to be some alterations, you may depend upon it, John."

"Father," said Kate, "you had better not argue with mother. She knows a deal more about the country than you think she does; and mother is always right."

"To be sure, Kate. To hear mother talk, she knows a lot; but if she would take my advice, she would forget a lot, and try and learn something better." Then touching his wife's hand, he continued, "Maude, I always did believe thou wert in favour of the land, and the law, and the King."

"I don't know that I ever said such a thing, John; but thou mayst have believed it. What I *thought*, was another matter. And I am beginning to think aloud now, that makes all the difference."

Such divided opinions were in every household; and yet, upon the whole, the death of the selfish, intolerant George was a hopeful event. When people are desperate, any change is a promise; and William had a reputation not only for good nature, but also for that love of fair play which is the first article of an Englishman's personal creed. He came to the throne on the twenty-sixth of June; and on the twenty-ninth Parliament resumed its sittings. Mr. Brougham led the opposition, and violent debates and unmeasured language distinguished the short session. The Duke of Wellington, representing the Government, was prominently bitter against Reform of every kind; and Mr. Brougham boldly declared that any Minister now hoping to rule either by royal favour or military power would be overwhelmed. In less than a month the King prorogued Parliament in person, and in so doing, congratulated his country on the tranquillity of Europe. Forty-eight hours afterwards, France was insurgent, and Paris in arms. Three days of most determined fighting followed; and then Charles the Tenth was driven from his throne, and the white flag of the Bourbon tyranny gave place to the Tri-colour of Liberty.

Now if there had been a direct electric or magnetic current between England and the Continent, the effect could not have been more sympathetically startling; and these three memorable "Days of July" in Paris impelled forward, with an irresistible impetus, the cause of freedom in England. The nobility and the landed gentry were gravely aware of this effect; and the great middle class, and the working men in every county, were stirred to more hopeful and united action. Far and wide the people began anew to express, in various ways, their determination to have the Tory Ministers dismissed, and a Liberal Government in favour of Reform inaugurated.

For the first time the Squire was anxious. For the first time he saw and felt positive symptoms of insubordination among his own people. Pickering's barns were burnt one night; and a few nights afterwards, Rudby's hay-ricks. Squire Atheling was a man of prompt action; one well disposed to do in his own manor what he expected the Government to do in the country, — take the Reform bull by the horns. He sent for all his labourers to meet him in the farm court at Atheling; and when they were gathered there, he stood up on the stone wall which enclosed one side of it and said in his strong, resonant voice, —

" Now, men of Atheling manor and village, you have been sulky and ugly for two or three weeks. You are n't sulky and ugly without

knowing *why* you are so. If you are Yorkshire-
men worth your bread and bacon, you will out
with your grievance — whatever it is. Tom Gisburn, what is it?"

"We can't starve any longer, Squire. We
want two shillings a week more wages. Me and
mine would hev been in t' churchyard if thy
Missis hed been as hard-hearted as thysen."

"I will give you all one shilling a week more."

"Nay, but a shilling won't do. Thy Missis is
good, and Miss Kate is good; but we want our
rights; and we hev made up our minds that two
shillings a week more wage will nobbut barely
cover them. We are varry poor, Squire! Varry
poor indeed!"

The man spoke sadly and respectfully; and the
Squire looked at him, and at the stolid, anxious
faces around with an angry pity. "I'll tell you
what, men," he continued; "everything in England is going to the devil. Englishmen are getting as ill to do with as a lot of grumbling,
contrary, bombastic Frenchers. If you'll promise
me to stand by the King, and the land, and the
laws, and give these trouble-making Reformers a
dip in the horse-pond if any of them come to
Atheling again — why, then, I will give you all —
every one of you — two shillings a week more
wage."

"Nay, Squire, we'll not sell oursens for two
shillings a week; not one of us — eh, men?" and
Gisburn looked at his fellows interrogatively.

"Sell oursens!" replied the Squire's black-smith, a big, hungry-looking fellow in a leather apron; "no! no, Squire! Thou oughtest to know us better. Sell oursens! Not for all the gold guineas in Yorkshire! We'll sell thee our labour for two shilling a week more wage, and thankful; but our will, and our good-will, thou can't buy for any money."

There was a subdued cheer at these words from the men, and the Squire's face suddenly lightened. His best self put his lower self behind him. "Sawley," he answered, "thou art well nick-named 'Straight-up!' and I don't know but what I'm very proud of such an independent, honour-able lot of men. Such as you won't let the land suffer. Remember, you were all born on it, and you'll like enough be buried in it. Stand by the land then; and if two shillings a week more wage will make you happy, you shall have it, — if I sell the gold buttons off my coat to pay it. Are we friends now?"

A hearty shout answered the question, and the Squire continued, "Then go into the barn, and eat and drink your fill. You'll find a barrel of old ale, and some roast beef, and wheat bread there."

In this way he turned the popular discontent from Atheling, and doubtless saved his barns and hay-ricks; but he went into his house angry at the men, and angry at his wife and daughter. They had evidently been aiding and succouring these discontents and their families; and — as

he took care to point out to Kate — evil and
not good had been the result. "I have to give
now as a right," he said, "what thee and thy
mother have been giving as a kindness!" And
his temper was not improved by hearing from
the barn the noisy "huzzas" with which the name
of "the young Squire" was received, and his
health drank.

"Wife, and son, and daughter! all of them
against me! I wonder what I have done to be
served in such a way?" he exclaimed sorrowfully.
And then Kate forgot everything about politics.
She said all kinds of consoling words without
any regard for the Reform Bill, and, with the
sweetest kisses, promised her father whatever she
thought would make him happy. It is an unreasonable, delightful way that belongs to loving
women; and God help both men and women when
they are too wise for such sweet deceptions!

Yet the Squire carried a hot, restless heart to
the Duke's meeting that night; and he was not
pleased to find that the tactics he had used with
his labourers met with general and great dis-
approval. Those men who had already suffered
loss, and those who knew that they had gone
beyond a conciliating policy, said some ugly
words about "knuckling down," and it required
all the Duke's wisdom and influence to represent
it as "a wise temporary concession, to be recalled as soon as the election was over, and the
Tory Government safely reinstalled."

Upon the whole, then, Squire Atheling had not
much satisfaction in his position; and every day
brought some new tale of thrilling interest. All
England was living a romance; and people got
so used to continual excitement that they set the
homeliest experiences of life to great historical
events. During the six weeks following the death
of King George the Fourth occurred the new
King's coronation, the dissolution of Parliament,
the " Three Days of July," and the landing of the
exiled French King in England; all of these
things being accompanied by agrarian outrages
in the farming districts, the destruction of machin-
ery in the manufacturing towns, and constant
political tumults wherever men congregated.

The next six weeks were even more restless
and excited. The French King was a constant
subject of interest to the Reformers; for was he
not a stupendous example of the triumph of
Liberal principles? He was reported first at
Lulworth Castle in Devonshire. Then he went
to Holyrood Palace in Edinburgh. The Scotch
Reformers resented his presence, and perpetually
insulted him, until Sir Walter Scott made a
manly appeal for the fallen tyrant. And while
the Bourbon sat in Holyrood, a sign and a
text for all lovers of Freedom, England was in
the direst storm and stress of a general election.
The men of the Fen Country were rising. The
Universities were arming their students. There
was rioting in this city and that city. The Tories

were gaining. The Reformers were gaining. Both sides were calling passionately on the women of the country to come to their help, without it seeming to occur to either that if women had political influence, they had also political rights.

But the end was just what all these events predicated. When the election was over, the Tory Government had lost fifty votes in the House of Commons; but Piers Exham was Member of Parliament for the borough of Gaythorne, and Squire Atheling was the Representative of the Twenty-two Tory citizens of the village of Asketh.

CHAPTER FIFTH

ANNABEL VYNER

THE first chapter of Kate's and Piers' love-story was told to these stirring events. They were like a *trumpet obligato* in the distance thrilling their hearts with a keener zest and a wider sympathy. True, the sympathy was not always in unison, for Piers was an inflexible partisan of his own order, yet in some directions Kate's feelings were in perfect accord. For instance, at Exham Hall and at Atheling Manor-house, there was the same terror of the mob's firebrand, and the same constant watch for its prevention. These buildings were not only the cherished homes of families; they were houses of national pride and record. Yet many such had perished in the unreasoning anger of multitudes mad with suffering and a sense of wrong; and the Squire and the Lord alike kept an unceasing watch over their habitations. On this subject, all were unanimous; and the fears, and frights, and suspicions relating to it drew the families into much closer sympathy.

After the election was over, there was a rapid subsidence of public feeling; the people had

6

taken the first step triumphantly; and they were willing to wait for its results. Then the Richmoor family began to consider an immediate removal to London, and, as a preparatory courtesy, gave a large dinner party at the Castle. As Kate was not yet in society, she had no invitation; but the Squire and Mrs. Atheling were specially honoured guests.

"The Squire has been of immense service to me," said Richmoor to his Duchess. "A man so sincere and candid I have seldom met. He has spoken well for us, simply and to the point, and I wish you to pay marked attention to Mrs. Atheling."

"Of course, if you desire it, I will do so. Who was Mrs. Atheling? Is she likely to be detrimental in town or troublesome?"

"She is the daughter of the late Thomas Hardwicke, of Hardwicke — as you know, a very ancient county family. She had a good fortune; in fact, she brought the Squire the Manor of Belward."

"In appearance, is she presentable?"

"She was very handsome some years ago. I have not seen her for a long time."

"I dare say she has grown stout and red; and she will probably wear blue satin in honour of her husband's Tory principles. These county dames always think it necessary to wear their party colours. I counted eleven blue satin dresses at our last election dinner."

" Even if she does wear blue satin, I should like you to be exceedingly civil to her."

" I suppose you know that Piers has been at Atheling a great deal. I heard in some way that — in fact, Duke, that Piers and Miss Atheling were generally considered lovers."

The Duke laughed. " I think I understand Piers," he said. " These incendiary terrors have drawn people together; and there has also been the election business as well. Many perfectly necessary natural causes have taken Piers to Atheling."

" Miss Atheling, for instance ! "

" Oh, perhaps so ! Why not? When I was a young man, I thought it both necessary and natural to have a pretty girl to ride and walk with. But riding and walking with a lovely girl is one thing; marrying her is another. Piers knows that he is expected to marry Annabel Vyner; he knows that for many reasons it will be well for him to do so. And above all other considerations, Piers puts his family and his caste."

The Duke's absolute confidence in his son satisfied the Duchess. She looked upon her husband as a man of wonderful penetration and invincible wisdom. If he was not uneasy about Piers and Miss Atheling, there was no necessity for her to carry an anxious thought on the subject; and she was glad to be fully released from it. Yet she had more than a passing curiosity about Kate's mother. The Squire she had frequently seen, both in the pink of the hunting-field and in the quieter dress of the dinner-table. But it so happened that she had never met Mrs. Atheling; and, on entering the great drawing-room, her eyes sought the only lady present who was a stranger to her.

Mrs. Atheling was standing at the Duke's side; and she went directly to her, taking note, as she did so, of the beauty, style, and physical grace that distinguished the lady. She saw that she wore a gown — not of blue — but of heavy black satin, that it fell away from her fine throat and shoulders, and showed her arms in all their exquisite form and colour. She saw also that her dark hair was dressed well on the top of the head in *bouillonés* curls, and that the only ornament she wore was among them, — a comb of wrought gold set with diamonds, — and that otherwise neither brooch nor bracelet, pendant nor ruffle of lace broke the noble lines of her figure or the rich folds of her gown. And the Duchess was both astonished and pleased with a toilet so distinguished; she assured herself in this passing investigation that Mrs. Atheling was quite " presentable," and also probably desirable.

The favourable impression was strengthened in that hour after dinner when ladies left to their own devices either become disagreeable or confidential. The Duchess and Mrs. Atheling fell into the latter mood, and their early removal to London was the first topic of conversation.

"We have no house in town," said Mrs. Atheling; "but the Squire has rented one that belonged to the late General Vyner. It is in very good condition, I hear, though we may have to stay a few days at ' *The Clarendon.*' "

"How strange! I mean that it is strange you should have rented the General's house. Did you make the arrangement with the Duke?"

"No, indeed; with a Mr. Pownell who is a large house agent."

"Mr. Pownell attends to the Duke's London property. I am sure he will be delighted to know his old friend's home is in such good hands. I wonder if you have heard that the Duke is General Vyner's executor and the guardian of his daughter?"

Mrs. Atheling made a motion indicative of her ignorance and her astonishment, and the Duchess continued, "It is quite a charge everyway; but there was a life-long friendship between the two men, and Annabel will come to us almost like a daughter."

"A great charge though," answered Mrs. Atheling, "especially if she is yet to educate."

"Her education is finished. She is twenty-two years of age. It is her wealth which will make my position an anxious one. It is not an easy thing to chaperon a great heiress."

"And if she is beautiful, that will add to the difficulty," said Mrs. Atheling.

"I have never seen Miss Vyner. I cannot tell

you whether she is beautiful or not so. She joins us in London, and my first duty will be to present her at the next drawing-room."

A little sensitive pause followed this statement, — a pause so sensitive that the Duchess divined the desire in Mrs. Atheling's heart; and Mrs. Atheling felt the hesitancy and wavering inclination weighing her wish in the thoughts of the Duchess. A sudden, straight glance from Mrs. Atheling's eyes decided the question.

"I should like to present Miss Atheling at the same time, if you have no objection," she added. And Mrs. Atheling's pleasure was so great, and her thanks so candid and positive, that the Duchess accepted the situation she had placed herself in with apparent satisfaction. Yet she wondered *why* she had made the offer. She felt as if the favour had been obtained against her will. She was half afraid in the very moment of the proposal that she was doing an imprudent thing. But when she had done it, she never thought of withdrawing from a position she must have taken voluntarily. On the contrary, she affected a great interest in the event, and talked of "the ceremonies Miss Atheling must make herself familiar with," of the probable date at which the function would take place, and of the dress and ornaments fitting for the occasion. "And the young people must meet each other as soon as possible," she continued.

Then the gentlemen entered the drawing-room,

and the groups **scattered**. The Duchess left Mrs.
Atheling; and Lord Exham took the chair she
vacated. **And** the happy mother was far too
simple, and too single-hearted to keep her pleasure to herself. She told Exham of the honour
intended Kate, and was a little dashed by the
manner in which he heard the news. He was
ashamed of it himself; but **he** could not at once
conquer the feeling of jealousy which assailed
him. It was the first time that the image of
Kate had been presented to him in company with
any but Piers Exham; and it gave **him real suf-**
fering to associate it with the attention and
admiration her beauty was sure to challenge
from all and sundry who would be present at
a court drawing-room. However, he made the
necessary assurances of pleasure, and Mrs.
Atheling was not a woman **who** went motive
hunting. **She** took a friend's words at their face
value.

Of course Kate was delighted, **and the Squire**
perhaps more so; for though he pretended to think
it "all a bit of nonsense," he opened his purse-
strings wide, and told his wife and daughter to
"help themselves." So the last few days at
Atheling were set to the dreams, and hopes,
and expectations of that gay social life which
always has a charm for youth. The clash of
party warfare, the wailing of want, the insistent
claims of justice, — all these voices were tempo-
rarily hushed. They had become monotonous

and, to Kate, suddenly uninteresting.   What was
the passing of a Reform Bill to a girl of nineteen,
when there was such a thing as a court drawing-
room in expectation?

It made her restless and anxious during the
two weeks occupied by their removal from
Atheling, and their settlement in London.   And
though the great city was full of wonder and
interest, and the new splendours of the Vyner
mansion very satisfactory, yet she could not
enjoy these things until there was some token
that the Duchess remembered, and intended to
fulfil her promise.   If only Piers had been in
London!   But Piers had been detained in Yorkshire, and was not expected until the formal
opening of Parliament, so that Kate could only
speculate, and wish, and fear, and in so doing
discount her present, and forestall her future
pleasures.   So prodigal is youth of happiness
and feeling!

However, at the end of October, Mrs. Atheling
received a letter from the Duchess.   It reminded
her of the drawing-room, and asked Miss Atheling's presence that evening in order to meet Miss
Vyner, and consult with her about the dresses to
be worn.   The visit was to be perfectly informal;
but even an informal visit to Richmoor House
was a great event to Kate.   And how pretty she
was when she came into her father's and mother's
presence, dressed for the occasion!   Mrs. Atheling looked at her with a smile of satisfaction, and

the Squire instantly rose, and took her on his
arm to the waiting carriage. This carriage was
the Squire's pet extravagance, and there was
not a more splendidly-appointed equipage in
London. Its horses were of the finest that Yorkshire breeds; the servant's liveries irreproachable
in taste; and when he saw his daughter's white
figure against its rich, blue linings he was satisfied
with his outlay.

Richmoor House was soon reached, and Kate
looked with wonder at its noble frontage, and its
stone colonnades. How much greater was her
wonder when she stepped into its interior vestibule! This vestibule was eighty-two feet long,
by more than twelve feet wide; it was orna-
mented with Doric columns and fine carvings,
and at each end there was a colossal staircase.
Up one of these stately ways Kate was con-
ducted into a gallery full of fine paintings, and
forming the corridor on which the one hundred
and fifty rooms appropriated to the use of the
family opened. Here, one servant after another
escorted her, until she was left with a woman-in-
waiting, who led her into a tiring-room and then
assisted Kate's own maid to remove her mistress's wrap and hood, and tie in pretty bows
her white satin sandals. The simple girl felt as
if she was in a dream, and she accepted all this
attention with the calm composure of a dream-
maiden. It was just like one of the old fairy
tales she used to live in. She was an enchanted

princess in an enchanted castle, and all she had to do, was to be passive in the hands of her destiny. Transient and illogical as this feeling was, it gave to her manner a singular air of serene confidence, and the Duchess noticed and approved it. She was relieved at once from any apprehension of anything *malapropos* in The Presence.

She went forward to meet Kate, and was both astonished and pleased at her *protégée's* appearance. The white llama in which she was gowned, its simple trimming of white satin, and its pretty accessories of white slippers and gloves satisfied both the pride and the taste of the Duchess. Any less attention to costume she would have felt as a want of respect towards herself; any more extravagant display would have indicated vulgar display and a due want of subordination to her own rank and age. But Kate offended no feeling, and she took her by the hand and led her down the long room. At its extremity there was a group of girls: one was standing; the others were sitting on a sofa before her. The eyes of all were fastened on Kate as she approached; but she was not disturbed by this scrutiny. She had all the strength and assurance which comes from a proper and moderate toilet; and she was even competent to do her own share of observation.

The three girls sitting on the sofa offered no points of remark or speculation. They were the three Ladies Anne, Mary, and Charlotte Warwick;

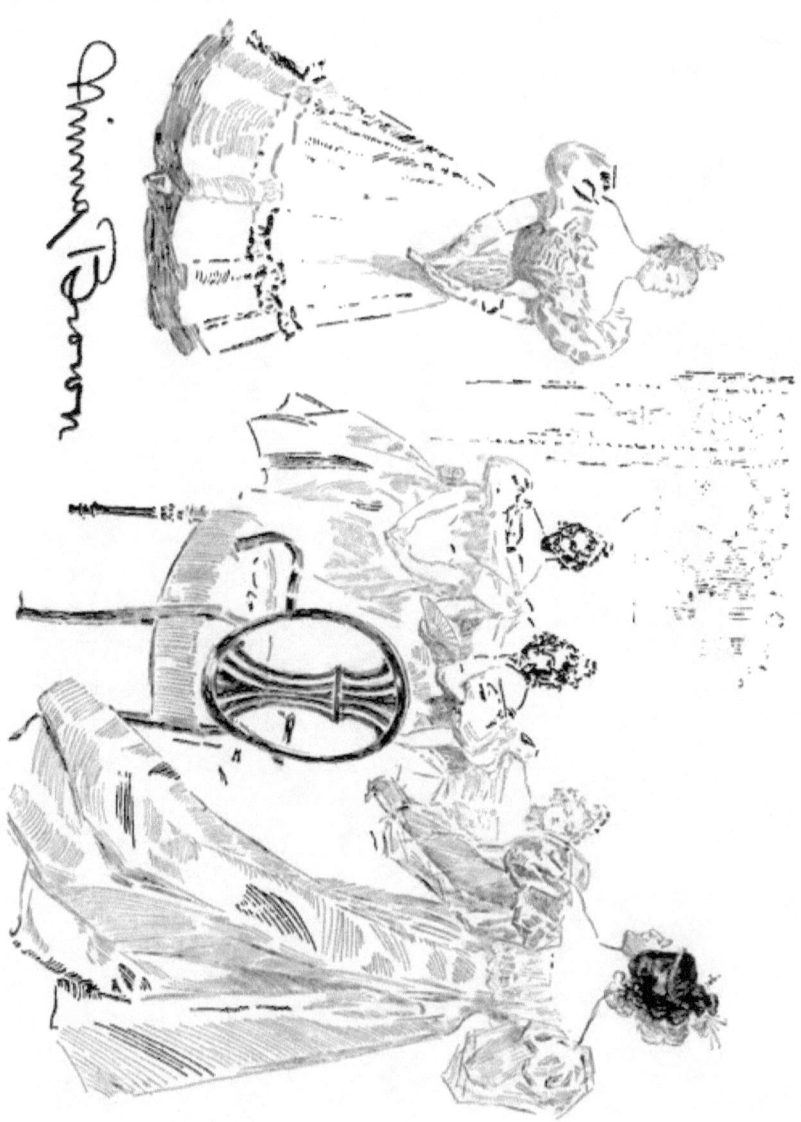

and all alike had the beauty of youth, the grace
of noble nurture, and the pretty garments indicative of their station. But the young lady standing was of a different character. Her personality
pervaded the space in which she stood; she
domineered with a look; and Kate knew instinctively that this girl was Annabel Vyner. The
knowledge came with a little shock, a sudden
failing of heart, a presentiment. She had given
her hand with a pleasant impulse, and without
consideration, to the Ladies Warwick; she did
not offer it to Annabel; and yet she was not
aware of the omission. All of these girls were
intending to make a Court *début*, and at that
moment were discussing its necessities. Kate
at first took little part in this discussion. Mrs.
Atheling had already decided on the costume
she thought most suitable for her daughter; and
Kate was quite satisfied with her choice. Miss
Vyner was however dictating to Lady Charlotte
Warwick what she ought to wear; and Kate
watched with a curious wonder this girlish oracle,
laying down laws for others her equal in age,
and far more than her equal in rank and social
position.

Miss Vyner was not beautiful; but she possessed an irresistible fascination. She was large,
and rather heavy. She reminded one of a rough-
hewn granite statue of old Egypt; and she was
just as magnificently imposing. Her hair was
long, and strong, and wavy; her eyes very black

and intrepid, but capable of liquid, languishing expressions, full of enchantment. Her nose, though thick and square at the end, had wide, sensitive nostrils; and her fine, red lips showed white and dazzling teeth. But it was the sense of power and plenitude of life which she possessed which gave her that natural authority, whose influence all felt, and few analysed or disputed.

She was quite aware that standing was a becoming posture, and that it gave to her a certain power over the girlish figures who seemed to sit at her feet. It was not long, however, before Kate felt an instinctive rebellion against the position assigned her; she knew that it put her in an unfair subordination; and she rose from her chair, and stood leaning against the Broadwood piano at her side. The action arrested Miss Vyner's attention. She stopped speaking in the middle of a sentence, and, looking steadily at Kate, said suavely, as she pushed the chair slightly, —

"Do sit down, Miss Atheling."

"No, thank you," answered Kate. "I have been sitting all day. I am tired of sitting."

Then Annabel gave her a still more searching look, and something came into Kate's eyes which she understood; for she smiled as she went on with her little dictation; but the thought in her heart was, "So you have thrown down the glove, Miss Atheling!"

Nothing however of this incipient defiance was noticeable; and Annabel's attention was almost immediately afterwards diverted from her companions. For in the middle of one of her fine descriptions of an Indian court, she observed a sudden loss of interest, and a simultaneous direction of every glance towards the upper end of the room. The Duchess was approaching, and with her, a young man in dinner costume. A crimson flush rushed over Kate's neck and face; she dropped her eyes, but could not restrain the faint smile that came and went like a flash of light.

"It is Lord Exham," she said in a low voice to Anne Warwick; and the Ladies nodded slightly, and continued a desultory conversation, they hardly knew what about. But Annabel stood erect and silent. She glanced once at Kate, and then turned the full blaze of her dazzling eyes upon the advancing nobleman. For once, their magnetic rays were ineffectual. The Duchess, on her son's arrival, had notified him of the ladies present; and Kate Atheling was the lodestar which drew his first attention. He had in the button-hole of his coat a few Michaelmas daisies, and after speaking to the other ladies, he put them into Kate's hand, saying, "I gathered them in Atheling garden. Do you remember the bush by the swing in the laurel walk? I thought you would like to have them." And Kate said "thank you" in the way that Piers perfectly understood and appreciated, though it seemed to be of the most formal kind.

The dinner was a family dinner, but far from being tiresome or dull. The Duke and Lord Exham had both adventures to tell. The latter in passing through a little market-town had seen the hungry people take the wheat from the grain-market by force, and said he had been delayed a little by the circumstance.

" But why? " asked the Duchess.

" There were some arrests made ; and after all, one cannot see hungry men and women punished for taking food." There was silence after this remark, and Kate glanced at Exham, whose veiled eyes, cast upon the glass of wine he held in his hand, betrayed nothing. But when he lifted them, they caught something from Kate's eyes, and an almost imperceptible smile passed from face to face. No one asked Exham for further particulars; and the Duke hurriedly changed the subject. " Where do you think I took lunch to-day? " he asked.

" At Stephen's," answered the Duchess.

" Not likely," he replied. " I am neither a fashionable officer, nor a dandy about town. If I had asked for lunch there, the waiters would have stared solemnly, and told me there was no table vacant."

" As you want horses, perhaps you went to Limmers," said Exham.

" No. I met a party of gentlemen and ladies

going to Whitbread's Brewery, and I went with them. We had a steak done on a hot malt shovel, and plenty of stout to wash it down. There were quite a number of visitors there; it has become one of the sights of London. Then I rode as far as the Philosophical Society, and heard a lecture on a new chemical force."

"The Archbishop does not approve of your devotion to Science," said the Duchess, reprovingly.

"I know it," he answered. "All our clergy regard Science as a new kind of sin. I saw the Archbishop later, at a very interesting ceremony, — the deposition in Whitehall Chapel of twelve Standards taken in Andalusia by the personal bravery of our soldiers."

"I wish I had seen that ceremony," said Kate.

"And I wish I had myself been one of the heroes carrying the Standard I had won," added Annabel.

The Duke smiled at the pretty volunteers, and continued, "It was a very interesting sight. Three royal Dukes, many Generals and foreign Ambassadors, and the finest troops in London were present. We had some good music, and a short religious service, and then the Archbishop deposited the flags on each side of the Altar."

"I like these military ceremonies," said the Duchess. "I shall not forget the Proclamation of Peace after Waterloo. What a procession of mediæval splendour it was!"

"I remember it, though I was only a little boy," said Exham. "The Proclamation was read three times, — at Temple Bar, at Charing Cross, and at The Royal Exchange. The blast of trumpets before and after each reading! — I can hear it yet!"

"And the Thanksgiving at St. Paul's after the procession was just as impressive," continued the Duchess. "The Prince Regent and the Duke of Wellington walked together, and Wellington carried the Sword of State. It was a gorgeous festival set to trumpets and drums, and the roll of organ music, and the seraphic singing of '*Lo! the conquering hero comes.*' The Duke could have asked England for anything he desired that day."

"Yet he is very unpopular now," said Kate, timidly. "Even my father thinks he carries everything with too high a hand."

"His military training must be considered, Miss Atheling," said the Duke. "And the country needs a tight rein now."

"He may hold it too tight," said Exham, in a low voice.

Then the conversation was turned to the theatres, and while they were talking, Squire Atheling was introduced. He had called to escort his daughter home; and after a short delay, Kate was ready to accompany him. The Duke and the Squire — who were deep in some item of political news — went to the entrance hall to-

gether; and Lord Exham took Kate's hand, and
led her down the great stairway. It was now
lighted with a profusion of wax candles in silver
candelabra. They were too happy to speak,
and there was no need of speech. Like two
notes of music made for each other, though dis-
similar, they were one; and the melody in the
heart of Piers was the melody in the heart of
Kate. The unison was perfect; why then should
it be explained? Very slowly they came down
the low broad steps, hardly feeling their feet
upon them; for spirit mingled with spirit, and
gave them the sense of ethereal motion.

When they reached the vestibule, Kate's maid
advanced and threw round her a wrap of pink
silk, trimmed with minever; and as Piers watched
the shrouding of her rose-like face in the pretty
hood, a sudden depression came like a cloud over
him. Oh, yes! True love has these moments of
deep gloom, in which intense feeling suspends
both movement and speech. He could only
look into the warm, secret foldings of silk and
fur which hid Kate's beauty; he had not even
the common words of courtesy at his command;
but Kate divined the much warmer "good-night"
that was masked by the formal bow and uncovered head.

After the departure of the Athelings, father
and son walked silently up the stairs together;
but at the top of them, the Duke paused and said,
" Piers, the King opens Parliament on the Second

7

of November. We have only three days' truce.
Then for the fight."

"We have foemen worthy of our steel. Grey
— Durham — Brougham — Russel and Graham.
They will not easily be put down."

"We shall win."

"Perhaps. The House of Lords is very near
of one mind. Will you come to my smoking-
room and have a pipe of Turkish?"

"I must see the ladies again; afterwards I may
do so."

With these words they parted, and Piers went
dreamily along the state corridor. In its dim,
soft light, he suddenly saw Miss Vyner approaching him. He was thinking of Kate; but he had
no wish to escape Annabel. He was even interested in watching her splendid figure in motion.
Only from some Indian loom had come that marvellous tissue of vivid scarlet with its embroidery
of golden butterflies. It made her look like
some superb flower. She smiled as she reached
Piers, and said, —

"I only am left to wish you a 'good-night
and happy dreams.' The Ladies Warwick were
sleepy, the Duchess longing to be rid of such a
lot of tiresome girls, and I — "

"What of 'I'?" he asked with a sudden, unaccountable interest.

"I am going to the Land where I always go
in sleep. I shut my eyes, and I am there."

"Then, 'Good-night.'"

" Good-night." She put her little, warm, brown hand, flashing with gems, into his; and then with one long, unwinking gaze — in which she caught Piers' gaze — she strangely troubled the young man. His blood grew hot as fire; his heart bounded; his face was like a flame; and he clasped her hand with an unconscious fervour. She laughed lightly, drew it away, and passed on. But as she did so, the Indian scarf she had over her arm trailed across his feet, and thrilled him like some living thing. He had a sense of intoxication, and he hurried forward to his own room, and threw himself into a chair.

"It is that strange perfume that clings around her," he said in a voice of controlled excitement. "I perceived it as soon as I met her. It makes me drowsy. It makes me feverish — and yet how delicious it is!" He threw his head backward, and lay with closed eyes, moving neither hand nor foot for some minutes. Then he rose, and began to walk about the room, lifting and putting down books, and papers, and odd trifles, as they came in the way of his restless fingers. And when at last he found speech, it was to reproach himself — his real self — the man within him.

"You, poor, weak, false-hearted lover!" he muttered bitterly. "Piers Exham! You hardly needed temptation. I am ashamed of you! Ashamed of you, Piers! Oh, Kate! I have been false to you. It was only a passing thought,

Kate; but you would not have given to another even a passing thought. Forgive me. *O Thou Dear One!*"

"Thou **Dear** One!" These three words had a meaning of inexpressible tenderness to him. For one night, — when as yet their Love was but learning to speak, — one warm, sweet July night, as they stood under the damask roses, he said to Kate, —

" How beautiful are the words and tones which your mother uses to the Squire. She does not speak thus to every one."

"No," replied Kate. "To strangers mother always says '*you.*' To those she loves, she says '*thou.*'"

And Piers answered, "Dear — if only—" and then he let the silence speak for him. But Kate understood, and she whispered softly, —

" *Thou Dear One!*"

It seemed to Piers as if no words to be spoken in time or in eternity could ever make those three words less sweet. They came to his memory always like a sigh of soft music on a breath of roses. And so it was at this hour. They filled his heart, they filled his room with soft delight. He stood still to realise their melody and their fragrance, the music of their sweet inflections, the perfume of their pure and perfect love.

" *Thou Dear One!*" He said these words again and again. " It has always been Kate and

Piers! Always *I* and *Thou* — and as for *the Other One* — "

This mental query, utterly unthought of and uncalled for, very much annoyed him. Who or What was it that suggested " The Other One"? Not himself; he was sure of that. He went to his father, and they talked of the King, and the Ministers, and the great Mr. Brougham, whom both King and Ministers feared — but all the time, and far below the tide of this restless conversation, Piers heard this very different one, —

"*I* and *Thou* !"

"And *the Other One*."

"There is no ' Other One.' "

"Annabel."

"No."

"If Annabel were Destiny?"

"Will is stronger than Destiny."

"If Annabel should be Will."

"Love is stronger than Will."

"It is Kate and Piers."

"And the Other One."

He grew impatient at this persistence of an idea that he had not evoked, that he had, in fact, denied. But he could not exorcise it. His very dreams were made and mingled of the two girls, — Kate, whom he loved, Annabel, who came like a splendid destiny to trouble love. In the pageant of sleep, he lost that will-power which controlled his life; he was tossed to-and-fro be-

tween blending shadows: Kate was Annabel;
Annabel was Kate; and the fretful, unreasonable
drama went on through restless hours, always
to the same tantalising refrain, —

"*I, Thou, and the Other One!*"

CHAPTER SIXTH

THE BEGINNING OF THE GREAT STRUGGLE

THERE is no eternity for nations. Individuals may be punished hereafter; nations are punished here. In the first years of the Nineteenth Century, Englishmen were mad on war; and though wise men warned them of the ruin that stalks after war, no one believed their report. The treasure that would have now fed the starving population of England, had been spent in killing Frenchmen. Bad harvests followed the war years, taxation was increased, wages were lowered and lowered, credit was gone, trade languished, hunger or scrimping carefulness was in every household. For the iniquitous Corn Laws of 1815, forbidding the importation of foreign grain, had raised English wheat to eighty shillings a quarter. And how were working men to buy bread at such a price? No wonder, they clamoured for a House of Commons that should represent their case, and repeal Acts that could only benefit one class, and inflict ruin and misery on all others.

A feeling therefore of intense anxiety pervaded the country on the Second of November, — the day on which the King was to open Parliament.

No one could work; every one was waiting for the King's speech.   He was as yet very popular; it was his first message to his people; and they openly begged him for some word of hope — some expression of sympathy for Reform.   He went in great state to Westminster, and was cheered by the city as he went.   "Will Your Majesty say a word for the poor?   God bless Your Majesty!   Stand by Reform!"   Such expressions assailed him on every hand; they were the prayers of a people wronged and suffering, yet disposed to be patient and loyal, and to seek Reform only to spare themselves and the country the ruth and ruin of Revolution.

Richmoor House was on the way of the royal procession, and Kate was there to watch it.   A little later, a great company began to assemble in its rooms; for the Duke had promised to bring, or to send, the earliest news of the event.   There was however an intense restlessness among these splendidly attired men and women.   They could not separate Reform from Revolution; and the French Revolution was yet red and bloody in their memories.   They still heard the thunder of those famous "Three Days of July," and there was constantly before their eyes, the heir of forty kings finding in a British palace an ignominious shelter.   Not only was this the case, but French noblemen, in poverty and exile, were earning precarious livings all around; and English noblemen and ladies looked forward with terror to a similar fate, if the Reformers obtained their desire. Indeed, Sir Robert Inglis had boldly prophesied, "Reform would sweep the House of Lords clear in ten years."

No wonder then the company waiting in Richmoor House were restless and anxious. Kate did not permit herself to speak, and Mrs. Atheling had very prudently remained in her own home. She had told the Squire she "must say what she thought, if she died for it!" and the Squire had answered, "To be sure, Maude. That is thy right; only, for goodness' sake, say it in thy own house!" But though Kate knew she would follow her mother's example, if she was brought to catechism on the subject, she did not have much fear of such a result; there were too many older ladies present, all of them desirous to express the hatreds and hopes of their class.

Yet it was these emotional, expressional women that Annabel Vyner naturally joined. She stood among them like a splendid incarnation of its spirit. She hoped vehemently that " Earl Grey and Lord John Russell would be beheaded as traitors;" she declared she would "go with delight to Tower Hill and see the axe fall." She flashed into contempt, when she spoke of Mr. Brougham. " Botany Bay and hard labour might do for him; and as for the waiting crowds in the streets, the proper thing was to shoot them down, like rabid animals." She wondered "the Duke of Wellington did not do so." These sentiments were vivified

by the passion that blazed in her black eyes and
flushed her brown face crimson, and by the gown
of bright yellow Chinese crape which she wore;
for it fluttered and waved with her impetuous
movements, and made a kind of luminous atmosphere around her.

"What a superb creature!" exclaimed Mr.
Disraeli to the Hon. Mrs. Norton. And Mrs.
Norton put up her glass and looked at Annabel
critically.

"Superb indeed — to look at. Would you like
to live with her?"

"It would be exciting."

"More so than your 'Vivian Grey,' which I
have just read. It is the book of the year."

"No, that honour belongs to a little volume of
poems by a young man called Tennyson. Get
it; you will read every word it contains."

"I am wedded to my idols, — Byron and Scott
and Keble. I am much interested at present
in those 'Imaginary Conversations' which that
queer Mr. Landor has given us. They are worth
reading, I assure you."

"But why read them? Listen to the 'Conversations' around us! They are of Revolution,
Civil War, Exile, and the Headsman. Could anything be more 'Imaginary'?"

"Who can tell? Here comes Richmoor. He
may be able to prognosticate. What a murmur
of voices! What invisible movement! Can you
divine the news from the messenger's face?"

"He thinks that he brings good news. He may be fatally wrong."

The Duke certainly thought that he brought good news. He was much excited. He came forward with his hands extended, palms upward.

"The King stands by us!" he cried. "God save the King!"

Twenty voices called out at once, "What did he say?"

"He said plainly that in spite of the public opinion expressed so loudly in recent elections, Reform would have no sanction from the Government. I only stayed until the end of the royal speech. Yet in some way rumours of its purport must have reached the street. In the neighbourhood, there was much agitation, and even anger."

Then Kate slipped away from the excited throng. Piers had evidently remained for the discussion on the King's speech; and it might be midnight when the House adjourned. The winter day was fast darkening; she ordered her chairmen, and the pretty sedan was brought into the vestibule for her. She had no fear, though the very gloom and silence of the waiting crowd was more indicative of danger than noise or threats would have been. When she reached Hyde Park corner, however, angry faces pressed around a little too close, and she was alarmed. Then she threw back her hood and looked out calmly at the crowd, and immediately a clear voice cried out, "It is Edgar Atheling's sister!

Take good care of her!"   And there was a cheer
and a cry, and about twenty men closed round
the chair, and saw it safely to its destination.

Then Cecil North stepped to the door and
opened it. "I knew it was you, Mr. North!"
cried Kate. "I knew your voice. How kind of
you to come all the way with me! How glad
mother will be to see you!"

"I cannot wait a moment, Miss Atheling. Can
you give me any news?"

"Yes. The King says the Government will
not sanction Reform."

"Who told you this?"

"The Duke of Richmoor — not an hour ago."

"Then 'good-night.' I am afraid there will be
trouble."

Mrs. Atheling and Kate were afraid also. The
murmur of the crowd grew louder and louder as
the tenor of the King's speech became known;
and many a time they wished themselves in the
safety and solitude of their Yorkshire home. So
they talked, and watched, and listened until the
night was far advanced. Then they heard the
firm, strong step of the Squire on the pavement;
and his imperative voice in denial of something
said by a group of men whom he passed. In a
few minutes he entered the drawing-room with
an angry light in his eyes, and the manner of a
man exasperated by opposition.

"Whatever is it, John? Is there trouble
already?" asked Mrs. Atheling.

"Plenty of it, and like to be more. The King has spoken like a fool."

"John Atheling! His Majesty!"

"His Imbecility! I tell you what, Maude, there has been enough said to-day, and to-night, to set all the dogs of civil war loose. Give me a bit of eating, and I will tell thee and Kitty what a lot of idiots are met together in Westminster."

The Squire always wanted a deal of waiting upon; and in a few minutes his valet was bringing him easy slippers and a loose coat, and two handmaidens serving a tray, bearing game pastry, and fruit tarts, and clotted cream. But he would take neither wine, nor strong ale, —

"Water is all a man wants that gets himself stirred up in the House of Commons," he said. "And if I had been in the Lords' House, I would have needed nothing but a strait-jacket."

He had hardly sat down to eat, when Piers Exham came in. No one could have been more welcome, and the young man's troubled face brightened in the sunshine of Kate's smile, and in the honest kindness of the Squire's greeting. "I was just going to tell Mrs. Atheling all I knew about to-night's blundering," he said; "but now we will have your report first, for you have seen the Duke, I'll warrant."

"Indeed, Squire, the Duke is not dissatisfied — though the general opinion is, that the Duke of Wellington has committed an egregious mistake."

"I should n't wonder. Wellington does not know the difference between a field-marshal and a Cabinet Minister. What did he say?"

"He said that as long as he held any office in the Government, he would resist Reform. He said there was no need of Reform; that we had the best government in the world. The Duke of Devonshire, whom I have just seen, told me that this statement produced a feeling of the utmost dismay, even in the calm atmosphere of the House of Lords."

"Calm!" interrupted the Squire. "You had better say, Incurable prosiness."

"Wellington noticed the suppressed excitement, the murmur, and the movement, and asked Devonshire in a whisper, 'What can I have said to cause such great disturbance?' And Devonshire shrugged his shoulders and answered candidly, 'You have announced the fall of your government, that is all.'"

"Wellington considers the nation as a mutinous regiment," answered the Squire. "He thinks the arguments for Reformers ought to be cannon balls; but Englishmen will not endure a military government."

"It would be better than a mob government, Squire. Remember France."

"Englishmen are not Frenchmen," said Kate. "You ought to remember *that*, Piers. Englishmen are the most fair, just, reasonable, brave, loyal, honourable people on the face of the earth!"

"Well done, Kitty!" cried the Squire. "It takes a little lass like thee to find adjectives plenty enough, and good enough, for thy own. My word! I wish thou couldst tell the Duke of Wellington what thou thinkest of his fellow-citizens. He would happen trust them more, and treat them better."

"There is Mr. Peel too," she continued. "Both he and the Duke of Wellington are always down on the people. And yet the Duke has led these same people from one victory to another; and Mr. Peel is one of the people. His father was a day-labourer, and he ought to be proud of it; William Cobbett is, and William Cobbett is a greater man than Robert Peel."

"Now then, Kitty, that is far enough; for thou art wrong already. Cobbett isn't a greater man than Peel; he isn't a great man at all, he is only a clever man. But the man for my money is Henry Brougham. He drives the world before him. He is a multitude. He had just one idea to-day,—Reform and again Reform. He played that tune finely to the House, and they danced to it like a miracle. Much good it will do them!"

"He was scarcely decent," said Piers. "He gave notice, as you must have heard, in the most aggressive manner that he should bring 'Reform' to an immediate issue."

"Yes," answered the Squire. "There is doubtless a big battle before us. But, mark my words, it will not be with Wellington and Peel. They signed their own resignation this afternoon."

"That is what my father thinks," said Piers.

"If Wellington could only have held his tongue!" said the Squire, bitterly.

"And if Daniel O'Connell would only cease making fun of the Government."

"That man!   He is nobody!"

"You mistake, Squire.   His buffoonery is fatal to our party.   I tell you that Ridicule is the lightning that kills.   Has not Aristophanes tossed his enemies for the scorn and laughter of a thousand cities for a thousand years?   I fear O'Connell's satire and joking, far more than I fear Grey's statesmanship, or Durham's popularity."

Then Piers turned to Kate, and asked if she had seen the royal procession. And she told him about her visit, and about Mr. North's interference for her safety, and his escort of her home. Piers was much annoyed at this incident. He begged her not to venture into the streets until public feeling had abated, or was controlled, and asked with singular petulance, "Who is this Mr. North? He plays the mysterious Knight very well. He interferes too much."

"I was grateful for his interference."

"Why did you not remain at Richmoor until I returned?   I expected it, Kate."

"I was afraid; and I knew my mother would

be anxious — and I felt so sad among strangers. You know, Piers, I have always lived among my own people — among those who loved me."

This little bit of conversation had taken place while the tray was being removed, and the Squire and Mrs. Atheling were talking about the engagements for the next day, so that definite orders might be given concerning the carriage and horses. The movements of the servants had enabled Piers and Kate, quite naturally, to withdraw a little from the fireside group; and when Kate made her tender assertion, about living with those who loved her, Piers's heart was full to overflowing. This girl of sweet nature, with her innocent beauty and ingenuous expressions, possessed his noblest feelings. He clasped her hands in his, and said, —

"Oh, Kate! I loved you when you were only twelve years old; I love you now beyond all measure of words. And you love me? Speak, Dear One!"

"I love none but thee!"

The next moment she was standing before her father and mother. Piers held her hand. He was talking to them in low but eager tones, yet she did not realise a word, until he said, —

"Give her to me, my friends. We have loved each other for many years. We shall love each other for ever. She is the wife of my soul. Without her, I can only half live." Then bending to Kate, he asked her fondly, "Do you love me,

Kate? Do you love me? Ask your heart about it. Tell us truly, do you love me?"

Then she lifted her sweet eyes to her lover, her father, and her mother, and answered, "I love Piers with all my heart."

The Squire was much troubled and affected. "This is taking a bit of advantage, Piers," he said. "There is a time for everything, and this is not my time for giving my little girl away."

"Speak for us, Mrs. Atheling," said Piers.

"Nay, I think the Squire is quite right," she replied. "Love isn't worth much if Duty does not stand with it."

"And there is far more, Piers," continued the Squire, "in such a marriage as you propose than a girl's and a lover's 'yes.' When the country has settled a bit, we will talk about love and wedding. I can't say more for my life, can I, Mother?"

"It is enough," answered Mrs. Atheling. "Why, we might have a civil war, and what not! To choose a proper mate is good enough; but it is quite as important to choose a proper time for mating. Now then, this is not a proper time, when everything is at ups-and-downs, and this way and that way, and great public events, that no one can foretell, crowding one on the neck of the other. Let things be as they are, children. If you only knew it, you are in the Maytime of your lives. I wouldn't hurry it over, if I was you. It won't come back again."

Then Kate kissed her father, and her mother, and her lover; and Piers kissed Kate, and Mrs. Atheling, and put his hand into the Squire's hand; and the solemn joy of betrothal was there, though it was not openly admitted.

In truth the Squire was much troubled at events coming to any climax. He would not suffer his daughter to enter into an engagement not openly acknowledged and approved by both families; and yet he was aware that at the present time the Duke would consider any subject — not public or political — as an interruption, perhaps as an intrusion. Besides which, the Squire's own sense of honour and personal pride made him averse to force an affair so manifestly to the pre-ferment of his daughter. It looked like taking advantage of circumstances — of presuming upon a kindness; in fact, the more Squire Atheling thought of the alliance, the less he was disposed to sanction it. Under no circumstances, could he give Kate such a fortune as the heir of a great Dukedom had a right to expect. She must enter the Richmoor family at a disadvantage — perhaps even on sufferance.

"No! by the Lord Harry, no!" he exclaimed. "I 'll have none of the Duke's toleration on any matter. I am sorry I took his seat. I wish Edgar was here — he ought to be here, looking after his mother and sister, instead of setting up rogues on Glasgow Green against their King and Country! Of course, there is Love to reckon

with, and Love does wonders — but it is money
that makes marriage."

With such reflections, and many others growing
out of them, the Squire hardened his heart, and
strengthened his personal sense of dignity, until he
almost taught himself to believe the Duke had already wounded it.   In this temper he was quite
inclined to severely blame his wife for not "putting a stop to the nonsense when it first began."

"John," she answered, "we are both of a
piece in that respect."

"On my honour, Mother."

"Don't say it, John.   You used to laugh at the
little lass going off with Edgar and Piers fishing.
You used to tease her about the gold brooch
Piers gave her.   Many a time you have called
her to me, ' the little Duchess.' "

"Wilt thou be quiet? "

"I am only reminding thee."

"Thou needest not.   I wish thou wouldst remind thy son that he has a sister that he might
look after a bit."

"I can look after Kate without his help.   He
is doing far better business than hanging around
Dukes."

"If thou wantest a quarrel this morning, Maude,
I'm willing to give thee one.   I say, Edgar ought
to be here."

"What for?   He is doing work that we will all
be proud enough of some day.   Thou oughtest to
be helping him, instead of abusing him.   I want

thee to open this morning's *Times*, and read the speech he made in Glasgow City Hall. Thou couldst not have made such a speech to save thy life."

" Say, I *would not* have made it, and then thou wilt say the very truth."

" Read it."

" Not I."

"Thou darest not. Thou knowest it would make thee turn round and vote with the Reformers."

" Roast the Reformers! I wish I could! I would not have believed thou couldst have said such a thing, Maude. How darest thou even think of thy husband as a turncoat? Why, in politics, it is the unpardonable sin."

" It is nothing of the kind. Not it! It is far worse to stick to a sin, than to turn from it. If I was the biggest of living Tories, and I found out I was wrong, I would stand up before all England and turn my coat in the sight of everybody. I would that. When I read thy name against Mr. Brougham bringing up Reform, I'll swear I could have cried for it!"

" I wouldn't wonder. All the fools are not dead yet. But I hear Kitty and her lover coming. I wonder what they are talking and laughing about?"

" Thou hadst better not ask them. I'll warrant, Piers is telling her the same sort of nonsense, thou usedst to tell me; and they will both of them, believe it, no doubt."

At these words Piers and Kate entered the room together. They were going for a gallop in the Park; and they looked so handsome, and so happy, that neither the Squire nor Mrs. Atheling could say a word to dash their pleasure. The Squire, indeed, reminded Piers that the House met at two o'clock; and Piers asked blankly, like a man who neither knew, nor cared anything about the House, "Does it?" With the words on his lips, he turned to Kate, and smiling said, "Let us make haste, my dear. The morning is too fine to lose." And hand in hand, they said a hasty, joyful "good-bye" and disappeared. The father and mother watched them down the street until they were out of sight. As they turned away from the window, their eyes met, and Mrs. Atheling smiled. The Squire looked abashed and disconcerted.

"Why didst not thou put a stop to such nonsense, John?" she asked.

Fortunately at this moment a servant entered to tell the Squire his horse was waiting, and this interruption, and a rather effusive parting, let him handsomely out of an embarrassing answer.

Then Mrs. Atheling wrote a long letter to her son, and looked after the ways of her household, and knit a few rounds on her husband's hunting stocking, and as she did so thought of Kate's future, and got tired of trying to settle it, and so left it, as a scholar leaves a difficult problem, for the Master to solve. And when she had reached this point Kate came into the room. She had removed her habit, and the joyous look which had been so remarkable two hours before was all gone. The girl was dashed and weary, and her mother asked her anxiously, " If she was sick? "

" No," she answered; " but I have been annoyed, and my heart is heavy, and I am tired."

" Who or what annoyed you, child? "

" I will tell you. Piers and I had a glorious ride, and were coming slowly home, when suddenly the Richmoor liveries came in sight. I saw the instant change on Piers's face, and I saw Annabel slightly push the Duchess and say something. And the Duchess drew her brows together as we passed each other, and though she bowed, I could see that she was angry and astonished. As for Annabel, she laughed a little, scornful laugh, and threw me a few words which I could not catch. It was a most unpleasant meeting; after it Piers was very silent. I felt as if I had done something wrong, and yet I was indignant at myself for the feeling."

" What did Piers say? "

" He said nothing that pleased me. He fastened his eyes on Annabel, — who was marvellously dressed in rose-coloured velvet and minever, — and she clapped her small hands together and nodded to him in a familiar way, and, bending slightly forward, passed on. And after that he did not talk much. All his love-making was over, and I thought he was glad when we reached home. I think Annabel will certainly take my lover from me."

"You mean that she has made up her mind to be Duchess of Richmoor?"

"Yes."

"Well, my dear Kate, a beautiful woman is strong, and money is stronger; but *True Love conquers all.*"

CHAPTER SEVENTH

THE LOST RING

"TO-MORROW some new light may come, and you will see things another way, Kitty." This was Mrs. Atheling's final opinion, and Kitty was inclined to take all the comfort there was in it. She was sitting then in her mother's room, watching her dress for dinner, and admiring, as good daughters will always do, everything she could find to admire about the yet handsome woman.

"You have such beautiful hair, Mother. I would n't wear a cap if I was you," she said.

"Your father likes a bit of lace on my head, Kitty. He says it makes me look more motherly."

She was laying the "bit of lace" on her brown hair as she spoke. Then she took from her open jewel case, two gold pins set with turquoise, and fastened the arrangement securely. Kitty watched her with loving smiles, and finally changed the whole fashion of the bit of lace, declaring that by so doing she had made her mother twenty years younger. And somehow in this little toilet ceremony, all Kitty's sorrow passed away, and she said, "I wonder where my fears are gone to,

Mother; for it does not now seem hard to hope
that all is just as it was."

"To be sure, Kitty, I never worry much about
fears. Fears are mostly made of nothing; and
in the long run they are often a blessing. Without fears, we could n't have hopes; now could
we?"

"Oh, you dear, sweet, good Mother! I wish I
was just like you!"

"Time enough, Kitty." Then a look of love
flashed from face to face, and struck straight from
heart to heart; and there was a little silence that
needed no words. Kitty lifted a ring and slipped
it on her finger. It was a hoop of fine, dark blue
sapphires, set in fretted gold, and clasped with a
tiny padlock, shaped like a heart.

"What a lovely ring!" she cried. "Why do
you not wear it, Mother?"

"Because it is a good bit too small now, Kitty."

"Miss Vyner's hands are always covered with
rings, and she says every one of them has a
romance."

"I've heard, or read, something like that.
There was a woman in the story-book, was
there not, who kept a tally of her lovers on a
string of rings they had given her? I don't
think it was anything to her credit. I should n't
wonder if that is a bit ill-natured. I ought not to
say such a thing, so don't mind it, Kitty."

"Is this sapphire band yours, Mother?"

"To be sure it is."

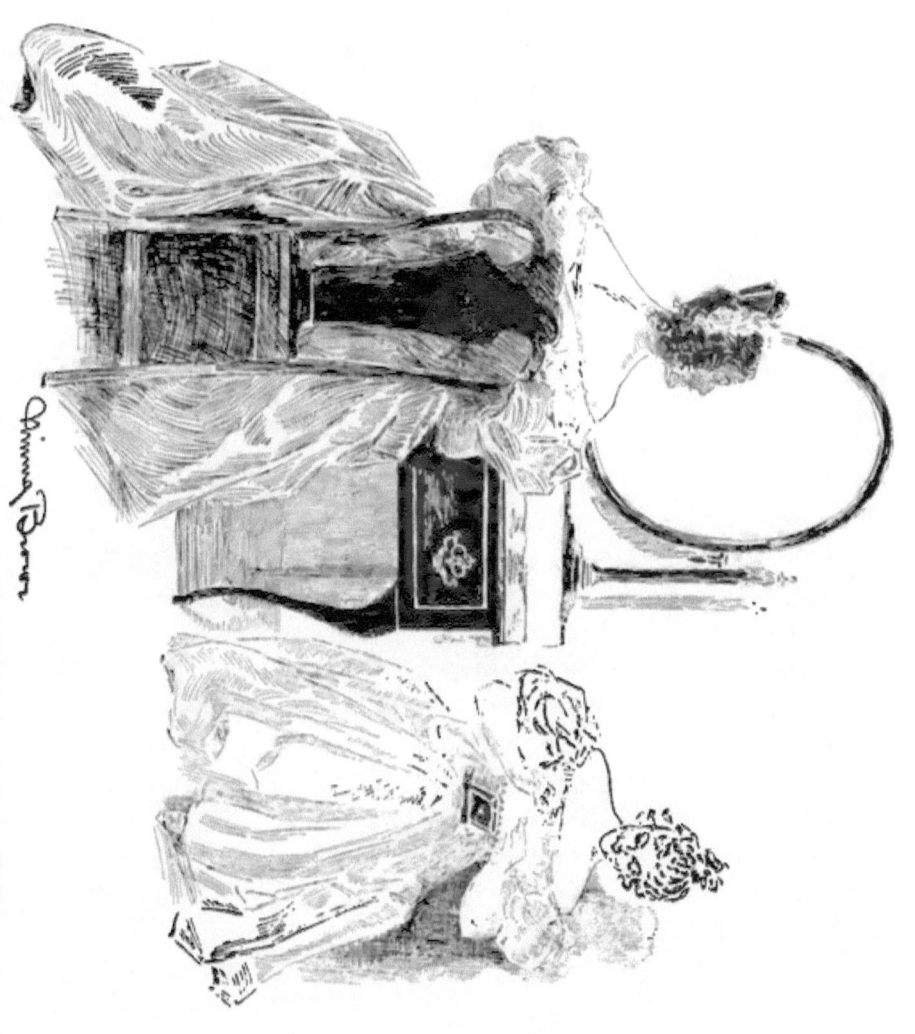

" May I wear it? "

" Well, Kitty, I think a deal of that ring. You must take great care of it."

"So then, Mother, one of your rings has a story too, has it?" And there was a little laugh for answer, and Kitty slipped the coveted trinket on her finger, and held up her hand to admire the gleam of the jewels, as she said, musingly, " I wonder what Piers is doing? "

" I would n't ' wonder,' dearie. Little troubles are often worrited into big troubles. If things are let alone, they work themselves right. I 'll warrant Piers is unhappy enough."

But Mrs. Atheling's warrant was hardly justified. Piers should have gone to the House; but he went instead to his room, threw himself among the cushions of a divan, and with a motion of his head indicated to his servant that he wanted his Turkish pipe. The strange inertia and indifference that had so suddenly assailed, still dominated him, and he had no desire to combat it. He was neither sick nor weary; yet he seemed to have lost all control over his feelings. Had the man within the man " gone off guard"? Have we not all — yes, we have all of us succumbed to just such intervals of supreme, inexpressible listlessness and insensibility? We are "not all there," but *where* has our inner self gone to? And what is it doing? It gives us no account of such lapses.

Piers asked no questions of himself. He was

like a man dreaming; for if his Will was not
asleep, it was at least quiescent. He made no
effort to control his thoughts, which drifted from
Annabel to Kate, and from Kate to Annabel, in
the vagrant, inconsequent manner which acknowl-
edges neither the guidance of Reason or Will.
And as the Levantine vapour lulled his brain, he
felt a pleasure in this surrender of his noblest
attributes. He thought of Annabel as he had
seen her the previous evening, dressed in a
shaded satin of blue and green, trimmed with
the tips of peacock feathers. The same resplendent ornaments were in her strong, wavy, black
hair, and round her throat was a necklace of
emeralds and amethysts. "What a Duchess of
Richmoor she would make!" he thought. "How
stately and proud! How well she would wear
the coronet and the gold strawberry leaves, and
the crimson robe and ermine of her state dress!
Yes, Annabel would be a proper Duchess; but
— but —" and then he was sitting with Kate
among the tall brackens, where the Yorkshire
hills threw miles of shadow. She was in her
riding dress; but her little velvet cap was in
her hand, and the fresh wind was blowing her
brown hair into bewitching tendrils about her
lovely face. How well he knew the sweet serious-
ness of her downcast eyes, the rich bloom of her
cheeks and lips, the tender smile with which she
always answered his "*Kate! Sweet Kate!*"

Even through all his listlessness, this vision

moved him, and he heard his heart say, " Oh,
Kate, wife of my soul! Oh, Beloved! Love of
my life, who can part us? Thou and I, Kate!
Thou and I — "

" And the Other One."

From *whom* or from *where* came the words?
Piers heard them with his spiritual sense plainly,
and their suggestion annoyed him. Now if we
stir under a nightmare, it is gone; and this faint
rebellion broke the chain of that mental inertia
which had held him at least three hours under
its spell. He moved irritably, and in so-doing
threw down the lid of the tobacco jar, and then
rose to his feet. In a moment, he was "all
there."

" I ought to be in the House," he muttered,
and he touched the bell for his valet, and dressed
with less deliberation than was his wont. And
during the toilet he was aware of a certain mental anger that longed to expend itself: " If Mr.
Brougham is as insufferably dictatorial as he was
last night, if Mr. O'Connell only plays the
buffoon again, we shall meet in a narrow path —
and one of us will fare ill," he muttered.

The hour generally comes when we are ready
for it; and Piers found both gentlemen in the
tempers he detested. He gladly accepted his
own challenge, and the Squire was so interested
in the wordy fight that he did not return home
to dinner. Mrs. Atheling neither worried nor
waited. She knew that the Squire's vote might

be wanted at any inconvenient hour; and, besides, the night had set stormily in, and she said
cheerfully to Kate, "It would n't do for father
to get a wetting and then be hours in damp
clothes. He is far better sitting to-day's business
out while he is there."

But the evening dragged wearily, in spite of
the efforts of both women to make little pleas-
antries. Kate's whole being was in her sense of
hearing. She was listening for a step that did
not come. On other nights there had been visitors; she heard the roll of carriages and the
clash of the heavy front door; but this dreary
night no roll of wheels broke the stillness of the
aristocratic Square; and she listened for the
sound of the closing door until she was ready to
cry out against the strain and the suspense.
However, the longest, saddest day wears to its
end; and though it does not appear likely that
a loving girl's anxiety about a coolness in her
lover should teach us how far deeper, even than
mother-love, is our trust in God's love, yet little
Kitty's behaviour on this sorrowful evening did
show forth this sublime fact.

For the girl left undone none of her usual
duties, left unsaid none of the pleasant words
she knew her mother expected from her; she
even followed her — as she always did when the
Squire was late — to her bedroom, and helped
her lay away her laces and jewels ere she bid
her a last "good-night." But as soon as she had

closed the door of her own room, she felt she
might give herself some release. If she did not
read the whole of the Evening Service, *God
would understand.* She could trust His love to
excuse, to pity, to release her from all ceremonies. She knelt down, she bowed her head, and
said only the two or three words which opened
her heart and let the rain of tears wash all her
anxieties away.

And though sorrow may endure for a night,
joy comes in the morning; and this is specially
true in youth. When Kate awoke, the sun was
shining, and the care and ache was gone from
her heart. " He giveth His Beloved sleep," and
thus some angel had certainly comforted her,
though she knew it not. With a cheerful heart
she dressed and went into the breakfast-room,
and there she saw her father standing on the
hearthrug, with *The Times* open in his hand. He
looked at her over its pages with beaming eyes,
and she ran to him and took the paper away,
and nestling to his heart, said, " she would have
no rival, first thing in the morning."

And the proud father stroked her hair, and
kissed her lips, and answered her, " Rival was not
born yet, and never would be born; and that he
was only seeing if them newspaper fellows had
told lies about Piers."

" Piers ! " cried Mrs. Atheling, entering the
room at the moment, " what about Piers ? "

" Well, Mother, the lad had his say last night;

but, Dal it! Mr. Brougham went at the Government and the Electors as if they were all of them wearing the devil's livery. I call it scandalous! It was nothing else. He let on to be preaching for Reform, but he was just preaching for Henry Brougham."

"What was Mr. Brougham talking about, Father?"

"Mr. Brougham can talk about nothing but Reform, Kitty, the right of every man to vote as seems good in his own eyes. He said peers and landowners influenced and prejudiced votes in a way that was outrageous and not to be borne, and a lot more words of the same kind; for Henry Brougham would lose his speech if he had anything pleasant to say. I was going to get up and give him a bit of my mind, when Piers rose; and the cool way in which he fixed his eye-glass, and looked Mr. Brougham up and down, and straight in the face, set us all by the ears. He was every inch of him, then and there, the future Duke of Richmoor; and he told Brougham, in a very sarcastic way, that his opinions were silly, and would neither bear the test of reason nor of candid examination."

"But, Father, I thought Mr. Brougham was the great man of the Commons, and held in much honour."

"Well, my little maid, he may be; but I'll warrant it is only by people who have their own reasons for worshipping the devil."

"Come, come, John! If I was thee, I would be silent until I could be just."

"Not thou, Maude! Right or wrong, thou wouldst say thy say. I think I ought to know thee by this time."

"Never mind me, John. We want to hear what Piers said."

"Brougham's words had come rattling off in full gallop. Piers, after looking at him a minute, began in that contemptuous drawl of his, — you 've heard it I 've no doubt, — ' Mr. Brougham affords an example of radical opinions degrading a statesman into a politician. He cannot but know that it is the positive, visible duty of every landowner to influence and prejudice votes. It is the business and the function of education and responsibility to enlighten ignorance, and to influence the misguided and the misled. If it is the business and the function of the clergy to influence and prejudice people in favour of a good life; if it is the business and function of a teacher to influence and prejudice scholars in favour of knowledge, — it is just as certainly the business and function of the landowner to influence his tenants in favour of law and order, and to prejudice them against men who would shatter to pieces the noblest political Constitution in the world.' "

The Squire read this period aloud with great emphasis, and added, " Well, Maude, you never heard such a tumult as followed. Cries of

'*Here! Here!*' and '*Order! Order!*' filled the
House; and the Speaker had work enough to
make silence. Piers stood quite still, watching
Brougham, and as soon as all was quiet, he went
on, —

"'If you take the peers, the gentry, the scholars, the men of enterprise and wealth, from our
population, what kind of a government should
we get from the remainder? Would they be
fit to select and elect?' Then there was another uproar, and Piers sat down, and O'Connell
jumped up. He put his witty tongue in his
laughing cheek, and, buttoning his coat round
him, held up his right hand. And the Reform
members cheered, and the Tory members
shrugged their shoulders, and waited for what
he would say."

"I don't want to hear a word from *him*,"
answered Mrs. Atheling. "Come and get your
coffee, John. A cup of good coffee costs a deal
now, and it's a shame to let it get cold and sloppy
over Dan O'Connell's blackguarding."

"Tell us what he said, Father," urged Kate,
who really desired to know more about Piers's
efforts. "You can drink your coffee to his
words. I don't suppose they will poison it."

"I wouldn't be sure of that," said Mrs.
Atheling, with a dubious shake of her head;
while the Squire lifted his cup, and emptied it
at a draught.

"What did he say, Father? Did he attack
Piers?"

"To be sure he did. He took the word 'Remainder,' and said Piers had called the great, substantial working men of England, Scotland, and Ireland *Remainders*. He said these '*Remainders*' might only be farmers, and bakers, and builders, and traders; but they were the backbone of the nation; and the honourable gentleman from Richmoor Palace had called them 'Remainders.' And then he gave Piers a few of such stinging, abusive names as he always keeps on hand, — and he keeps a good many kinds of them on hand, — and Piers was like a man that neither heard nor saw him. He looked clean through the member for Kilkenny as if he was n't there at all. And then Mr. Scarlett got up, and asked the Speaker if such unparliamentary conduct was to be permitted? And Mr. Dickson called upon the House to protect itself from the browbeating, bullying ruffianism of the member for Kilkenny; and Dan O'Connell sat laughing, with his hat on one side of his head, till Dickson sat down; then he said, he 'considered Mr. Dickson's words complimentary;' and the shouts became louder and louder, and the Speaker had hard work to get things quieted down."

"Why, John! I never heard tell of such carryings on."

"Then, Maude, I thought *I* would say a word or two; and I got the Speaker's eye, and he said peremptorily, 'The member for Asketh!' and I rose in my place and said I thought the honourable member for Kilkenny — "

" John !   I would n't have called him ' honourable.' "

" I know thou wouldst not, Maude. Well, I said honourable, and I went on to say that Mr. O'Connell had mistaken the meaning Lord Exham attached to the word ' Remainder.' I said it was n't a disrespectful word at all, and that there were plenty of ' remainders,' we all of us thought a good deal of; but, I said, I would come to an instance which every man could understand, — the remainder of a glass of fine, old October ale. The rich, creamy, bubbling froth might stand for the landowners; but it was part of the whole; and the remainder was all the better for the froth, and the more froth, and the richer the froth, the better the ale below it. And I went on to say that Lord Exham, and every man of us, knew right well, that the great body of the English nation was n't made up of knaves, and scoundrels, and fools, but of good men and women. And then our benches cheered me, up and down, till I felt it was a good thing to be a Representative of the Remainder, and I said so."

Then Mrs. Atheling and Kitty cheered the Squire more than a little, with smiles, and kisses, and proud words; and he went on with increased animation, " In a minute O'Connell was on his feet again, and he called me a lot of names I need n't repeat here; until he said, 'My example of a glass of ale was exactly what anybody might expect from such a John Bull as the member for Asketh.' And, Maude and Kitty, I could not stand that. The House was shouting, 'Order! Order!' and I cried, 'Mr. Speaker!' and the Speaker said, 'Order, the member for Kilkenny is speaking!' 'But, Mr. Speaker,' I said, 'I only want to say to the member for Kilkenny that I would rather be a John Bull, than a bully.' And that was the end. There was no 'Order' after it. Our side cheered and roared, and, Maude, what dost thou think?—the one to cheer loudest was thy son Edgar. He must have got in by the Speaker's favour; but there he was, and when I came through the lobby, with Piers and Lord Althorp, and a crowd after me, he was standing with that young fellow I threw on Atheling Green; and he looked at me so pleased, and eager, and happy, that I thought for a moment he was going to shake hands; but I kept my hands in my pockets—yet I'll say this,—he has thy fine eyes, Maude,—I most felt as if thou wert looking at me."

"John! John! How couldst thou keep thy hands in thy pockets? How couldst thou do such an unfatherly thing? I'm ashamed of thee! I am."

"Give me a slice of ham, and don't ask questions. I want my breakfast now. I can't live on talk, as if I was a woman."

Fortunately at this moment a servant entered
with the morning's mail. He gave Mrs. Atheling a letter, and Kate two letters; and then
offered the large salver full of matter to the
Squire. He looked at the pile with indignation.
"Put it out of my sight, Dobson," he said angrily.
"Do you think I want letters and papers to
my breakfast? I'm astonished at you!" He was
breaking his egg-shell impatiently as he spoke,
and he looked up with affected anger at his companions. Kitty met his glance with a smile. She
could afford to do so, for both her letters lay
untouched at her side. She tapped the upper
one and said, "It is from Miss Vyner, Father;
it can easily wait."

"And the other, Kitty? Who is it from?"

"From Piers, I don't want to read it yet."

"To be sure." Then he looked at Mrs. Atheling, and was surprised. Her face was really shining with pleasure, her eyes misty with happy
tears. She held her letter with a certain pride
and tenderness that her whole attitude also expressed; and the Squire had an instant premoni-
tion as to the writer of it.

"Well, Maude," he said, "I would drink my
coffee, if I was thee. A cup of coffee costs a
deal now; and it's a shame to let it get cold and
sloppy over a bit of a letter — nobody knows
who from."

"It is from Edgar," said Mrs. Atheling, far
too proud and pleased to keep her happiness to

herself. "And, John, I am going to have a little lunch-party to-day at two o'clock; and I do wish thou wouldst make it in thy way to be present."

"I won't. And I would like to know who is coming here. I won't have all kinds and sorts sitting at my board, and eating my bread and salt — and I never heard tell of a good wife asking people to do that without even mentioning their names to her husband — and — "

"I am quite ready to name everybody I ask to thy board, John. There will be thy own son Edgar Atheling, and Mr. Cecil North, and thy wife Maude Atheling, and thy daughter Kitty. Maybe, also, Lord Exham and Miss Vyner. Kitty says she has a letter from her."

"I told thee once and for all, I had forbid Edgar Atheling to come to my house again until I asked him to do so."

"This is n't thy house, John. It is only a rented roof. Thou mayst be sure Edgar will never come near Atheling till God visits thee and gives thee a heart like His own to love thy son. Thou hast never told Edgar to keep away from the Vyner mansion, and thou hadst better never try to do so; for I tell thee plainly if thou dost — "

"Keep threats behind thy teeth, Maude. It is n't like thee, and I won't be threatened either by man or woman. If thou thinkest it right to set Edgar before me, and to teach him *not* to 'Honour his father' — "

"Did n't he 'honour' thee last night! Was n't he proud of thee? And he wanted to tell thee so, if thou wouldst have let him. Poor Edgar!" And Edgar's mother covered her face, and began to cry softly to herself.

"Nay, Maude, if thou takest to crying I must run away. It is n't fair at all. What can a man say to tears? I wish I could have a bit of breakfast in peace; I do that!" — and he pushed his chair away in a little passion, and lifted his mail, and was going noisily out of the room, when he found Kitty's arms round his neck. Then he said peevishly, "Thou art spilling my letters, Kitty. Let me alone, dearie! Thou never hast a word to say on thy father's side. It 's too bad!"

"I am all for you, father, — you and you first of all. There is nobody like you; nobody before you; nobody that can ever take your place." Then she kissed him, and whispered some of those loving, senseless little words that go right to the heart, if Love sends them there. And the Squire was comforted by them, and whispered back to her, "God love thee, my little maid! I 'll do anything I can to give thee pleasure."

"Then just think about Edgar as you saw him last night, think of him with mother's eyes watching you, listening to you, full of pride and loving you so much — oh, yes, Father! loving you so much."

"Well, well, — let me go now, Kitty. I have

all these bothering letters and papers to look at; they are enough to make any man cross."

"Let me help you."

"Go to thy mother. Listen, Kitty," and he spoke very low, "tell her, thou art sure and certain thy father does not object to her seeing her son, if it makes her happy — thou knowest my bark is a deal worse than my bite — say — thou believest I would like to see Edgar myself — nay, thou needest not say that — but say a few words just to please her; thou knowest what they should be better than I do," — then, with a rather gruff "good-morning," he went out of the room; and Kitty turned to her mother.

Mrs. Atheling was smiling, though there were indeed some remaining evidences of tears. "He went without bidding me 'good-morning,' Kitty. What did he say? Is he very angry?"

"Not at all angry. All put on, Mother. He loves Edgar quite as much as you do."

"He can't do that, Kitty. There is nothing like a mother's love."

"Except a father's love. Don't you remember, that God takes a father's love to express His own great care for us? And when the Prodigal Son came home, Christ makes his father, not his mother, go to meet him."

"That was because Christ knew children were sure and certain of their mother's love and forgiveness. He was n't so sure of the fathers. So he gave the lesson to them; he knew that

mothers did not need it. Mothers are always
ready to forgive, Kitty; but there is nothing to
forgive in Edgar."

"Is he really coming to-day?"

"Listen to what he says, Kitty. 'Darling
Mother, I cannot live another day without seeing you. Let me come to-morrow at two o'clock,
and put my arms round you, and kiss you, and
talk to you for an hour. Ask father to let me
come. London is not Atheling. If he counts
his passionate words as forever binding between
him and me, surely they are not binding between
you and me. Let me see you anyway, Mother.
Sweet, dear Mother! When father forgives the
rest, he will forgive this also. Your loving son,
Edgar.' Now, Kitty, if Edgar was your son, what
would you say?"

"I would say, Come at once, Edgar, and
dearly welcome!"

"To be sure you would. So shall I. What is
Miss Vyner writing about?"

Then Kitty lifted the squarely folded letter
with its great splash of white wax stamped with
the Vyner crest, and after a rapid glance at its
contents said, "There is likely to be a great
House to-night; and the Duchess has three seats
in the Ladies Gallery. One is for Annabel, the
other for me; and she asks you to take her place.
Do go, Mother."

"I'll think about it."

"Don't say that."

"It is all I will say just yet. Did you have a letter from Piers?"

"Yes."

"I knew you would. Go and read it, and tell Dobson to send the cook to me. We want the best lunch that can be made; and put on a pretty dress, Kitty. Edgar must feel that nothing is too good for him."

In accordance with this intent, Mrs. Atheling took particular pains with her own dress; and Kitty thought she had never seen her mother so handsome. Soft brown satin, and gold ornaments, and the bit of lace on her head set off her large, blonde, stately beauty to perfection; while the look of love and anxiety, as the clock moved on to two, gave to her countenance that "something more" without which beauty is only flesh and blood.

She had said to herself that Edgar might be detained, that he might not be able to keep his time, and that she would not feel disappointed if he was a bit behind two o'clock. But fully ten minutes before the hour, she heard his quick, firm knock; and as she stood trembling with joy in the middle of the room, he took her in his arms, and, between laughing and crying, they knew not, either of them, what they said. And then Kitty ran into the room, all a flutter with pale-blue ribbons, and it was a good five minutes before the two women found time to see, and to speak to Cecil North, who stood watching the scene with his kind heart in his face.

Evidently the meeting had bespoke a fortunate hour. The weather, though it was November, was sunny; the lunch was perfection, and they were in the midst of the merriest possible meal when Annabel Vyner and Piers Exham joined them. Annabel had expected nothing better from this visit than an opportunity to show off her familiar relations with Lord Exham, and torment Kitty, as far as she thought it prudent to do so; but Fate had prepared motives more personal and delightful for her, — two handsome young men, whom she at once determined to conquer. Cecil North made no resistance; he went over heart and head in love with her. Her splendid vitality, her manner, — so demanding and so caressing, — her daring dress, and dazzling jewelry, her altogether unconventional air charmed and vanquished him, and he devoted himself to pleasing her.

During the lunch hour the conversation was general, and very animated. Annabel excelled herself in her peculiar way of saying things which appeared singularly brilliant, but which really derived all their point from her looks, and shrugs, and flashing movements. The good mother was in an earthly heaven, watching, and listening, and attending to every one's wants, actual and possible. Laughter and repartee and merry jests mingled with bits of social and parliamentary gossip, though politics were instinctively avoided. Piers knew well the opinions of the two men with whom he was sitting; and he was quite capable of respecting them. Besides, he had an old friendship for Edgar Atheling; and he loved his sister, and was well aware that she had much sympathy with her brother's views. So all Annabel's attempts to make a division were futile; no one took up the little challenges she flung into their midst, and the parliamentary talk drifted no nearer dangerous ground than the Ladies Gallery. Piers knew of the invitation given to the Athelings, and he proposed to meet the ladies in the courtyard near the entrance to the exclusive precinct.

"Too exclusive by far," said Annabel. "Why do English ladies submit to that grating? It is a relic of the barbarous ages. I intend to move in the matter. Let us get up a petition, or an act, or an agitation of some kind for its removal. I think we should succeed. What do you say, Lord Exham?"

"I think you would *not* succeed," answered Piers. "I have heard the Duke say that the proposition is frequently made in the House; that it is always enthusiastically cheered; but that every time the question comes practically up, there is a dexterous count out."

"Well, then, I will propose that the front Treasury Bench be taken away, and twenty-four ladies' seats put in its place. Do you see, Mr. North, what I intend by that?"

"I am sure it is something wise and good, Miss Vyner."

"My idea is, that twenty-four ladies should sit there as representatives of the women of England. Twenty-four bishops in lovely lawn sit as representatives of the clergy of England; why should not English women have their representation? I hope while Reformers are correcting the abuses of Representation, they will consider this abuse. Mr. Atheling, what do you say?"

"I am at your service, Miss Vyner."

"Indeed, sir, just at present you are hand and heart in the service of Mrs. Atheling. I must turn to Mr. North."

Then Mrs. Atheling perceived that in her interesting conversation with Edgar, she was keeping her guests at table; and she rose with an apology, and led the way into the parlour. There was a large conservatory opening out of this room, and Kate and Piers, on some pretext of rosebuds, went into it.

"My dear Kate, I have been so unhappy!" he said, taking her hand.

"But why, Piers?"

"We parted so strangely yesterday. I do not know how it happened."

"We were both tired, I think. I was as much in fault as you. Is not this an exquisite flower?" That was the end of the trouble. He drew her to his side, and kissed the hand that touched the flower; and so all explanations were over; and

they took up their love-story where the shadow
of yesterday had broken it off. And as their
hands wandered among the shrubs, it was natural
for Piers to notice the ring on Kate's finger. "It
is a very singular jewel," he said; "I never saw
one like it."

"It is my mother's," answered Kate. "She
told me this morning it was her betrothal ring
and that father bought it in Venice."

"Kate dear, I wish to get you a ring just like
it. Let us ask Mrs. Atheling if I may show it to
my jeweller, and have one made for you."

"I am sure mother will be willing," and she
slipped the shining circle from her finger, and
gave it to Piers; and he whispered fondly, as he
placed it on his own hand, "Will you take it from
me, Kate, as a love gage?—never to leave your
finger until I put the wife's gold ring above it?"

And what she said need not be told. Many
happy words grew from her answer; and they
forgot the rosebuds they had come to gather, and
the company they had left, and the flight of time,
until Edgar came into the conservatory to bid his
sister "good-bye." There had been a slight for-
mality between Piers and Edgar at their first
meeting; but with Kate standing between them,
all the good days on the Yorkshire hills and
moors came into their memories, and they
clasped hands with their old boyish fervour, and
it was "Piers" and "Edgar" again. So the
parting was the real meeting; and they went

back to the parlour in an unmistakable enthusiasm of good fellowship.

Annabel was then quite ready to leave, and the
question of the Ladies Gallery came up for settlement.   Mrs. Atheling declared she was too
weary to go out; and Kate preferred her own
happy thoughts to the tumult of a political quarrel.   Annabel was equally indifferent.   She had
discovered that Mr. North was a son of the Earl
of Westover, and might with propriety be asked
to the Richmoor opera-box, that there was even
an acquaintance strong enough between the
families to enable her new lover to pay his
respects to the Duchess in the interludes, and, in
fact, an understanding to that effect had been
made for that very night, if the offer of the seats
in the Ladies Gallery was not accepted.   So
their refusal caused no regret; for when politics
come in competition with youth and love, they
have scarcely a hearing.   But during the slight
discussion, Piers found time to speak to Mrs.
Atheling about the ring; and the direction of
three pair of eyes to the trinket caught Annabel's attention.   Her face flamed when she saw
that it had passed from Kate's hand to the hand
of Exham; and for the first time, she had a feeling of active dislike against Kate.   Her sweet,
calm, innocent beauty, her happy eyes and ingenuous girlish expression, offended her, and set
all the worst forces of her soul in revolt.

She did not dare to trust herself with Piers.

In her present mood, she knew she would be sure to say something that would hamper her future actions. She declared she would only accept Mr. North's escort to Richmoor House; for she was sure the Duke was expecting Piers to be in his place in the Commons when the vote was taken.

Piers had a similar conviction, and he looked at his watch almost guiltily, and went hurriedly away. Then the little party was soon dispersed; but Mrs. Atheling and Kate were both far too happy to need outside aids. They talked of Edgar and Cecil North, and Annabel's witcheries, and Piers's great and good qualities, and the promised ring, and the excellent lunch, and the general success of the impromptu little feast. Everything had been pleasant, and the Squire's absence was not thought worth worrying about.

"He will come round, bit by bit," said the happy mother. "I know John Atheling. The first thing Edgar does to please him, will put all straight; and Edgar is on the very road to please him most of all."

"What road is that, Mother?"

"Nay, I can't tell you, Kitty; for just yet it is a secret between Edgar and me. He was glad to meet Piers again; and, if I am any judge, they will be better friends than ever before."

Thus the two women talked the evening away, and were by no means sorry to be at their own fireside. "We could have done no good by

going to the House," said Kate. " If we were
men, it would be different. They like it. Father
says the House is the best club in London."

"It gives men a lot of excuses," said Mrs.
Atheling, with a sigh. "I dare say your father
won't get home till late. You had better go to
bed, Kitty."

" Perhaps Piers may come with him."

" I don't think he will. He looked tired when
he left here ; he will be worse tired when he gets
away from the Commons. He said he was going
to speak again, if he got the opportunity, — that
is, if he could find anything to contradict in Mr.
Brougham's speech. Piers likes saying, No, sir !'
his spurs are always in fighting trim. Go to bed,
Kitty. Piers won't be back to-night, and I can
say to father whatever I think proper."

Mrs. Atheling judged correctly. Piers sat a
long time before his opportunity came, and then
he did not get the best of it. Brougham's fol-
lowers overflowed the Opposition benches, the
Government side, and the gangway, and Piers
exhausted himself vainly in an endeavour to get
a hearing. It was late when he returned to Richmoor House, but the Duke was still absent, and
the Duchess and Annabel at the opera. He
went to the Duke's private parlour, for there
were some things he felt he must discuss before
another day's sitting; and the warmth and stillness, added to his own mental and physical
weariness, soon overcame all the resistance he

could make. The couch on which he had thrown himself was also a drowsy place; it seemed to sink softly down, and down, until Piers was far below the tide of thought, or even dreams.

It was then that Annabel returned. She came slowly and rather thoughtfully along the silent corridor. She had exhausted for the time being her fine spirits, her wit, almost her good looks. She hoped she would *not* meet Piers, and was glad in passing the door of his apartments to see no man in attendance, nor any sign of wakeful life. A little further on she noticed a band of light from the Duke's private parlour; the door was a trifle open, left purposely so by Piers in order that his father might not be tempted to pass it. Tired as she was, she could not resist the opportunity it offered. She liked to show herself in her fineries to her guardian, for he always had a compliment for her beauty; and although she had listened for hours to compliments her vanity was still unsatiated. With a coquettish smile she pushed wider the door and saw Lord Exham. There could be no doubt of his profound insensibility; his face, his attitude, his breathing, all expressed the deep sleep of a thoroughly-exhausted man.

For one moment she looked at him curiously, then, at the instigation of the Evil One, her eyes saw the ring upon his hand, and her heart instantly desired it; for what reason she did not

ask.   At the moment she perhaps had no reason,
except the wicked hope that its loss might make
trouble between Kitty and her lover.   With the
swift, noiseless step that Nature gives to women
who have the treachery and cruelty of the feline
family, she reached Piers's side.   But rapid as her
movement had been, her thought had been more
rapid.   " If I am caught, I will say I won a pair
of gloves, and took the ring as the gage of my
victory."

She stooped to the dropped hand, but never
touched it.   The ring was large, and it was only
necessary for her to place her finger and thumb
on each side of it.   It slipped off without pressing against the flesh, and in a moment it was in
her palm.   She waited to see if the movement
had been felt.   There was no evidence of it, and
she passed rapidly out of the room.   Outside the
door, she again waited for a movement, but none
came, and she walked leisurely, and with a certain air of weariness, to her own apartments.
Once there all was safe; she dropped it into
the receptacle in which she kept the key of her
jewel-case, and went smiling to bed.

Not ten minutes after her theft the Duke entered the room.   He did not scruple to awaken
his son, and to discuss with him the tactics of a
warfare which was every day becoming more
bitter and violent.   Piers was full of interest, and
eager to take his part in the fray.   Suddenly he
became aware of his loss.   Then he forgot every

other thing. He insisted, then and there, on calling his valet and searching every inch of carpet in the room. The Duke was disgusted with this radical change of interest. He went pettishly away in the middle of the search, saying, —

"The Reformers might well carry all before them, when peers who had everything to lose or gain thought more of a lost ring than a lost cause."

And Piers could not answer a word. He was confounded by the circumstance. That the ring was on his hand when he entered the room was certain. He searched all his pockets with frantic fear, his purse, the couch on which he had slept. There was no part of the room not examined, no piece of furniture that was not moved; and the day began to dawn when the useless search was over. He went to his room, sleepless and troubled beyond belief. Government might be defeated, Ministers might resign, Reform might spell Revolution, the estates and titles of nobles might be in jeopardy, — but Kitty's ring was lost, and that was the first, and the last, and the only thought Piers Exham could entertain.

CHAPTER EIGHTH

WILL SHE CHOOSE EVIL OR GOOD?

ANNABEL had a very good night. Her conscience was an indulgent one, and she easily
satisfied its complaining. " It was after all only
a joke," she said. " In the morning I can restore
the ring. The Duke will have a good laugh at
his son's discomfiture, and will praise my clever-
ness. The Duchess will either knit her brows, or
else take it merrily; and Piers will owe me a forfeit, and that will be the end of the affair. What
is there to make a fuss over?" Annabel's conscience thought, in such case, there was nothing
to fuss about; and it let her sleep comfortably on
the prevaricating promise.

She considered the matter over as she was
dressing. She had slept well, was refreshed
and full of life, and therefore full of selfish
wilfulness: —

" I will restore the ring to Piers." She said
this to please one side of her nature.

" I will not restore the ring." She said this to
please the other side. " As a thing of worth, it is
by no means costly. I will give Kate Atheling a

ring of twice its value. As a thing of power it is mine, the spoil of my will and my skill; and I will not part with it." Still she kept the first decision in reserve; she promised herself to be influenced by the circumstances which the affair induced.

But the way out of temptation is always very difficult, and circumstances are rarely favourable to it. They were not in this case. Before Annabel was dressed she received a message that overthrew all her intentions. The Duchess was going to breakfast in her own parlour, and she desired Annabel's company at the meal. The desires of the Duchess were commands, and the young lady reluctantly obeyed them; for she anticipated the reproof that came, as soon as they were alone, regarding her attitude towards Cecil North.

" It will not do, Annabel," said the Duchess, severely. " The Norths are a fine family, but poor, even in the elder branches. This young man can look forward to nothing better than some diplomatic or military appointment, and that in an Indian Presidency."

" What could be better?" asked Annabel, with an affectation of delight. " An Indian Court is a court. It has the splendour, the ceremony, the very air of royalty."

" But with your fortune — "

" I assure you, Duchess, any man who marries me will need all my fortune. He will in fact deserve it. You know that I am *not* amiable, and that I *am* extravagant and luxurious."

" But you may avoid such a foolish, unwomanly thing as flirtation, even if you are not amiable. It seems to me the world has forgotten how to be amiable. This morning, the Duke is touchy and disagreeable; and Piers has not come to ask after my health, though it is his usual custom when I remain in my room. He angered the Duke also last night."

"Did you see him last night?" asked Annabel, with an air of indifference.

"The Duke did. Piers seems to have behaved in an absurd way about a ring he has lost. The Duke says, he turned his room topsy-turvy, and went on as if he had lost his whole estate."

" Was it the ring with the ducal arms that he always wears? "

" No, indeed! Only a simple band of sapphires, or some other stone. The Duke thinks it must have been the gift of some woman. Were you the donor, Annabel?"

"I! I should think not! I do not give rings away. I prefer to receive them. He wore no sapphire band yesterday when he and I went to the Athelings —" and she looked the rest of the query, over her coffee-cup, straight into the eyes of the Duchess.

"What is it you mean to ask, Annabel?"

" Do you think that Miss Atheling —"

" Miss Atheling! That girl! What an absurd

idea! Why should she give Lord Exham a ring?"

"*Why!* There are so many '*whys*' that nobody can answer." And with this remark, Annabel felt that her opportunity for confession had quite lapsed. For if the Duchess had thought it right to reprove her for such freedom as she had shown towards Cecil North, what would she say about an act so daring, so really improper in a social sense, as the removal of a ring from her son's hand? Annabel had no mind to bring on herself the disagreeable looks and words she merited. She gave the conversation the political turn that answered all purposes, by asking the Duchess if she was not afraid Piers's principles might be influenced by his friendship with young Atheling. "They were David and Jonathan yesterday," she said; "and as for Cecil North, he is a Radical of the first water."

"Lord Exham is not so easily persuaded," answered the Duchess, loftily. "He could as readily change his nose as his principles. But I am seriously annoyed at this intercourse with a family distinctly out of our own caste. The Duke has been very foolish to encourage it."

"You have also encouraged Miss Atheling."

"I have been too good-natured. I admit that. But as I have promised to present her, I must honourably keep my word; that is, if any opportunity offers. It now appears as if there would be no court functions. The King declined the

Lord Mayor's feast, — a most unprecedented thing, — and it is said the Queen is averse to receive while the Reform agitation continues. When it will end, nobody knows."

"It will end when it succeeds, not before," said Annabel. "I am only a woman, but I see that conclusion very clearly." It gave her pleasure to make this statement. It was her way of returning to the Duchess the disagreeable words she had been obliged to take from her; and she was not at all dismayed by the look of anger she provoked.

"I am astonished at you, Annabel. Are you also in danger of changing your opinions?"

"I am astonished at myself, Duchess. My opinions are movable; but I have not yet changed them. Truth, however, belongs to all sides, and I cannot avoid seeing things as they are."

"That is, as young Atheling and Cecil North show them to you."

"Lord Exham has still more frequent opportunities of showing me the course of events. I have 'influences' on both sides, you see, Duchess; but, after all, I form my own opinions."

"Reform will never be accomplished. The people must follow the nobles, as surely as the thread follows the needle."

"I have ceased to prophesy. Anything can happen in a long enough time; and I often heard my father say that, 'They who *care* and *dare*

may do as they like.' I think the Reform party
both '*care*' and '*dare*.'"

"Have you fallen in love with Cecil North, or
with Mr. Atheling?"

"I am in love with Annabel Vyner. I worship
none of the idols that have been set up, either by
Tories or Reformers. Men who talk politics are
immensely stupid. I shall marry a man who is a
good fighter. Mere talkers are like barking dogs.
Why don't these Reformers stop whimpering,
and fly like a bull dog at the throat of their
wrongs? Then I should go with them, heart and
soul and purse."

"You are talking now for talking's sake,
Annabel. You are actually advocating civil
war."

"Am I really? Well, war is man's natural
condition. It takes churches, and priests, and
standing armies, and constables always on hand,
to keep peace in any sort of fashion. We are all
barbarians under our clothes, — just civilised on
the top."

"Such assertions are odious, and you cannot prove them."

"I can. The other evening I was reading to
Lord Tatham a most exquisite poem by that
young man Tennyson; and he seemed to be en-
joying it, until Algernon Sydney showed him his
watch, and said something about 'the Black Boy.'
Then his face fairly glowed, and he went off with
a compliment that meant nothing. The next

morning I found out 'the Black Boy' was a famous pugilist. We are all of us, in some way or other, in this mixed condition."

" I think you are particularly disagreeable this morning, Miss."

" Pardon, Duchess. We have fallen on a disagreeable subject. Let us change it. Are we to drive to Richmond to-day ? "

"If Piers will accompany us. Ay! that is his knock." She turned a radiant face to meet her son, but received a sudden chill. Piers was pale and sombre-looking; he said he had not slept, and politely declined the Richmond excursion. Annabel was sure he would. " He will have an explanation at the Athelings instead," she thought; and she waited curiously for some remark which might open the way for her confession — or else close it. But Lord Exham did not allude to his loss, and the Duchess either attached no importance to the subject, or else thought it too important to bring forward. The tone of the room was not brightened by the young lord's advent, and Annabel quickly excused herself from further attendance.

" He will tell his mother when I am not there; and I shall get his opinions, with commentaries from her," she thought, as she hurried to her own rooms. Once there, she dismissed her maid, and sat down to realise herself. She doubled her little hands, and beat her knees softly with them. It was her way of summoning her mental forces, and of collecting vagrant and undecided thought.

"I am just here," she said to her own consciousness. "I have taken a ring from Lord Exham's finger. What for? Mischief or a joke? Which? Probably mischief. I wanted to turn it into a joke, and my opportunity is gone. Not my fault. If the Duchess had been in a good humour, I should have told her all about it. If Exham's manner had not frozen everything but the commonplaces of propriety, I would have teased him a little, and then given up the ring. It is their own fault. If people are cross at breakfast, they deserve a disagreeable day. I am not sorry to give them their deserts."

Then she rose and went to her jewel-case, and took the ring out and put it on her finger. "It is a poor little thing after all," she said as she turned it round and round. "The stones are not very fine; I have sapphires of far finer colour. If I give Kate Atheling my diamond locket, she will have reason to be grateful, — the setting is, however, really beautiful; that is the point, I suppose. I would like to have a ring set in the same way; but it would be dangerous —" and she laughed as if she enjoyed the thought of the danger. She took off the ring at this point, and looked at it more critically. "What must I do with the troublesome thing?" she asked herself. "Justine is a curious, suspicious creature, and when she hears the talk in the servants' hall, if

she got but a glimpse of it, she would put two
and two together." A momentary resolve to
throw it into the fire-place of the Duke's parlour came into her mind. "If it is found there,"
she argued, "the only supposition will be that
Piers dropped it on the hearth. If it is not
found, there will be no suppositions at all."

This resolve, however, received no real encour-
agement. There is a perverse disposition in
human nature to keep with special care things
that incriminate, or which might become sources
of suspicion or trouble; and the ring exercised
over the girl this fatal fascination. She closed her
jewel-case deliberately, holding the lid a trifle open
for a moment or two of last consideration; then
she dropped it with decision, and took from her
pocket a small purse, made of gold as flexible as
leather or satin. There were a few sovereigns in
one compartment, and a Hindoo charm in another. She put the ring with the charm, and
closed the purse with a smile of satisfaction.
For the time being, at any rate, it was out of
her way; and there were yet possibilities of
turning the whole matter into a pleasantry.

"I may even take it to Kate Atheling and tell
her to claim my forfeit." This very improbable
solution satisfied Annabel's conscience; she was
at peace after it, and able to consider more
personal affairs.

In order to do this under the most favourable
conditions, she placed herself comfortably on

her lounge. Her fine, tall form lay at length, supine and indolent, the feet, in their crimson sandals, crossed at the ankles. Her dark, powerful head, with its masses of strong, black hair, looked almost handsome on the pale amber cushions, with the hands and arms — jewelled though it was only morning — clasped above it. She was going to examine herself, and she was not one to shirk even the innermost chamber of her heart.

"First," she thought, "there is Lord Exham. Do I really want to marry him? Let me be sure of this, and then there is nothing for him to do, but make out the settlements. He cannot resist my influence when I choose to exert it. As yet I have not troubled him much; but I can trouble him — and I will, if I want to. Do I? Be honest, Annabel. There is no use lying to yourself. Well, then, I want to be Duchess of Richmoor; but I do *not* want to be Exham's wife. And if I marry him, the present Duke may live ten, twenty, even thirty years. I would not wait for the crown of England thirty years, with a husband I rather despised; only — only what? I do not want that Atheling girl to marry him. Jane Warwick, or Helen Percy, or Margaret Gower, I would not mind — but Kate Atheling! No! Why? I cannot tell." Nor could she. It was one of those apparently unreasonable dislikes we bring into the world with us, and which, probably, are the most reasonable dislikes of all. "Very well, then," she continued, "I will not marry Piers, nor shall Kate Atheling marry him. That is fair enough. If I manage to make her give him up, I give him up myself also. I am only doing to her as I do to myself.

"Now there is Wynn, and Sidmouth, and Russell — and others. Every one of them have appraised my value, and made inquiries about my wealth. No one has told me this, but I know it. I know it with that invincible certainty with which women know things they are never told. Cecil North? Yes, I like Cecil North. He really fell in love with me, — with *me, myself*. A woman knows; she is never deceived about that unless she wants to be deceived. He is poor, — the Westovers are all poor, — I do not care if he is as poor as Job. I am tired to death of rich people. If Cecil North would get a military commission in India, I could be his wife. I could follow the drum, or live in quarters with him, and I should be a better and a happier woman than I am here. This life is too small for me."

She was right in this estimation of herself. Her nature was one fitted to respond to great emergencies. She was a woman for frontiers and forts, for strife with men or elements, for days of danger in the shadow of suffering or death; and she was living in a society so artificial that any real cry of nature and needless familiarity, any sign of genuine passion was startling and distasteful to it. The soldierly temper inherited from her father demanded an adventurous life, because people made for overcoming obstacles cannot be morally healthy without obstacles to overcome. And, therefore, it was a poor life for Annabel Vyner that offered her no difficulty to surmount but the claims of Kate Atheling. She was quite aware of this, and the ring in her purse was no real triumph. It was rather one of those irreparable facts, the very thought of which gives pain.

If she had been morally stronger, she would have dominated her environment, and defied the circumstances that so easily prevented her from doing the right thing. She would have been obedient to Duty; and that grand, immutable principle would have given her strength to resist temptation, or, having fallen into it, to make the obvious reparation; for

> " So nigh is grandeur to our dust,
>   So near is God to man,
>   When Duty whispers low, '*Thou Must,*'
>   The Soul replies, ' *I Can.*' "

This morning, though she was far from diagnosing her feelings correctly, Annabel soon began to suffer from that nervous and even that physical fatigue which is bred of moral indifference. For nothing is more certain than that moral strength is the very *Life* of life. She yawned;

she felt the hours too long to be endured, while she pictured to herself the scene in the Atheling parlour, when Piers would confess the loss of the ring, and Kate lovingly excuse it. Finally, she became nervously angry at the persistence of the vision. In every possible way she tried to banish it, but though she fetched memories from farthest India, the exasperating phantasm would not be driven away.

In reality the affair produced very little apparent effect. Piers made his confession to Mrs. and Miss Atheling with so much genuine emotion that they could not but make light of the loss while he was present. Yet it troubled both women very much. Mrs. Atheling cried over it when she was alone; and Kate took it as a sign of some untoward event in the course of love between Piers and herself. No one is able to put aside such inferences and presentiments; and, quite unconsciously, it worked towards the end Kate feared. Piers began to fancy — perhaps unjustly — that he never entered Kate's or Mrs. Atheling's presence without seeing in their first glance an unspoken inquiry after the lost ring. In some measure he was to blame, if this was so. He had employed detectives to watch such servants of the Richmoor household as could have had access to the Duke's parlour on that unhappy night; and as the ladies were aware of this movement, it was only natural they should desire to know if any result came from it.

Of course there was no result; and the real culprit remained absolutely unsuspected. As the days wore away, her conscience grew accustomed to the situation; it made no troublesome demands; and Annabel even began to feel a certain pleasurable excitement in holding in her hands what might prove to be a power for great good, or great evil, — for she was not yet ready to admit an entirely evil intention; she chose rather to regard it as a practical jest which she might undo, or explain, in some future, favourable hour.

She kept the jewel always in her purse; she went frequently to the Athelings; and once or twice she had a transitory impulse to tell Kate the whole circumstance, and be guided by her advice in the matter. But the Evil One, who had prompted her in the first instance to take it, always met these intents or impulses with some plausible excuse; and every good impulse which does not crystallise into a good action, only tends towards the strengthening of the evil one. Then outside events made delay more easy. On the fifteenth of November, there was a short, decided argument in the House of Commons on the Civil List; a division was promptly taken, and the Government was found to be in a minority of twenty-nine. The Squire and Lord Exham returned home together, both very much annoyed at this result.

"All this election business will be to go over again," the Squire said, wearily. "Wellington and Peel are sure to take this opportunity to resign."

"Why should they resign, John?" asked Mrs. Atheling.

"Well, Maude," he answered, "they are bound to resign sooner or later; and I should think, if they have any sense left, they will go out as champions of the royal prerogative, rather than be driven out by a Reform division, which is sure to come. They will go out, my word for it, Maude!"

"And what then, John?"

"Well, then, we shall have all the bother of another election; and Earl Grey will form a new Ministry, and Lord Brougham will bully the new Ministry, as he has done the old one, about this Reform Bill. He intended to have begun that business this very night; but there was n't any Ministers, nor any Administration to arraign, and so he said, in his domineering way, that he would put the question of Reform off until the twenty-fifth of this month, and not a day longer, no matter what circumstances prevailed, nor who were His Majesty's Ministers. I can tell you the city was in a pretty commotion as we came home. We shall have a Reform Government now, with Earl Grey at the head, and the real fight will then begin."

"Earl Grey!" said Mrs. Atheling; "that is Edgar's friend."

"Well, I would n't brag about it, Mother, if I was thee. I shall have to go back to Yorkshire,

and so will Exham; and there will be no end of
bother, and a Reform Ministry at the end of it.
It is too bad! What they will do with Mr.
Brougham, I am sure I don't know. No Ministry can live without him; and it will be hard
work for any Ministry to live with him; for if he
drew up a bill himself, he would find faults in it,
and never rest until he had torn it to pieces."

Piers was sitting in the embrasure of a window,
holding Kate's hands, and talking to her in those
low, sweet tones that women love; and at this
remark he rose, and, coming towards the Squire,
said with a grave smile, " For such dilemmas,
Squire, there are remedies made and provided.
If it is a clever clergyman who arraigns the
church, or his superiors, he is made a bishop;
and thereafter, he sees no faults. If it is a clever
Commoner who arraigns the Government, the
Government makes him a peer; and in the
House of Lords, he finds the grace of silence.
Earl Grey will have Mr. Brougham made Lord
High Chancellor, and then *Lord* Brougham will
only have the power to put the question."

Exham's prophecy proved to be correct.
Brougham had declared that under any circumstances he would bring up Reform on the
twenty-fifth of November; but on the twenty-
second of November, he took his seat as Chancellor in the House of Lords. It was said the
Great Seal had been forced upon him; but the
Squire wondered what pressure, never before

known, had been discovered to make Henry
Brougham do anything, or take anything, he did
not want to do or take.

However the feat was an accomplished one;
and with Earl Gray, Lord Durham, Sir James
Graham, Viscounts Melbourne and Palmerston,
and other great leaders, Brougham kissed the
King's hand on his appointment just three days
before his threatened demonstration for Reform.
Soon after Parliament adjourned for the re-elec-
tion of Members in the Lower House; and the
Duke, with Lord Exham and Squire Atheling,
went down into Yorkshire.

Edgar and Cecil North also disappeared.
"They have gone into the country on business,
and I'll tell you what it is, Kitty," said Mrs.
Atheling, with a little happy importance. "A
friend of Earl Grey has a close borough, and
Edgar is to have it. I am sure I don't know
what will happen, if he should clash with
father in the House. Father cannot bear con-
tradicting."

"Nothing wrong will happen, Mother."

"To be sure, the floor of the House of Commons is a bit different from his own hearthstone.
When Edgar is a Parliament man, father will give
him his place."

"And Edgar will never forget to give father his
place, I am sure of that."

"I wouldn't stand a minute with him if he did.
What a father and son say to each other in their

homestead, is home talk; but Edgar must not
threep his father before strangers. No, indeed!"

"I would n't wonder if father comes round a
little to Edgar's views. He listened very patiently to Cecil North, the last time they talked
on politics."

"He *has* to listen in Parliament, and so he is
getting used to listening. He never listened
patiently at home — not even to me. But we
can hope for the best anyhow, Kitty."

"To be sure, Mother. Hoping for the best is
far better than looking for the worst."

"I should think it was. Do you believe Piers
will be in London at Christmas?"

"I fear not. Mother, he is going to send us
each a ring at Christmas; then we will forget the
other ring — shall we not?"

"I don't know, Kitty. I think a deal of that
other ring. No new one can make up for it.
Why, my dear, your father gave it to me the
night I promised to marry him. We were standing under the big white hawthorn at Belward.
I 'll never forget that hour."

"It is so long ago, Mother — you cannot care
very much now about it."

"Now, Kitty, if you think only young people
can be in love, get that idea out of your mind at
once. You don't know anything about love yet.
After twenty-five years bearing, and forbearing,
and childbearing, you will smile at your gentle-
shepherding of to-day. Your love is only a

fancy now, it will be a fact then that has its foundations in your very life. You do not love Piers Exham, child, as I love your father. You can't. It is n't to be expected. And it is a good thing, love is so ordered; for if it did not grow stronger, instead of weaker, marrying would be a poor way of living."

"That weary ring! I am so sorry that I ever put it on."

"I did not ask you to put it on, Kitty. I did not want you to put it on."

"Mother, please don't be cross."

"Kitty, don't be unjust; it is not like you."

Then Kitty laid her cheek against her mother's cheek, and said sadly, "I fear, somehow, that ring will make trouble between Piers and me."

"Nonsense, dearie! The ring is lost and gone. It can't make trouble now."

"Its loss was a bad omen, Mother."

"There is no omen against true love, Kitty. Love counts every sign a good sign."

"The Duke was very formal with me at my last visit. The Duchess dislikes me; and Miss Vyner has so many opportunities; it seems nearly impossible that Piers should ever marry me."

"If Piers loves you, there is no impossibility. Love works miracles. You cannot say ' impossible ' to Love. Love will find out a way."

CHAPTER NINTH

A FOOLISH VIRGIN

PARLIAMENT was adjourned on the twenty-third of December, and did not re-assemble until the third of February. The interval was one of great public excitement and of great private anxiety. The country had been assured of a Government pledged to Reform; and, in the main, were waiting as patiently as men, hungry and naked, and burning with a sense of injury and injustice, could wait. But no one knew what hour a spark might be cast into such inflammable material, — that would mean Revolution instead of Reform.

Consequently life was depressed, and not disposed to any exhibition of wealth or festivity; the most heartless and reckless feeling that it would not be endured by men and women on the very verge of starvation. The Queen also was unpopular, and the great social leaders were, as a general thing, bitter political partisans; in theatres and ball-rooms and even on the streets, the Whig and Tory ladies, when they met, looked at one another as Guelphs and Ghibellines, instead of christened English gentlewomen.

Both the Duchess of Richmoor and Miss Vyner were women of strong and irrepressible prejudices; and, before Parliament adjourned, they had made for themselves an environment of active, political enemies. And women carry their politics into their domestic and social life; the Duchess had wounded many of her oldest friends; and Annabel, with the haughty intolerance of youth and wealth, had succeeded in making herself a person whom all the ladies of the Reform party delighted either to positively offend, or to scornfully ignore.

These circumstances, with all her audacity and advantages, she was unable to control. Her brilliant beauty, her clever tongue, her ostentatious dress and display were as nothing against the united disposition of a score of other women to make her understand that they neither desired her friendship nor felt her influence; and she had at least the sense to retire from a conflict "whose weapons," she said contemptuously, "were not in her armory." This condition of affairs naturally threw her very much upon the Athelings for society. While the Duchess sat with a few old ladies of her own caste and political persuasion, talking fearfully of the state of English society and of the horrors Reform would inaugurate for the nobility, Annabel spent her time with Mrs. and Miss

Atheling, and learned to look hopefully into a future in which, perhaps, there would be neither dukes nor lords. Besides, Cecil North had a habit of visiting the Athelings also; and, without expressed arrangement, both Cecil and Annabel looked forward to those charming lunches which Mrs. Atheling dispensed with so little ceremony and so much good nature. It had been Cecil's intention to go with Edgar into the country; but when the hour for departure arrived, he had not been able to leave Annabel's vicinity, and, in some of those mysterious ways known to Love, she understood, and was pleased with this evidence of her power.

Cecil's mother had been particularly prominent in that social ostracism the Reform ladies had meted out to her; and it gave to the real liking which she had for Cecil a piquant relish to parade the young man as her devoted servant in all places where his noble mother would be likely to see or hear tell of her son's "infatuation." But Cecil North's affection, and the favour it received, did not much influence Kate. With the perversity of a woman in love, she believed Annabel to be only amusing herself during Lord Exham's absence; and she accepted, without a doubt, all the little innuendoes, and half-truths, and half-admissions which Annabel suffered herself, as it were, without intent, to make.

Thus the dreary winter days passed slowly

away. In January Edgar returned. His election had been a mere walk over the ground.
The patron of the borough of Shereham had
spoken the word, and Edgar Atheling was its
lawful representative. It was a poor little
place, but it gave Edgar a vote on the right side;
and Earl Grey also hoped much from his power
as a natural orator. He might take Brougham's
place, and be far more amenable to directions
than Brougham had ever been. Mrs. Atheling
considered none of these things. She took in
only the grand fact that her son was in Parliament, and that he must have won his place there
by some transcendent personal merit. True,
she had some little qualms of fear as to how
Edgar's father would treat the new representative of Englishmen; but her invincible habit of
hoping and her cheerful way of looking into the
future did not suffer these passing doubts to
seriously mar her glory and pride in her son's
dignity.

In fact, even in Annabel's eyes, Edgar Atheling was now an important person. Women do
not consider causes, they look at results; and
in Edgar Atheling's case the result was satisfactory. On the day the new member for Shereham
returned home, she was lunching with the Athelings, eating her salad and playing with Cecil
North's heart, when Edgar entered the room.
His honour sat well on him; he neither paraded,
nor yet affectedly ignored it. His mother's

pride, his sister's pleasure, and the congratulations of his friends made him happy, and he showed it. The lunch that was nearly finished was delayed for another hour. No one liked to break up the delightful meal and conversation; and when Annabel got back to Richmoor House the short day was over, and the Duchess had sent an escort to hurry her return.

"You are exceedingly imprudent, Annabel," she said, when the girl entered her presence; "and I do think it high time you stopped visiting so much at one house."

"Duchess, will you say what other house equally charming is open to me? You know how little of a favourite I am. To-day I was delayed by an event, — the return of young Atheling after his election. He is now an M. P., — a great honour for so young a man, I think."

"Honour, indeed! Grey or Durham, or some of those renegades to their own caste, have given him a seat. Grey would give a seat to a puppy if it could bark 'aye' for him."

"Well, I should not think Atheling will be a dumb dog; he has a ready tongue. Mr. North says he will take Brougham's place."

"He will do nothing of the kind. Young Atheling is a fine talker when he has to face a mob of grumbling men on a Yorkshire moor or a city common. It is a different thing, Annabel, to stand up before the gentlemen of England. As for Mr. North, I have told you before

that both the Duke and myself seriously object
to that entanglement."

Annabel laughed.   "There is no entanglement, Duchess, — that is, on my part."

"Then why throw yourself continually in the
young man's way?"

"You are scarcely polite.   He throws himself
in my way."

"Pardon.   I meant nothing disrespectful."

"And I have reasons."

"May I know them?"

"Yes.   Mr. North's mother was particularly
insulting to me at the last Morning Concert I
attended.   I heard also that she had spoken of
me as 'an Indian girl of doubtful parentage.'
She is particularly fond of Cecil, who is her
youngest child, and she is trying to make a marriage between him and that enormously rich
Miss Curzon.   I am going to defeat her plans."

Then the Duchess laughed.   "I never interfere with any woman's retributions," she said.
"But do not burn yourself at the fire you kindle
for others."

"I am fire-proof."

"I must think so, or surely Piers would have
influenced you."

"Lord Exham never tried to 'influence' me;
and only one woman in the world can 'influence'
him."

"You mean Miss Atheling, of course; and I
have already told you that there is not even a

supposition in that case.   Miss Atheling is out
of the question.   The Duke would never consent
to such a marriage; and I would never forgive
it.   Never!   I should prefer to lose my son
altogether."

"Then you ought to let Miss Atheling know
how you feel.   She is a very honourable, yes,
a very proud girl.   She would not force herself
into your family, no matter how much she loved
your son.   Now, I would.   If I had thought
you did *not* want me to marry Lord Exham, I
should probably have been his wife to-day."

The Duchess glanced at the speaker a little
scornfully, and said, " Perhaps you over-estimate
your abilities.   However, Annabel, your suggestion about Miss Atheling has much likelihood.   I shall make an opportunity to speak to
her.   Will you go out to-night?   There will be
the usual crush at Lady Paget's."

"Excuse me, I do not wish to go."   The
statement was correct.   She had begun to
weary of a routine of visiting that lacked deci-
sive personal interest.   She had many lovers;
but even love-making grows tiresome unless it
is reciprocal, or has some spice of jealousy, or
some element of the chase in it.   Cecil North
did interest her, and Piers Exham did stimulate
her desire for conquest; but Cecil was most
pleasantly met at the Athelings, and Lord
Exham was in Yorkshire.

So, after dining alone with the Duchess, she

went to a little drawing-room that was her favourite resort. The great ash logs burned brightly on the white marble hearth, and threw shifting lights on the white-and-gold furnishings, on the pictured walls, on the ferns and flowers, and on the lovely marble forms of two wood nymphs among them. She placed herself comfortably in a large easy-chair, with her back to the argand lamp, and stretched out her sandalled feet before the blaze, and nestled her head among the soft white cushions. The delicious drowsy atmosphere was a physical satisfaction of the highest order to her, quite as much so as it was to the splendid Persian cat that grumblingly resigned, at her order, the pleasantest end of the snow-white rug.

"Now I can think," she said with lazy satisfaction, as she closed her restless eyes and began the operation. "In the first place, I have set a ball rolling that I may not be able to manage. It is in the hand of the Duchess, and she will have no scruples — she never has, if she is fighting for her own side. Perhaps I ought not to have given her such a ' leader,' for Kate Atheling has always been kind to me — thoughtful about Cecil, ready at making excuses to let us have a little solitude, arranging shopping excursions in his presence, so that he would know where he could ' accidentally ' meet us — and so on. No, it was not exactly kind; but then, in love and war, all things are fair — and I dare say Miss Kate's motives were probably selfish enough. She would give me Cecil to make her own way clear to Piers; and, also, Cecil is a favourite with the Athelings and young Atheling's friend; and they know that he is poor, and doubtless wish to help him to a rich wife. Every one works out their own plan, why should not I do the same? But I must find out something about that ring, and, as the straight way is the best way, I will ask Kate the necessary questions. She will be sure to betray herself."

Then she opened her purse, took out the ring, and placed it upon her finger, holding up her hand to the blaze to catch its reflections. "It is a pretty little thing, but I have bought it two or three times over with my diamond locket. I wonder why Kate never wears that locket! Is it too fine? Or has she some feeling against me? I gave her it at Christmas, and I have only seen it once on her neck — that is strange! I never thought of it before — it really is not much of a ring — I have twenty finer ones — and I dare say I shall give it back some day: yes, of course I shall give it back — but at present — " and she stopped thinking of the demands of the present, and taking the ring off her finger laid it in the palm of her hand, and softly tossed it and the Hindoo charm up and down together ere she replaced them in their receptacle.

Evidently she had arranged things comfortably

with herself, for, after closing the purse, she began to swing it by its golden chain before the cat's eyes, until the creature became thoroughly annoyed, and tried to catch the gleaming, tantalising worry with its claws. The play delighted her; she gave herself up to its tormenting charm, and for once lost, in the momentary amusement, all consciousness of herself and her appearance. It was then the great white door swung noiselessly open, and Lord Exham stood within it. The sensuous little drama, so full of colour and life, instantly arrested him; and he stood motionless to watch it. The girl's strong, vivid face, her black hair, her dress of bright scarlet, her arms and hands flashing with gems, were thrown into dazzling prominence by the chair of white brocade in which she sat, and the white rug at her feet, and the lamp shining behind her. She waved the golden purse before the cat's eyes, and let it almost fall into the eager paws, and then drew it backward with a little laugh, and was not aware that she was, in the act, an absolutely bewitching type of mere physical beauty.

But Piers was aware of it. He forgot everything but delight in the moving picture; and, as he advanced, he cried, in a voice full of pleasure, "*Annabel! Annabel!*" And the girl answered her name with an instantaneous movement towards him. Her radiant face looked into his face, and ere they were aware they had met in each other's arms and Piers had kissed her.

She was silent and smiling, and he instantly recovered himself. "I ask your pardon," he said, releasing her and bowing gravely; "but you are one of the family, you know, and I have been long away, and am so glad to get home again that some liberty must be excused me."

"Oh, indeed!" she answered, with a pretty pout, "I think the apology is the worst part of the business," and she looked into his eyes with that steady, unwinking gaze which none withstand. Then he drew her closer, and said softly, "You are simply bewildering to-night, Annabel. How have you made yourself so beautiful?" As he spoke he led her to her seat, and drew a chair close to her side; and the cat leaped to his knee and began to loudly purr her satisfaction in her master's return.

"Are you alone to-night?" he asked. "Or perhaps you are expecting company?"

"I am alone. I expected no company; but Destiny loves surprises, and to-night she has surpassed herself. The Duchess has gone to Lady Paget's. I could not sacrifice myself so far. You know what her political nights are. And if it is not Relief Bills, and Reform Bills, then it is Mr. Clarkson and Anti-Slavery; and we are solemnly told to make little petticoats for the negro children if we desire to go to heaven." She laughed, and dropped her eyes, and was silent; and the silence grew dangerous. Fortunately, she herself broke the spell by asking Piers if he had seen Squire Atheling in Yorkshire.

"We came from Yorkshire together," he said. Then he began to talk about the election, and in a few minutes a butler announced his dinner, and Annabel's hour was over.

She was not disappointed. "We went far enough," she thought. "I am not yet ready to put my hand out further than I can draw it back. I cannot give up Cecil now; he is the only private pleasure I have. Every other thing I share with the Duchess, or somebody else. And Piers I should have to share with her and the Duke. As heir to the dukedom, they will always retain a right in his time and interests. No, Lord Exham, not yet — not yet."

She rose with the words, and went to the piano and dashed off in splendid style that famous old military fantasia, "The Battle of Prague." And the drift of her uncontrolled thoughts during it may be guessed by the first query she made of her intelligence when the noisy music ceased: —

"I wonder what the Athelings are doing? Piers says the Squire is at home. I suppose Mrs. Atheling and Kate are coddling, and petting, and feeding him."

In some respects Annabel judged fairly well. The Squire reached his home about the same

time that Lord Exham arrived at Richmoor
House, and found Mrs. Atheling waiting to
receive him. He made no secret of his joy in
seeing her again.   "I was afraid thou mightst be
gadding about somewhere, Maude," he said.
"It is pleasant to find thee at home."

"John Atheling!"

"Well, it is too bad to say such a thing,
Maude. I knew well I would find thee at home
when there was either chance or likelihood of my
getting back there. But where is little Kitty?
It is n't right without Kitty."

"Well, John, Squire Pickering's family came
to London a few days ago, and Kitty has gone
to the theatre with them."

"I 'll tell thee a good joke about Squire
Pickering, Maude," said the Squire, laughing
heartily as he spoke. "He was feared young
Sam Pickering was going to vote for Reform,
and he served a writ on him for a trespass, or
something of that sort, and got him put safely in
jail till voting time was over. Then he quashed
the writ and let the lad out. But, my word!
young Sam is fighting furious, and he has
treated his father nearly as bad as Edgar treated
me."

"Edgar is going to Parliament now. I told
thee he would. John, for goodness' sake, don't
quarrel with him before all England!"

"Maude Atheling! I never quarrelled with
Edgar. Never! He quarrelled with me. If

he had done his duty by his father, we would have been finger and thumb, buckle and strap, yesterday, and to-day, and to-morrow, and every other day. The Duke says my anger at Edgar is quite reasonable and justifiable."

" *The Duke!* So then thou art framing thy opinions to what *he* says. Dear me! I would n't have believed such a thing could ever come to pass."

"Wait till it *does* come to pass. Why, Richmoor and I very near came to quarrelling point because I would *not* frame my opinions by his say-so. I have been looking into things a bit, Maude, more than I ever did before, and I have learned what I am not going to deny for anybody. I met Philip Brotherton of Knaseborough, and he asked me to go home with him for two or three days— You know Philip and I have been friends ever since we were lads, and our fathers before us."

"I know that."

"So I went with him, and he showed me how working men live and labour in such towns as Leeds and Manchester; and I am not going to say less than it is a sin and a shame to keep human beings alive on such terms. I do not believe any Reform Bill is going to help them; but they ought to be helped; and they must be helped; or else government is nothing but blunderment, and legislating nothing but folly. And I said as much to Richmoor, and he asked

me if my son had been lecturing me; and I told
him I had been using my own eyes, and my own
ears, and my own conscience."

"What did he say to that?"

"He said, ' Squire, I do not like your asso-
ciating with Philip Brotherton. The man has
radical ideas, though he does not profess them.'
And I said, ' I like Philip Brotherton, and I
shall associate with him whenever I can make
it convenient to do so; and as for his ideas, if
they are radical, then Christianity is radical;
and as for professing them, Philip Brotherton
does better than that, he lives them;' and I
went on to say that I thought it would be a
right and righteous thing if both landlords and
loomlords would do the same."

"My word, John! Thou didst speak up! I'll
warrant Richmoor was angry enough."

The Squire laughed a little as he answered,
"Well, Maude, he got as red in the face as a
turkey-cock, and he asked me if I was really
going to be Philip Brotherton's fool. And I
answered, ' No, I am like you, Duke, I do my
own business in that line.' And he said, ' *Squire
Atheling!*' and turned on his heel and walked
one way; and I said, ' *Duke Richmoor!*' and
turned on my heel and walked the other way.
Now then, Maude, dost thou think he orders my
opinions for me?"

And Mrs. Atheling smiled understandingly
in her lord's face, and cut him a double portion

from the best part of the haunch of venison she was carving.

A few days after this event Annabel called one morning at the Athelings. She expected Cecil North to be there, and he was not there; she waited for him to come, and he did not come; she tried in many devious ways to get Kate to express an opinion about his absence, and Kate seemed entirely unconscious of it. It provoked her into an ill-natured anger; and, casting about in her mind for something disagreeable to say, she remembered her resolve to find out how the sapphire ring came to be in Lord Exham's possession. Even if "the straight way had not been the best way," she was by nature inclined to direct inquiries; and she had just proven in her mental manœuvring about Cecil North that indirect methods were not satisfactory. So she said bluntly:—

"Kate, did you ever hear about Lord Exham losing a ring he valued very much?"

"Yes," answered Kate, without the slightest embarrassment; "it was my mother's ring."

"Your mother's ring?"

"Yes."

"But Lord Exham had it on his finger."

"My mother loaned it to him. He admired it very much, and wished to have one made like it."

"The Duchess was sure that some lady had given it to him as a love gage. Do you know

that he has fretted himself sick about its loss?"

"Oh, no! I am sure he is not sick. My mother made light of the loss to him, though she really was very much attached to that particular ring."

"Have I ever seen her wear it?"

"No.   It was too small for her."

"Then it was a simple souvenir?"

"It was more than that; it was her betrothal ring.   Father bought it in Venice."

"Oh!"

"But she had a slim little hand, then — like mine is now — " said Kate, laughing, and spreading out her hand for Annabel to observe.

"Then you must have been talking of rings, and shown it to him."

"I was wearing it. I had it on during the lunch hour, and you were present. It is a wonder you did not notice it, for you are so curious about finger-rings."

"Yes, I am quite a ring collector."

"It was rather a singular ring."

"Will you describe it to me?"

Kate did so, and Annabel listened with apparent curiosity. "I wonder what Exham could want with such a queer ring," she said in answer.

"Perhaps he is also a ring collector."

"Perhaps!" But the one word by no means explained the thoughts forming in her mind.

She rose, and, lifting her bonnet, went to a mirror and carefully tied the satin ribbons under her chin, in the big bows then considered vastly becoming. Kate tried to arrest her hands. "Stay and take lunch with us," she urged. "Edgar is sure to be here; and I should like him to see you in that pretty cloth pelisse."

"Mr. Atheling never notices me; then why should he notice my pelisse? I heard Lady Inglis say that he is very much in Miss Curzon's society. If so, he will clash with his friend Mr. North, who is also her devoted slave."

"Now, Annabel! You know that Cecil North loves no one but you."

"How can you be so wise about his love-affairs?"

"No great wisdom is needed to see what he cannot hide."

"Was he here yesterday?"

"He was here last night. He called to tell us he was going to Westover on some business for his father. I suppose he wanted you to know."

"But you never thought of telling me. How selfish girls in love are! They cannot think a thought beyond their own lover. I declare I was going without giving you my news, — the Duchess has a large dinner party on the first of March. The Tory ladies will wait in her rooms the reading of this famous Reform Bill that Lord John Russell is concocting, and there will

be a great crowd. Kate, if I was you, I would
wear your court dress. It is very unlikely that
the Queen will receive at all this season."

"Perhaps we shall not be invited to the
dinner."

"You certainly will be invited. I heard the
list read, and as your name begins with ' A ' it
was almost the first. If Mr. Atheling does
come to lunch, give him my respects and describe my pelisse to him."

She went away with this mocking message,
and was driven first to a famous jeweller's, where
she bought a sapphire band sufficiently like the
one Lord Exham had lost to pass for it, if the
view was cursory and at a distance. Kate's
confidence had made one course exceedingly
plain to Annabel. She said to herself as she
drove through the city streets, "My best plan is
evidently to arouse Squire Atheling's suspicions.
I will let him see the ring on my hand. I will
lead him to think Piers gave it to me. He will
of course make inquiries, and I wonder what
Mrs. Atheling and Kate will say. It is a
pretty piece of confusion — and, if the matter
goes too far, I reserve the power to play the good
fairy and put all right. This is a complication
I shall enjoy thoroughly, and I am sure, with
nothing on earth but Reform and Revolution in
my ears, I deserve some little private amusement. All I have to do is to be constantly ready
for opportunities."

Opportunities, however, with Squire Atheling, were few and far between. It was not until the day before the first of March she found one. On that afternoon she called at the Athelings, and found Mrs. and Miss Atheling out. The Squire was walking from the fire-place to the window, and from the window to the fire-place, and grumbling at their absence. Miss Vyner's entrance diverted him for a few minutes; and as they were talking a servant brought in a small package. The Squire took it up, and laid it down, and then took it up again, and was evidently either anxious or curious concerning its contents.

"Why do you not open your package, Squire?" asked Annabel.

"Well, young lady, I am not going to act as if your presence was not entertainment enough and to spare."

"Nonsense! Please do not stand on ceremony with me. It may contain important papers — something relating to Church or State. I am only a young woman. Open it, Squire."

"Well, then, if you say so, I will open it," and he began fumbling at the well-tied string. Annabel saw her opportunity. In a moment she had slipped on to the forefinger of her right hand the lost ring, and the next moment she had gently pushed aside the Squire's hands, and was saying, "Let me unfasten the knots. I am cleverer at that work than you."

"To be sure you are. There is work little fingers do better than big ones, and this is that kind of a job. But I will get my knife and cut the knots; that is the best and quickest way."

He began to hunt in his pockets for his knife, but could not find it. "Dobson never does put things where they ought to be," he said fretfully; and then he pulled the bell-rope for Dobson with a force that fully indicated his annoyance. In the mean time, Annabel was quietly untying the string, and the Squire naturally watched her efforts. He was complaining and scolding his servant and his womenkind, and Annabel did not heed him; but when he suddenly stopped speaking, in the middle of a sentence, she looked into his face. It expressed the blankest wonder and curiosity. His eyes were fixed upon her hands, and he would probably have asked her some inconvenient question if Dobson had not entered at the moment. Then Annabel retired. Dobson had taken the parcel in charge, and she excused herself from further delay.

"I have several things to do," she said, "and I shall only be in the way of the parcel and its contents. Tell Mrs. Atheling and Kate that I called, will you, Squire?"

"To be sure! To be sure, Miss Vyner," he answered; but his eyes were on the papers Dobson was unfolding, and his mind was vaguely wandering to the ring he had seen on her finger. When he had satisfied his curiosity concerning the papers, his thoughts returned with persistent wonder to it. "I'll wager my best hunter, yes, I'll wager *Flying Selma* that was the ring I bought in Venice and gave to Maude. How did that girl get it? Maude would never sell it or give it away. Never! *Dal it!* there is something queer in her having it. I must find out how it comes to pass."

When he arrived at this decision Mrs. Atheling came into the room. She was rosy and smiling, and put aside with sweet good nature the Squire's complaints about both her and Kitty being out of the house when he was in it. "Not a soul to say a word to me, or to see that I had a bit of comfortable eating," he said in a tone of injury.

"Never mind, John!"

"Oh, but I do mind! I mind a great deal, Maude."

"You see, it was Kitty wanted me. She had to have a new clasp to the pearl necklace your mother left her; and she was sure you would like me to choose it, so I went with her. I thought we should certainly be home before you got back."

"Well, never mind, then. Nothing suits me so much as to see Kitty suited. I hope you bought a clasp good enough for the necklace."

"I did not forget that she was going with you to-morrow night."

"But you are going too, Maude?"

"Nay, I am not. When I can shut my ears as easy as my eyes, I can afford to be less particular about the company I keep. I know beforehand what the women in that crowd will say about their own danger, and about the murmuring poor who won't starve in peace, and I know that I would be sure to answer them with a little bit of plain truth."

"And the truth is not always pleasant, eh, Maude?"

"In this case I'm sure it would n't be pleasant. So, then, the outside of Richmoor House is the best side for me."

"I must say I'm getting a bit tired myself of the Duke's masterful way, and of his everlasting talk about the 'noble memories of the past.'"

"Then tell him, John, that the noble hopes of the future are something better than the noble memories of the past. The country is in a bad condition as ever was. Something must be done, and done quickly."

"I'm saying nothing to the contrary, Maude. But even if Reform was right, it cannot be carried. We must drive the nail that will go. That is only good common-sense, Maude."

"Mark my words, John. Reform will *have* to come, and better now than later. That which fools do in the end, wise men do in the beginning. I know, I know."

"On this subject thou knowest nothing what-

ever, Maude.   Now, then, I am going to have a
bit of sleep.   But I will say thus far — as soon
as ever I am sure that I am on a wrong road I
won't go a step further.   John Atheling is not
the man to carry a candle for the devil."

With these words he threw his bandana
handkerchief over his head, adding, "He hoped
now he had a ' right ' to a bit of sleep."   Then
Mrs. Atheling went softly out of the room.
There was a tolerant smile on her face, for she
was not deceived by the Squire's habit of digni-
fying his self-assertions and his self-indulgences
with the name of "rights."

CHAPTER TENTH

TROUBLE COMES UNSUMMONED

NEVER had the ducal palace of Richmoor been more splendidly prepared for festivity than on the night of the first of March, 1831. And yet every guest present knew that it was not a festival, but a gathering of men and women moved by the gravest fears for the future. The long suites of parlours, brilliantly lighted, were crowded with peers and noble ladies, wearing, indeed, the smiles of conventional pleasure; but all of them eager to discuss the portentous circumstances by which they were environed.

Annabel stood at the right hand of the Duchess, but was strangely distrait and silent. Everything had gone wrong with her. It had been a day of calamity. She began it with a fret and a scold, and her maid Justine had been from that moment in a temper calculated to provoke to extremities her impatient mistress. Then her costume did not arrive till some hours after it was due; and when examined, it was found to be very unbecoming. She had been persuaded to select a pale-blue satin, simply because she had tired of every other colour; and she was disgusted with the

13

effect of its cold beauty against her olive-tinted
skin. She wore out Justine's temper with the
variety of her suggestions, and her angry impa-
tience with every effort. The girl became sulkily
silent, then defiantly silent, then, after a most
unreasonable burst of anger, actively impertinent,
so much so that she left Annabel only one way
of retaliation — an instant dismissal. She lifted
her purse passionately, counted out the money
due, and, pushing it contemptuously towards the
girl, told her " to leave the house instantly."

To her utter amazement, Justine pushed back
the money. "I will not take it," she said. "I
have no intention of leaving the house until I see
the ring in your possession — the ring in your
purse, Miss — returned to the owner of it."

If Annabel had been struck to the ground, she
could not have been more confounded and be-
wildered ; and Justine saw and pushed her advantage. "Miss knows," she continued, "that police
detectives are watching night and day the innocent men whose duties are on this corridor.
Any hour some little thing may cause one of
them to be suspected and arrested; and then
who but I could save him from the gallows?
No, Miss, I shall not leave till you give up the
ring — till the real th — the real taker of it is
known."

These words terrified Annabel. She felt her
heart stop beating; a strange sickness overwhelmed her; she sunk speechless into a chair,

and closed her eyes. With an attention utterly devoid of sympathy, Justine put between her lips a tea-spoonful of aniseed cordial which she brought from her own apartment.

In a few minutes Annabel recovered herself physically; but her prostration, and the hysterical mood which followed it, were admissions she could not by any future word, or act, contradict. She had been taken by surprise, and surrendered. If she had had but ten minutes to survey the situation, she would have defied it; but such an emergency had never occurred to her. Over and over again she had supposed every other likelihood of discovery; this one, never! She was at the mercy of her maid; but for the time being the maid was not inclined to extremities. She only insisted that Annabel should use her influence to place the men under suspicion out of the danger of arrest; and when Annabel had explained, with a wretched little laugh, that the ring had been taken "as a means of forwarding her love-affair with Lord Exham," the maid assured her "she was on her side in that matter." Then she pocketed the sovereigns Annabel offered as a peace gift, and "hoped Miss would think no more of what she had said."

But Annabel could not dismiss the subject. Under her magnificent but singularly unbecoming gown, she carried a heart heavy with apprehension. The shadow of the gallows, which Justine had evoked for the suspected culprit, fell upon her own consciousness. In those days, the most trifling theft was punished with death; and Annabel had a terror of that mysterious Law of which she was so profoundly ignorant. How it would regard her position, she could not imagine. Would even her confession and restoration exonerate her? In this respect, she suffered from fright, as an ignorant child suffers. Besides which, when the subject of "confession" came close to her, she felt that it was impossible. Constantly she had flattered her conscience with this promise; but if it was to come to actuality, she thought she would rather die.

So it was with a wretched heart she took the place the Duchess had assigned her at her own right hand. This position associated her intimately with Lord Exham, and it was for this very reason the Duchess had decided upon it. She knew the value of the popular voice; she wished the popular voice to unite Lord Exham and her rich and beautiful ward; and she felt sure that their association at her right hand would give all the certainty necessary to such a belief. Heart-sick with her strange, new terror, Annabel stood in that brilliant throng. Just before the dinner hour, she saw Squire Atheling and Kate approaching to pay their respects to the Duchess. She saw also the quick, joyful lifting of Exham's eyelids, the bright flush of pleasure that gave sudden life to his pale cheeks, and the irrepressible gladness that made his voice musical, as he said softly, "How beautiful she is!"

"Miss Atheling?"

"Yes."

Then Annabel considered her rival's approach. Her eyes fell first on the Squire, whose splendid physique arrested every one's attention. He wore a coat of dark-blue broadcloth, trimmed with gold buttons, a long, white satin vest, and exquisitely fine linen, rather ostentatiously ruffled. On his arm Kate's hand just rested. Her gown of rich white silk was soft as lawn, and resplendent as moonbeams; and around her throat lay one string of Oriental pearls. Her bright, brown hair was dressed high, without any ornament; but there were silver buckles, set with pearls, on the front of her white satin sandals. A pause, a murmur of admiration was perceptible; for conversation ceased a moment as a creature so fresh, so pure, so exquisite, and so suitably protected, moved among them. Lord Exham, forgetting all ceremonies, went eagerly forward to meet these favoured guests; and the Duchess also had a momentary pleasure in Kate's well-gowned loveliness. She was very friendly to the Squire; and she took his daughter under her own protection.

After dinner — which was specially early for that night — the majority of the gentlemen went to the House. The Reform Bill, about which all England was in agonising suspense, was to be read for the first time. Never, within the memory of Englishmen, had there been so great a crowd eager to get into the House. Every inch of space on the floor was filled; and troops of eager politicians, from all parts of the country, were waiting at the doors of the various galleries. When they were opened, the clamour, the struggle, and the confusion was so indescribable that the Speaker threatened to have all the galleries cleared. Even among the members, there was great confusion and complaining; for their seats, though marked with their cards, had in many instances been taken by others.

Outside, the streets were packed with men wrought up to feverish excitement and anxiety; and in all the great centres of society, and in every club in London, there were restless crowds waiting for news from Westminster. The Duchess of Richmoor's parlours were the central point of Tory interest. Not one of the company there present but believed with Sir Robert Inglis — an orator of their party — that "Reform would sweep the House of Lords clear in ten years." This night was, to them, their salvation or their ruin. Below their jewelled bodices, their hearts trembled with anxious terror. After the departure of the members for the House, they gathered in little knots, wondering, and fearing, and listening to the noises in the crowded streets, with an agitation not quite devoid of pleasurable stimulation. For they were not without comforters and encouragers. The Duke of Wellington went from group to group, assuring them that Lord Grey's Ministry must go down, and that no Reform Bill which could injure the nobility would be permitted to pass the House of Lords.

Annabel was almost glad to see every one so unhappy. She had a perverse desire to say contradictious things. Her heart was heavy with fear, and it was burning with envy and jealousy. Kate's beauty, and Lord Exham's undisguised admiration, made her realise all the bitterness of failure. She wandered about making evil prophecies, or saying irritating truths, and watching Kate the while, till she was ready to cry out with mental pain and mortification. For the great Duke — never insensible to female loveliness — had given Kate his arm, and was walking about the parlours with her. Why had such honour not fallen to her lot? Never had she been so desirous to lead, to be admired, to enforce her eminent fitness to wear the Richmoor coronet. Never had she so signally failed. Even her wit had deserted her; she said *malapropos* clever things, and got snubbed for them. In her anger, and fear, and disappointment, she wished Reform *might* make a clean sweep of such a selfish crowd of so-called nobility. She had arrived at that point when her misery demanded company.

About ten o'clock, the Duke and Lord Exham returned. The large lofty rooms, with their moving throngs of splendidly attired men and women, were yet crowded; but their atmosphere was charged with an electric tension, generated by the unusual pitch to which every one's thoughts, and feelings, and words were set. Many were almost hysterical; some had subsided into mere waiting, conscious of requiring all their strength for simple endurance of the suspense; others, more hopeful, were restless and watching, — but all alike became instantly and breathlessly silent as the two men appeared. For a moment no one spoke; then the Duke of Wellington asked, with an assumption of cheerfulness, "What news? Has the Bill been read?"

"It has been read," answered Richmoor. "Lord John Russell introduced it in a speech lasting more than two hours."

"And pray what are its provisions."

"This infamous Bill proposes that every borough of less than two thousand inhabitants shall lose the right to send a member to Parliament."

"What a scandalous robbery of our privileges!" ejaculated some one of the listeners.

"It is nothing else!" answered the Duke. "It robs me of the gift of seven boroughs."

"What excuse did he make for such an act?"

"He supposed the case of a stranger, coming to England to investigate our method of representation, being taken to a green mound, and told that green mound sent two members to Parliament; or to a stone wall with three niches in it, and told that those three niches sent two

members to Parliament; or to a green park with
no signs of human habitation, and told that green
park sent two members to Parliament; and then
pictured the amazement of the stranger at this
condition of things. 'But,' he cried, 'how much
greater would be his amazement if he were then
taken to large and populous cities, full of in-
dustry, enterprise, and intelligence, and containing vast magazines of every kind of manufactures,
and was then told that these cities did not send
a single man to represent their rights and their
necessities in the great national council.' It was
really a very effective passage."

"We have heard that argument before; it is
stale and unprofitable," said the Duchess.

"Listen! This Bill proposes to give every
man paying taxes for houses of the yearly value
of ten pounds and upward — *a vote.*"

"What an absurdity!"

"It proposes to give Manchester, Birmingham,
Leeds, Sheffield, and three other large towns,
each two members, and London eight additional
members."

"Infamous! It will give us a mob government."

"This so-called Reform Bill gives the fran-
chise to one hundred and ten thousand people
in the counties of England who never had it
before; in the provincial towns, it gives it to fifty
thousand; in London, it gives it to ninety-five
thousand; in Scotland, to fifty thousand; and in
Ireland, to forty thousand: in all, half a million

of persons are to be added to the constituency of the House of Commons."

At this information the tendency of the whole company was to laughter. Indeed the Duke's face, and voice, and manner was that of a man telling an utterly absurd story. Such sweeping alterations were not conceivable; their very excess doomed them to ridicule and failure, in the opinion of the privileged class; but the Duke of Wellington's face expressed an anxiety not consonant with this feeling; and he asked gloomily:

"Did Lord John Russell *dare* to read the names of the boroughs he intends to disfranchise, with their members present?"

"He read them with the greatest emphasis and deliberation."

"And the result? What was the result? How did they take being robbed of their seats in this summary way?"

"The excitement in the House was incredible. He was derisively interrupted by shouts of laughter, and by cries of "Hear! Hear!" and by constant questions across the table from the members of those boroughs. The wisest statesmen in the House were aghast at proposals so sweeping and so revolutionary."

"What did Peel say?"

"Nothing. He sat rigid as a statue, his face working with emotion, his brow wrinkled and sombre. His supporters, who were gathered round him, burst again and again into uncontrollable laughter. Peel tried to make them behave like gentlemen, and could not. Every one is sure such a measure predicts a speedy downfall of Grey's Ministry."

"Of course it does," said the Duchess, with a contemptuous laugh. The laugh was contagious, and the majority of the company burst into merriment and ridicule.

"It is really a good joke," said an aged Marquis who had the idea that England was the birthright of her nobles.

"A good joke!" answered the Duke of Wellington, sternly. "I can tell you it is no joke. You will find it no laughing matter."

"I am weary of it all," whispered Annabel to Kate; "let us go into the conservatory." Kate was willing also, and as they entered the sweet, green place, with its tender lights and restful peace, she sighed with pleasure and said, "I wonder, Annabel, if the roses and camellias think themselves better than the violets and daisies."

"I dare say they do. Let us sit down here. I have had such a wretched day, and I am worn out;" and for a moment, as she looked in Kate's gentle face, she had a mind to tell her the whole truth about the unfortunate ring. But while she hesitated, there was a footstep; and in a moment, Piers pushed aside the fronds of the gigantic ferns and joined them.

"It is allowable," said Annabel, "provided you do do not mention Reform."

"There is no necessity here," he answered gallantly. "How could perfection be reformed?" Gradually the conversation fell into a more serious mood, and they began to speak of York-shire, and to long after its breezy wolds and lovely dales; and Annabel listened and said, "She would be delighted when they went down there." Kate also acknowledged that she was impatient to return to Atheling; and Piers watched her every movement, — the smile parting her lips, the light coming and going on her cheeks from dropped or lifted eyes, the graceful movements of her hands, the noble poise of her head, — all these things were fresh enchantments to him. What was the noisy, dusty Senate chamber to this green spot filled with the charming presence of the woman he adored?

Very quickly Annabel perceived that she was the one person *not* necessary; and she was too depressed to resent this position. With a whisper to Kate, she went away, promising to return in ten minutes. She did not return; but in half an hour — which had seemed as five minutes — the Duchess came in her stead, and said blandly, "Annabel has a headache, and has gone to sleep it away. I have sent the Squire home, Miss Atheling; I told him I should keep you here to-night. Indeed he was glad for you to remain; the streets are not in a very pleasant condition. London has lost its senses. It has gone mad; in the morning it may be saner."

So the sweet interval was over; but one secret glance between the lovers showed how delicious it had been. Kate went away with the Duchess; and waiting women led her to a splendid sleeping apartment. There, all night long, she kept the sense of Piers holding her hand in his; and, faintly smiling with this interior bliss, she dreamed away the hours until late in the morning.

Her first thought on awakening was, "What shall I wear? I cannot go to breakfast in a white silk gown." Then, as she rose, she saw a street costume laid ready for her use. "Mrs. Atheling sent it very early this morning," said the maid; and Kate thought with a blessing of the good mother who never forgot her smallest necessities. At breakfast, the Duchess was particularly gracious to her; she affected an entire oblivion of Piers's evident devotion, and talked incessantly of the stupidity of the Grey Ministry; but as she rose from the table, she said, —

"My dear Miss Atheling, will you do me the favour to come to my private parlour before you leave?"

Kate stood up, curtsied slightly, and made the required promise. But she did not at once attend the Duchess, as that lady certainly expected. She had promised Piers to walk with him in the conservatory, and finish their interrupted conversation of the previous night; and a gentle pressure of her hand reminded her of this previous engagement. So it was near the noon hour when she went to the room which the Duchess had selected for their interview.

She entered it without a suspicion of the sorrow waiting there for her, though the first glance at the cold, haughty face that greeted her made her a little indignant. "I expected you an hour ago, Miss Atheling," said the Duchess.

"I am sorry if I have detained you, Duchess. I did not think my interview with you could be of much importance."

"Perhaps not as important to you as the interview you put before it—and yet, perhaps, far more so. For I must tell you that such entirely personal companionship with Lord Exham, must cease from this very hour."

Kate had taken the seat the Duchess indicated on her entering the room; she now rose to her feet, and answered, "If so, Duchess, it is proper for me to leave your home at once. My mother is waiting to see me. She will tell me what it is right for me to do."

"In this case, I am a better adviser than your mother. I believe you to be a girl of noble principles, so I tell you frankly that Lord Exham is bound, by every honourable tie, to marry Miss Vyner. When you are not present, he is quite happy in her society; when you are present, you seem to exert some unaccountable influence over him. Miss Vyner has often complained of this. I thought it was simple jealousy on her part,

until I observed you with Lord Exham last night.
I am now compelled, by my duty to my son and
his affianced wife, to tell you how impossible a marriage between you and Lord Exham is and must
be. I believe this information to be all that is
necessary to a girl of your birth and breeding."

" What information, Duchess? " She asked the
question with a dignity that irritated a woman
who thought her word, without her reasons, was
quite sufficient.

" If you persist in having the truth, I must give
it to you. Remember, I would gladly have
spared you and myself this humiliation. Know,
then, that many years ago the late General
Vyner rendered the Duke a great service. When
Annabel was born, the Duke offered himself as
her godfather and guardian, and his son as her
husband. It is not necessary to go into details;
the facts ought to be sufficient for you. There
are circumstances which make the fulfilment of
this promise imperative; and, if you do not interfere, my son will very willingly perform his part
of it. Pardon me if I also remind you that your
birth and fortune make any hopes you may entertain of being the future Duchess of Richmoor
very presumptuous hopes. I assure you that I
have spoken reluctantly, and with sincere kindness; and I do not desire this conversation to interfere with our future intercourse. If you will
give me your promise, I know that I may trust
you absolutely."

"What do you wish me to promise?"

"That you will allow no love-making between Lord Exham and yourself; that you will not in any way interfere between Lord Exham and Miss Vyner, — in fact, promise me, in a word, that you will never marry Lord Exham. I assure you, such a marriage would be most improper and unfortunate."

Kate stood for a moment still and white as a marble statue; and when she spoke, her words dropped slowly and with an evident effort. And yet her self-control and dignity of manner was remarkable, as she answered, —

"Duchess, I have always done exactly what my dear wise father and mother have told me to do. I shall ask their advice on this matter before I make any promise. If they tell me to do as you wish me to do, I shall know that they are right, and obey them. I do not recognise any other human authority than theirs."

She was leaving the room after these words; but the Duchess cried angrily, "Your father must not at present be asked to interfere. There are interests — grave, political interests — between him and the Duke that cannot be imperilled for some love-nonsense between you and Lord Exham."

"There are no grave political interests between my mother and the Duke; and I shall, at all events, take my mother's counsel."

She had stood with the door open in her hand;

she now passed outside. So far she had kept
herself from any exhibition of feeling; but, oh,
how wronged and unhappy and offended she felt!
She went down and down the splendid stairway,
erect as a reed; but her heart was like a wounded
bird: it fluttered wildly in her bosom, and would
not be comforted until she reached that nest of
all nests, — her mother's breast.

There she poured out all her grief and indignation; and Mrs. Atheling never interrupted the
relation by a single word. She clasped the weeping girl to her heart, and stroked her hands, and
soothed her in those tender little ways that are
closer and sweeter than any words can be. But
when Kate had wept her passionate sense of
wrong and affront away, the good mother withdrew herself a little, and began to question her
child.

"Let me understand plainly, Kitty dear," she
said. "Her Grace — Grace indeed! — wishes
you to promise her that you will give up Piers
to Annabel."

"Yes, Mother."

"And that you will never marry Piers under
any circumstances?"

"Yes, Mother."

"And she thinks you 'presumptuous' in hoping to marry her son?"

"Yes, dear Mother. She said 'presumptuous.'
Am I; ought I to do as she wishes me? Oh, I
cannot give up Piers! Only this morning he

14

told me that he would never marry any woman
but me."

"Have I or your good father told you to give
up Piers?"

"No, Mother."

"When we do, you will of course know we
have good reasons for such an order, and you
will give him up. But as yet, father hasn't said
such a word; and I haven't. Kitty darling, the
Fifth Commandment only asks you to obey your
own father and mother. Let the Duchess put the
'giving up' where it ought to be. Let her tell
her son to give you up — that is quite as far as
her authority extends. She has nothing to say
to Kate Atheling; nor has my little Kitty any
obligation to obey her. She must give such
orders to Piers Exham. It is the duty of his
heart and conscience to decide whether he will
obey or not."

"Then I can go on loving him, Mother, without wronging myself or others?"

"Go on loving him, dearie."

"He said he was coming to ride with me at
three o'clock."

"Ride with him, and be happy while you can,
dear child. Let mother kiss such foolish tears
away. I can tell you father was proud of your
beauty last night. He said you were the loveliest
woman in London."

"The Duke of Wellington told me I was a
beautiful girl; and he said many wise and kind

things to me, Mother. What did father think about the Reform Bill?"

"It troubled him, Kitty; it troubled him very much. He said, 'It meant civil war;' but I said, 'Nonsense, John Atheling, it will prevent civil war.' And so it will, dearie. The people will have it, or else they will have far more. Your father said all London was shouting till day-break, 'The Bill! The whole Bill! Nothing but the Bill!' Now then, run away and wash your eyes bright, and put on your habit. I'll warrant Piers outruns the clock."

"Have you seen Edgar this morning?"

"For a few minutes just before you came. Cecil was with him. They had been up all night; but Cecil would have stayed if Annabel had been here. How he does love that girl!"

"I think she loves him. She looked ill last night, and I did not see her this morning. What a tangle it is! Annabel loves Cecil — Piers loves me — and the Duchess — "

"Never mind the Duchess, nor the tangle either, Kitty. To-day is yours; to-morrow is not born; and you are not told to unravel any tangle. There are *them* whose business it is; and they know all the knots and snarls, and will wind the ball all right in the end."

"Oh, Mother, how I love you!"

"Oh, Kitty, how I love you!"

"Piers loves me too, Mother."

"I'll warrant he does. Who could help loving

thee, Kitty? But men's love isn't mother's love; it is a good bit more selfish. God Almighty made thy father, John Atheling, of the best of human elements; but John Atheling has his shabby moments. Piers Exham won't be different; so don't expect it." Then the two women looked at each other and smiled. They understood.

CHAPTER ELEVENTH

"LIFE COMES AND GOES THE OLD, OLD WAY!"

ANNABEL had purposely kept out of Kitty's way. She had more than a suspicion of the probable interview between the Duchess and Kitty; and she wished to avoid any unpleasant-ness with the Athelings. They gave her the most reliable opportunities with Cecil North; and besides, she was so little of a general favourite as to have no other acquaintances as intimate. She was also really sick and unhappy; and the first occurrence of the day did not tend to make her less so. She wished to see the Duke about some matter relating to her finances; and, as soon as she left her room, she went to the apart-ment in which she was most likely to find him.

The Duke was not there, but Squire Atheling was waiting for him. He said he "had an appointment at two o'clock," and then, looking at the time-piece on the mantel, added, "I always give myself ten minutes or so to come and go on." Annabel knew this peculiarity of the Squire, and made her little joke on the matter; and then the conversation turned a moment on Kitty, and her probable return home. Annabel assured the

Squire she had already gone home, and then, offering her hand in adieu, was about to leave the room. The little brown-gemmed hand roused a sudden memory and anxiety in his heart. He detained it, as he said, "Miss Vyner, I have a question to ask you. Do you remember untying a parcel for me the other day?"

"I should think so," she replied with a laugh. "A more impatient man to do anything for I never saw."

"I am a bit impatient. But that is not what I am thinking of. You wore a ring that day — a sapphire ring with a little sapphire padlock — and that ring interests me very much. Will you tell me where you got it?"

"No, sir. Even if I knew, I might have excellent reasons for not telling you. Why, Squire, I am astonished at your asking such a question! Rings have mostly a story — a love-story too; you might be asking for secrets!"

"I beg pardon. To be sure I might. But you see a ring exactly like the one you wore, holds a secret of my own."

"Perhaps you are mistaken about the ring. So many rings look alike."

"I could not be mistaken. I do wish you would tell me — I am afraid you think me rude and inquisitive — "

"Indeed I do, sir! And, if you please, we will forget this conversation. It is too personal to be pleasant."

With these words she bowed and withdrew, and the Squire got up and walked about the room until the Duke entered it. By that time, he had worried himself into an impatient, suspicious temper, and was touchy as tinder when his political chief asked him to sit down and discuss the situation with him.

"Exham has gone to see a number of our party; but I thought I would outline to you personally the course we intend to pursue with regard to this infamous Bill." The Squire bowed but said not a word; and the Duke proceeded, "We have resolved to worry and delay it to the death. In the Commons, the Opposition will go over and over the same arguments, and ask again, and again, and again, the same questions. This course will be continued week after week — month after month if necessary. Obstruction, Squire, obstruction, that is the word!"

"What do you mean exactly by 'obstruction'?"

"I will explain. Lord Exham will move, 'That the Speaker do now leave the Chair.' When this motion is lost, some other member of the Opposition will move, 'That the debate be now adjourned.' That being lost, some other member will again move, 'That the Speaker do now leave the Chair,' and so, with alternations of these motions, the whole night can be passed — and night after night — and day after day. It is quite a legitimate parliamentary proceeding."

"It may be," answered the Squire; "but I am

astonished at your asking John Atheling to take
any part in such ways. I will fight as well as
any man, on the square and the open; if I
cannot do this, I will not fight at all. I would
as soon worry a vixen fox, as run a doubling
race of that kind. No, Duke, I will not worry,
and nag, and tease, and obstruct. Such tactics
are fitter for old women than for reasoning men,
sure of a good cause, and working to win it."

"I did not expect this obstruction from you,
Squire; and, I must say, I am disappointed—
very much disappointed."

"I don't know, Duke Richmoor, that I have
ever given you cause to think I would fight in
any other way than in a square, stand-up, face-
to-face manner. Wasting time is not fighting,
and it is not reasoning. It is just tormenting an
angry and impatient nation; it is playing with
fire; it is a dangerous, deceitful, cowardly bit of
business, and I will have nothing to do with it."

"You remember that I gave you your seat?"

"You can have it back and welcome. I took
my seat from you; but when it comes to right and
wrong, I take orders only from my own conscience."

"Advice, Squire, advice; I did not think of
giving you orders."

"Well, Duke, I am perhaps a little hasty; but
I do not understand obstructing warfare. I am
ready to attack the Bill, tooth and nail. I am
ready to vote against it; but I do not think what
you call 'obstructing' is fair and manly."

"All things are fair in love and war, Squire; and this is a war to the knife-hilt for our own caste and privileges."

Here there was a light tap at the door, and, in answer to the Duke's "enter," Annabel came in. She said a few words to him in a low voice, gave him a paper, and disappeared. But, short as the interview was, it put the Duke in a good temper. He looked after her with pride and affection, and said pleasantly,—

"Fight in your own way, Squire Atheling; it is sure to be a good, straight-forward fight. But the other way will be the tactics of our party, and you need not interfere with them. By-the-bye, Miss Vyner is a good deal at your house, I think."

"She is always welcome. My daughter likes her company. We all do. She is both witty and pretty."

"She is a great beauty — a particularly noble-looking beauty. She will make a fine Duchess, and my son is most fortunate in such an alliance; for she has money, — plenty of money, — and a dukedom is not kept up on nothing a year. Perhaps, however, this Reform Bill will eventually get rid of dukedoms and dukes, as it proposes to do with boroughs and members."

The Squire did not immediately answer. He wanted a definite assertion about Lord Exham and Miss Vyner, and could not decide on words which would unsuspiciously bring it. Finally, he blurted out an inquiry as to the date of a marriage between them; and the Duke answered carelessly, —

"It may occur soon or late. We have not yet fixed the time. Probably as soon as this dreadful Reform question is settled. But as the ceremony will surely take place at the Castle, Atheling Manor will be an important factor in the event."

He was shifting and folding up papers as he spoke, and the Squire *felt*, more than understood, that the interview had better be closed. Ostensibly they parted friends; but the Squire kept his right hand across his back as he said "good-morning," and the Duke understood the meaning of this action, though he thought it best to take no notice of it.

"What a fractious, testy, touchy fellow this is!" he said irritably to himself, when he was alone. "A perfect John Bull, absolutely sure of his own infallibility; sure that he knows everything about everything; that he is always right, and always must be right, and that any one who doubts his always being right is either a knave or a fool. *Tush!* I am glad I gave him that thrust about Piers and Annabel. It hurt. I could see it hurt, though he kept his hand to cover the wound."

The Duke was quite right. Squire Atheling was hurt. He went straight home. In any trouble, his first medicine was his wife; for though he pretended to think little of her advice, he always took it — or regretted that he had not taken it. He found her half-asleep in the chair by the window which she had taken in order to watch Lord Exham and Kitty ride down the street together. She was at rest and happy; but the Squire's entrance, at an hour not very usual, interested her. "Why, John!" she asked, "what has happened? I thought you went to the House at three o'clock."

"I have some questions to ask in my own house, first," he answered. "Maude, I am sure you remember the ring I gave you one night at Belward, — the ring you promised to marry me on, the sapphire ring with the little padlock?"

"To be sure I remember it, John."

"You used to wear it night and day. I have not seen it on your hand for a long time."

"It became too small for me. I had to take it off. Whatever has brought it into your thoughts at this time?"

"I saw one just like it. Where did you put your ring?"

"In my jewel-case."

"Is it there now."

She hesitated a moment, but a life-time of truth is not easily turned aside. "John," she answered, "it is not there. It is gone."

"I thought so. Did you sell it for Edgar, some time when he wanted money?"

"Edgar never asked me for a shilling. I never gave him a shilling unknown to you. And I did not sell the ring at all.   I would never have done such a thing."

"But I have seen the ring on a lady's hand."

"Do you know the lady?"

"I think I could find her."

"I will tell you about it, John.   I loaned it to Kitty, and Piers saw it and wanted one made like it for Kitty, and so he took it away to show it to his jeweller, and lost it that very night.   He has moved heaven and earth to find it, but got neither word nor sight of it.   You ought to tell him where you saw it."

"Not yet, Maude."

"Tell me then."

"To be sure!   I saw it on Miss Vyner's hand."

"Impossible!"

"Sure!"

"But how?"

"Thou mayst well ask 'how.'   Piers gave it to her."

"I wouldn't believe such a thing, not on a seven-fold oath."

"Thou knowest little about men.   There are times when they would give their souls away. Thou knowest nothing about such women as Miss Vyner.   They have a power that while it lasts is omnipotent.   Antony lost a world for Cleopatra, and Herod would have given half, yes, the 'whole of his kingdom to a dancing woman, if she had asked him for it."

"Those men were pagans, John, and lived in foreign countries. Christian men in England —"

"Christian men in England, in proportion to their power, do things just as reckless and wicked. Piers Exham has never learned any control; he has always given himself, or had given him, whatever he wanted. And I can tell thee, there is a perfect witchery about Miss Vyner in some hours. She has met Exham in a favourable time, and begged the ring from him."

"I cannot believe it. Why should she do such a thing? She must have had a reason."

"Certainly she had a reason. It might be pure mischief, for she is mischievous as a cat. It might be superstition; she is as superstitious as an Hindoo fakir. She has charms and signs for everything. She orders her very life by the stars of heaven. I have watched her, and listened to her, and never trusted her about Kitty — not a moment. Now this is a secret between thee and me. I asked her to-day about the ring, and she would say neither this nor that; yet somehow she gave me to understand it was a love token."

"She is a liar, if she means that Piers gave it to her as a love token. I saw the young man half an hour ago. If ever a man loved a maid, he loves our Kitty."

"Yet he is going to marry Miss Vyner."

"He is not. I am sure he is not. He will marry Kate Atheling."

"The Duke told me this afternoon that Lord

Exham would marry Miss Vyner as soon as this Reform question is settled. He said the marriage would take place at the Castle."

"The Duke has been talking false to you for some purpose of his own."

"Not he. Richmoor has faults — more than enough of them; but he treads his shoes straight. A truthful man, no one can say different."

"I wouldn't notice a thing he said for all that. Pass it by. Leave Kitty to manage her own affairs."

"No, I will not! Thou must tell Kitty to give the man up. He is going to marry another woman."

"I don't believe a word of it."

"His father said so. What would you have?"

"Fathers don't know everything."

"Now, Maude Atheling, my girl shall not marry where she is not wanted. I would rather see her in her death shroud than in her wedding gown, if things were in that way."

"John, I have always been open as the day with you, and I will not change now. The Duchess said something like it to Kitty this morning, so you see there has been a plan between the Duke and Duchess to make trouble about Piers. Kitty came home very troubled."

"And you let her go out with the man! I am astonished at you!"

"She asked me what she ought to do, and I told the dear girl to be happy until *you* told her to be miserable. If you think it is right to do so, tell her when she comes home never to see Piers again."

" You had better tell her. I cannot."

" I cannot, and I will not, for the life of me."

" Don't you believe what I say?"

" Yes — with a grain of salt. Piers is to hear from yet."

" Well, you must speak to her, Mother. My heart is too soft. It is *your* place to do it."

" My heart is as soft as yours, John. I say, let things alone. We are going to Atheling soon — we cannot go too soon now. If it must be told her, Kate will hear it, and bear it best in her own home; and, besides, he will not be within calling distance. John, this thing cannot be done in a hurry. God help the dear girl — to find Piers false — to give him up — it will break her heart, Father!"

" Kitty's heart is made of better stuff. When she finds out that Piers has been false to her, she will despise him."

" She will make excuses for him."

" No good woman will care about an unworthy man."

" Then, God help the men, John! If that were so, there would be lots of them without any good woman to care for them."

" Show Kitty that Piers is unworthy of her love, and I tell you she will put him out of her heart very quickly. I think I know Kitty."

"Women do not love according to deserts, John. If a woman has a bad son or daughter, does she take it for comfort when they go away from her? No, indeed! She never once says, 'They were nothing but a sorrow and an expense, and I am glad to be rid of them.' She weeps, and she prays all the more for them, just because they were bad. And one kind of love is like another; so I will not speak ill of Piers to Kate; besides, I do not think ill of him. If she has to give him up, it will not be his fault; and I could not tell her 'he is no loss, Kate,'—and such nonsense as that, — for it would be nonsense."

"What will you say then?"

"I shall help her to remember everything pleasant about him, and to make excuses for him. Even if you put comfort on the lowest ground possible, no woman likes to think she has been fooled and deceived, and given her heart for worse than nothing. Nine hundred and ninety-nine women out of a thousand would rather blame Fate or father or Fortune, or some other man or woman, than their own lover."

"Women are queer. A man in such a case whistles or sings his heartache away with the thought, —

> " 'If she be not fair for me,
> What care I how fair she be?'"

"You are slandering good men, John. Plenty of men would not give heart-room to such selfish love. They can live for the woman they love,

and yet live apart from her. My advice is that
we go back to Atheling at once. My heart is
there already. Kitty and I were talking yesterday of the garden. The trees will soon be in
blossom, and the birds busy building in them.
Oh, John, —

> " ' The Spring's delight,
> In the cowslip bright,
> As she laughs to the warbling linnet!
> And a whistling thrush,
> On a white May bush,
> And his mate on the nest within it!'"

And both caught the joy of the spring in the
words, and the Squire, smiling, stooped and kissed
his wife; and she knew then that she had permission to carry her daughter out of the way
of immediate sorrow. As for the future, Mrs.
Atheling never went into an enemy's country
in search of trouble. She thought it time enough
to meet misfortune when it came to her.

Kate was not averse to the change. Her conversation with the Duchess naturally affected her
feeling towards Annabel. She could not imagine
her quite ignorant of it; and it was, therefore, a
trial to have the girl intruding daily into her life.
Yet self-respect forbade her to make any change
in their relationship to each other. Annabel,
indeed, appeared wishful to nullify all the
Duchess had said by her behaviour to Cecil
North. Never had she been so familiar and so
affectionate towards him, and she evidently de-

sired Mrs. Atheling and Kate to understand that she was sincerely in love, and had every intention of marrying for love.

But yet she was unable to disguise her pleasure when she was suddenly told of their proposed return to the country. A vivid wave of crimson rushed over her face and throat; and though she said she "was sorry," there was an uncontrollable note of satisfaction in her voice. She was really sorry in one respect; but she had become afraid of the Squire. He asked such point-blank questions. His suspicions were wide awake and veering to the truth. He was another danger in her situation, and she felt Justine to be all she could manage. Mrs. Atheling and Kate being gone, her visits to the Vyner house could naturally cease; and, as the winter was nearly over, she could arrange some other place for her meetings with Cecil North. Indeed, he had already joined her in a few early morning gallops; and, besides which, she reflected, "Love always finds out a way." Cecil was a quite manageable factor.

About the middle of March, one fine spring evening, Mrs. Atheling and Kate came once more near to their own home. The road was a beautiful one, bordered with plantations of feathery firs on each side; and the pure resinous odour was to these two northern women sweeter than a rose garden. And, oh, what a home-like air the long, rambling old Manor House had, and how

Minna Brown.

bright and comfortable were its low-ceiled rooms!
When Kate went to her own chamber, a robin
on a spray of sweet-briar was singing at her
window. She took it for her welcome back to
the happy place. To be sure, the polished oak
floor with its strips of bright carpet, the little
tent-bed with its white dimity curtains, and the
low, latticed windows, full of rosemary pots and
monthly roses, were but simple surroundings;
yet Kate threw herself with joyful abandon into
her white chair before the blazing logs, and
thought, without regret, of the splendid rooms
of the Vyner mansion, and the tumult of men
and horses in the thousand-streeted city outside it.

Certainly Piers was in the city, and she had no
hope of his speedy return to the country. But,
equally, she had no doubts of his true affection;
and the passing days and weeks brought her no
reasons for doubting. She had frequent letters
from him, and many rich tokens of his constant
remembrance. And, as the spring advanced, the
joy of her heart kept pace with it. Never before
had she taken such delight in the sylvan life
around her. The cool sweetness of the dairy;
the satiny sides of the milking-pails; the trig
beauty of the dairymaids, waiting for the cows,
coming slowly out of the stable, — the beautiful
cows, with their indolent gait and majestic tramp,
their noble, solemn faces, and their peaceful
breathing, — why had she never noticed these

things before? Was it because we must lose
good things — though but for a time — in order
to find them? And very soon the bare, brown
garden was aflame with gold and purple crocus
buds, and the delicious woody perfume of wall-
flowers, and the springtide scent of the sweet-
briar filled all its box-lined paths. The trees
became misty with buds and plumes and tufts
and tassels; and in the deep, green meadow-
grass the primroses were nestling, and the
anemones met her with their wistful looks.

And far and wide the ear was as satisfied as
the eye with the tones of waterfalls, the inland
sounds of caves and woods, the birds twittering
secrets in the tree-tops, and the running waters
that were the tongue of life in many a silent
place. Oh, how beautiful, and peaceful, and happy
were these things! Often the mother and daughter wondered to each other how they could ever
have been pleased to exchange them for the gilt
and gewgaws and the social smut of the great
city. Thus they fell naturally into the habit of
pitying the Squire, and Edgar, and Piers, and
wishing they were all back at Atheling to share
the joy of the spring-time with them.

One night towards the close of April, Kate
was very restless. "I cannot tell what is the
matter, Mother," she said. "My feet go of their
own will to the garden gates. It is as if my
soul knew there was somebody coming. Can it
be father?"

"I think not, Kitty. Father's last letter gave
no promise of any let-up in the Reform quarrel.
You know the Bill was read for the second time
as we left London; and Earl Grey's Ministry
had then only a majority of one. Your father
said the Duke was triumphant about it. He was
sure that a Bill which passed its second reading
by only a majority of one, could be easily mutilated in Committee until it would be harmless.
The Lords mean to kill it, bit by bit, — that will
take time."

"But what then, Mother?"

"God knows, child! I do not believe the
country will ever settle to work again until it
gets what it wants."

"Then will the House sit all summer?"

"I think it will."

At these words a long, cheerful "*hallo!*" —
the Squire's own call in the hunting-field — was
heard; and Kate, crying, "I told you so!" ran
rapidly into the garden. The Squire was just
entering the gates at a gallop. He drew rein,
threw himself off his horse, and took his daughter
in his arms.

"I am so glad, Father!" she cried. "So happy,
Father! I knew you were coming! I knew you
were coming! I did that!"

"Nay, not thou! I told nobody."

"Your heart told my heart. Ask mother.
Here she comes."

Then, late as it was, the quiet house suddenly

became full of noise and bustle; and the hubbub
that usually followed the Squire's advent was
everywhere apparent.   For he wanted all at once,
— his meat and his drink, his easy coat and his
slippers, his pipe and his dogs, and his serving
men and women.   He wanted to hear about the
ploughing, and the sowing, and the gardening;
about the horses, and the cattle, and the markets;
the farm hands, and the tenants of the Atheling
cottages.   He wanted his wife's report, and his
steward's report, and his daughter's petting and
opinions.   The night wore on to midnight before
he would speak of London, or the House, or the
Bill.

"I may surely have a little bit of peace, Maude,"
he said reproachfully, when she ventured to in-
troduce the subject; "it has been the Bill, and
the Bill, and the Bill, till my ears ache with the
sound of the words."

"Just tell us if it has passed, John."

"No, it has *not* passed; and Parliament is dis-
solved again; and the country has taken the bit
in its teeth, and the very mischief of hell is let
loose.   I told the Duke what his 'obstructing'
ways would do.   Englishmen like obstructions.
They would put them there, if they were absent,
for the very pleasure of getting over them.   Many
a man that was against the Bill is now against the
'obstructions' and bound to get over them."

"Did Piers come down with you, Father?"
asked Kate.   She had waited long and patiently,

and the Squire had not named him; and she felt
a little wounded by the neglect.

"No. He did not come down with me, Kitty.
But I dare say he is at the Castle. The Duke
spoke of returning to Yorkshire at once."

"He might have come with you, I think."

"I think not. A man's father and mother
cannot always be put aside for his sweetheart.
Lovers think they can run the world to their own
whim-whams. 'T would be a God's pity if they
could!"

"What are you cross about, Father? Has
Piers vexed you?"

"Am I cross, Kitty? I did not know it. Go to
bed, child. England stands where she did, and
Piers is yet Lord of Exham Hall. I dare say he
will be here to-morrow. I came at my own pace.
He would have to keep the pace of two fine
ladies. And I'll be bound he fretted like a race-
horse yoked in a plough."

And Kitty was wise enough to know that she
had heard all she was likely to hear that night;
nor was she ill-pleased to be alone with her hopes.
Piers was at hand. To-morrow she might see
him, and hear him speak, and feel the tenderness
of his clasp, and meet the love in his eyes. So
she sat at the open casement, breathing the sweetness and peace of the night, and shaping things
for the future that made her heart beat quick
with many thoughts not to be revealed. The
faint smile of the loving, dreaming of the loved

one, was on her lips; and if a doubt came to her,
she put it far away.   In fear she would not dwell,
and, besides, her heart had given her that insight
which changes faith into knowledge.   She *knew*
that Piers loved her.

The Squire had no such clear confidence.
When Kitty had gone away, he said plainly, "I
am not pleased with Piers.   I do not like his
ways; I do not like them at all.   After Kate left
London, he was seen everywhere, and constantly,
with Miss Vyner."

"Why not? She is one of his own household."

"They were very confidential together.   I
noticed them often for Kitty's sake."

"I do wish, Squire, that you would leave Kitty's
love-affairs alone."

"*That* I will not, Maude.   If I have any business now, it is to pay attention to them.   I have
taken your 'let-alone' plan, far too long.   My
girl shall not be courted in any such underhand,
mouse-in-the-corner way.   Her engagement to
Lord Exham must be publicly acknowledged, or
else broken entirely off."

"The man loves Kate.   He will do right to her."

"Loves Kate! Very good.   But what of the
Other One?   He cannot do right to both."

"Yes, he can.   Their claims are different.
You may depend on that.   Kate is the love of
his soul; the Other One is like a sister."

"I do not trust either Piers or the Other One
— and I wish she would give me my ring."

" You do not certainly know that she has your
ring. "

" I will ask her to let me see it."

" Now, John Atheling, you will meddle with
things that concern you, and let other things
alone. It may be your duty to interfere about
your daughter. You may insist on having her
recognised as the future Duchess of Richmoor, —
it will be a feather in your own cap; you may
say to the Duke, you must accept my daughter,
or I will — "

" Maude! You are just trying to stand me
upon my pride. You cannot do that any longer.
If you are willing to let Kate 'drift,' I am not. It
is my duty to insist on her proper recognition."

" Then do your duty. But it is *not* your duty
to catechise Miss Vyner about *my* ring. When
that inquiry is to be made, I will make it myself.
If Piers has to give up Kate, it will be to him a
knock-down blow; it will be a shot in the backbone; you need not sting him at the same time."

" I will speak to him to-morrow, and see the
Duke afterwards. I owe my little Kate that
much."

" And the Duke and yourself will be the
upper and the nether millstones, and your little
Kate between them. I know! I know!"

" I will do what is right, Maude, and I will be
as kind as I can in doing it. Who loves Kitty as
I do? There is a deal said about mother love;
but, I tell thee, a father's love is bottomless. I

would lay my life down for my little girl, this
minute."

"But not thy pride."

"Not my honour — which is her honour also.
Honour must stand with love, or else — nay, I
will not give thee any more reasons. I know my
decision is right; but it is thy way to make out
that all my reasons are wrong. I wish thou
wouldst prepare her a bit for what may come."

"There is no preparation for sorrow, John.
When it comes it smites."

Then the Squire lit his pipe, and the mother
went softly upstairs to look at her little girl.
And, as she did so, Kate's arms enfolded her, and
she whispered, "Piers is coming to-morrow. Are
you glad, Mother?"

Then, so strange and contrary is human nature,
the mother felt a moment's angry annoyance.
"Can you think of no one but Piers, Kate?" she
asked. And the girl was suddenly aware of her
selfish happiness, and ashamed of it. She ran
after her mother, and brought her back to her
bedside, and said sorrowfully, "I know, Mother,
that about Piers I am a little sinner." And then
Mrs. Atheling kissed her again, and answered,
"Never mind, Kitty. I have often seen sinners
that were more angel-like than saints — " and
the shadow was over. Oh, how good it is when
human nature reaches down to the perennial!

·CHAPTER TWELFTH

THE SHADOW OF SORROW STRETCHED OUT

WHEN the Squire entered the breakfast parlour, Kate was just coming in from the garden. The dew of the morning was on her cheeks, the scent of the sweet-briar and the daffodils in her hair, the songs of the thrush and the linnet in her heart. She was beautiful as Hebe, and fresh as Aurora. He clasped her face between his large hands, and she lifted the bunch of daffodils to his face, and asked, "Are they not beautiful? Do you know what Mr. Wordsworth says about them, Father?"

"Not I! I never read his foolishness."

"His 'foolishness' is music; I can tell you that. Listen sir, —

> "'A smile of last year's sun strayed down the hills,
> And lost its way within yon windy wood;
> Lost through the months of snow — but not for good :
> I found it in a clump of daffodils.'

Are they not lovely lines?"

"They sound like most uncommon nonsense, Kitty. Come and sit beside me, I have something far more sensible and important to tell you."

"About the Bill, Father?"

" Partly about the Bill and partly about Edgar.
Which news will you have first? "

" Mother will say 'Edgar,' and I go with
mother."

" I do not think you can tell me any news
about Edgar, John."

" Go on, Father, mother is only talking. She
is so anxious she cannot pour the coffee straight.
What about Edgar? "

" I must tell you that I made a speech two
days before the House closed; and the papers
said it was a very great speech, and I think it
was a tone or two above the average. Did you
read it ? "

" You never sent us a paper, Father."

" You would n't have read it if I had sent it.
I knew Philip Brotherton would read every word,
so it went to him. I was a little astonished at
myself, for I did not know that I could bring out
the very truth the way I did ; but I saw Edgar
watching me, and I saw no one else; and I just
talked to him, as I used to do, — good, plain,
household words, with a bit of Yorkshire now
and then to give them pith and power. I was
cheered to the echo, and if Edgar, when I used
to talk to him for his good, had only cheered me
on my hearthstone as he cheered me in the
Commons, there would n't have been any ill
blood between us. Afterwards, in the crush of
the lobby, I saw Edgar a little before me; and
Mr. O'Connell walked up to him, and said, ' Athel-

ing, you ought to take lessons from your father,
he strikes every nail on the head. In your case,
the old cock crows, but the young one has not
learnt his lesson.' I was just behind, and I heard
every word, and I was ready to answer; but
Edgar did my work finely."

"He should not have noticed him," said Mrs.
Atheling.

"Ah, but he did! He said, 'Mr. O'Connell, I
will trouble you to speak of Squire Atheling respectfully. He is not old; he is in the prime of
life; and, in all that makes youth desirable, he is
twenty-five years younger than you are. I think
you have felt his spurs once, and I would advise
you to beware of them.' And what O'Connell
answered I cannot tell, but it would be up to
mark, I can warrant that! I slipped away before
I was noticed, and I am not ashamed to say I
was pleased with what I had heard. 'Not as old
as O'Connell by twenty-five years!' I laughed
to myself all the way home; and, in the dark of
the night, I could not help thinking of Edgar's
angry face, and the way he stood up for me. I
do think, Maude, that somehow it must have been
thy fault we had that quarrel — I mean to say,
that if thou hadst stood firm by me, — that is, if
thou hadst — "

"John, go on and do not bother thyself to
make excuses. Was that the end of it?"

"In a way. The next afternoon I was sitting
by the fireside having a quiet smoke, and think-

ing of the fine speech I had made, and if it would
be safe to try again, when Dobson came in and
said, ' Squire, Mr. Edgar wishes to see you,' and
I said, ' Very well, bring Mr. Edgar upstairs.' I
had thrown off my coat; but I had on one of my
fine ruffled shirts and my best blue waistcoat, and
so I didn't feel so very out of the way when
Edgar came in with the loveliest young woman
on his arm — except Kitty — that I ever set eyes
on; and I was dumfounded when he brought
her to me and said, ' My dear Father, Annie
Curzon, who has promised to be my wife, wants
to know you and to love you.' And the little
thing — for she is but a sprite of a woman —
laid her hand on my arm and looked at me; and
what in heaven's name was I to do?"

"What did you do?"

"I just lifted her up and kissed her bonny
face, and said I had room enough in my heart
and home for her; and that she was gladly welcome, and would be much made of, and I don't
know what else — plenty of things of the same
sort.   My word! Edgar was set up."

" He may well be set up," answered Mrs. Atheling; "she is the richest and sweetest girl in
England; and she thinks the sun rises and sets
in Edgar Atheling. He ought to be set up with
a wife like that."

" He was, with her and me together. I don't
know which of us seemed to please him most.
Maude, they are coming down to Lord Ashley's

on a visit, and I asked them *here*. I could not do any different, could I?"

"If you had you would have been a poor kind of a father. What did you say?"

"I said, when you are at Ashley Place come over to Atheling, and I gave Edgar my hand and looked at him ; and he looked at me and clasped it tight, and said, 'We will come.'"

"That was right."

"I am glad I have done right for once, Maude. Do you know that Ashley is one of the worst Radicals in the lot of them?"

"Never mind, John. I have noticed that, as a general thing, the worse Radical, the better man ; but a Tory cannot be trusted to give a Radical a character. The Tories are very like the poor cat who said, 'If she only had wings, she would gladly extirpate the whole race of those troublesome sparrows.'"

"There are to be no more Tories now, we have got a new name. Lord John Russell called us 'Conservatives,' and we took to the word, and it is as like as not to stick to us. It will be Conservatives and Reformers in the future."

"But you said the Reform Bill was lost."

"I said it had not passed. What of that? The rascals have only been downed for this round ; they will be up to time, when time is called June the twenty-first; and they will fight harder than ever."

"How was the Bill lost? By obstructions?"

" Yes; when it was ready to go into Committee,
General Gascoigne moved that, ' The number of
members returned to Parliament ought not to be
diminished ; ' and when the House divided on this
motion, Gascoigne's resolution had a majority of
eight."

" Then Grey's Ministry have retired? " said
Mrs. Atheling, in alarm.

" No, they have not ; they should have done
so by all decent precedents ; but, instead of be-
having like gentlemen, they resolved to appeal
to the country. We sat all night quarrelling on
this subject ; but at five in the morning I was
worn out with the stifling, roaring House, and
sick with the smell of dying candles, and the reek
and steam of quarrelling human beings, so I
stepped out and took a few turns on Westminster
Bridge. It was a dead-calm, lovely morning, and
the sun was just rising over the trees of the Abbey and the Speaker's house, and I had a bit of
heart-longing for Atheling."

" Why did you not run away to Atheling,
Father? "

" I could not have done a thing like that, Kitty,
not for the life of me. I went back to the House ;
and for three days we fought like dogs, tooth and
nail, over the dissolution. Then Lord Grey and
Lord Brougham did such a thing as never was:
they went to the King and told him, plump and
plain, he must dissolve Parliament or they would
resign, and he must be answerable for conse-

quences; and the King did not want to dissolve
Parliament; he knew a new House would be still
fuller of Reform members; and he made all kinds
of excuses. He said, 'The Crown and Robes
were not ready, and the Guards and troops had
not been notified;' and then, to his amazement
and anger, Lord Brougham told him that the
officers of State had been summoned, that the
Crown and Robes were ready, and the Guards
and troops waiting."

"My word, John! That was a daring thing to
do."

"If William the Fourth had been Henry the
Eighth, Lord Brougham's head would n't have
been worth a shilling; as it was, William flew
into a great passion, and cried out, 'You! You,
my Lord Chancellor! You ought to know that
such an act is treason, is high treason, my lord!'
And Brougham said, humbly, that he did know it
was high treason, and that nothing but his solemn belief that the safety of the State depended
on the act would have made him bold enough to
venture on so improper a proceeding. Then the
King cooled down; and Brougham took from his
pocket the speech which the King was to read;
and the King took it with words; that were partly
menace, and partly joke at his Minister's audacity,
and so dismissed them."

"I never heard of such carryings on. Why
did n't Brougham put the Crown on his own
head, and be done with it?"

"I do not like Brougham; but in this matter, he acted very wisely. If the King had refused to dissolve a Parliament that had proved itself unable to carry Reform, I do think, Maude, London would have been in flames, and the whole country in rebellion, before another day broke."

"Were you present at the dissolution, John?"

"I was sitting beside Piers, when the Usher of the Black Rod knocked at the door of the Commons. It had to be a very loud knock, for the House was in a state of turbulence and confusion far beyond the Speaker's control; while Sir Robert Peel was denouncing the Ministry in the hardest words he could pick out, and being interrupted in much the same manner. I can tell you that a good many of us were glad enough to hear the guns announcing the King's approach. The Duke told me afterwards that the Lords were in still greater commotion. Brougham was speaking, when there were cries of 'The King! The King!' And Lord Londonderry rose in a fury and said, 'He would not submit to —' Nobody heard what he would not submit to; for Brougham snatched up the Seals and rushed out of the House. Then there was terrible confusion, and Lord Mansfield rose and was making a passionate oration against the Reform Bill, when the King entered and cut it short. Well, London went mad for a few hours. Nearly every house was illuminated; and the Duke of Wellington, and the Duke of Richmoor, and other great Tories had their windows broken, as a warning not to obstruct the next Parliament. I really don't know what to make of it all, Maude!"

"Well, John, I think statesmen ought to know what to make of it."

"I rode down from London on my own nag; and in many a town and village I saw things that made my heart ache. Why, my dears, there has been sixty thousand pounds put into — not bread and meat — but peas and meal to feed the starving women and children; the Government has given away forty thousand garments to clothe the naked; and the Bank of England — a very close concern — is lending money, yes, as much as ten thousand pounds, to some private individuals, in order to keep their factories going. Something is far wrong, when good English workmen are paupers. But I don't see how Parliamentary Reform is going to help them to bread and meat and decent work."

"John, these hungry, naked men know what they want. Edgar says a Reform Parliament will open all the ports to free trade, and tear to pieces the infamous Corn Laws, and make hours of work shorter, and wages higher and —"

"Give the whole country to the working men. I see! I see! Now, Maude, men are not going to run factories for fun, nor yet for charity; and farmers are not going to till their fields just to see how little they can get for their wheat."

"Father, what part did Piers take in all this trouble?"

"He voted with his party. He was very regular in his place."

"I will go now and put on my habit. Piers sent me word that he would be here soon after eleven o'clock;" and Kate, with a smile, went quickly out of the room. The Squire was nonplussed by the suddenness of her movement, and did not know whether to detain her or not. Mrs. Atheling saw his irresolution, and said, —

"Let her go this time, John. Let her have one last happy memory to keep through the time of trouble you seem bound to give her."

"Can I help it?"

"I don't know."

"You speak as if it was a pleasure to me."

"What for are you so set on interfering just at this time?"

"Because it is the right time."

"Who told you it was the right time?"

"My own heart, and my own knowledge of what is right and wrong."

"You are never liable to make a mistake, I suppose, John?"

"Not on this subject. I never saw such an unreasonable woman! Never! It is enough to discourage any man;" and as Mrs. Atheling rose and began to put away her silver without answering him a word, he grew angry at her want of approval, and put on his hat and went towards the stables.

He had no special intention of watching for
Lord Exham, and indeed had for the moment
forgotten his existence, when the young man
leaped his horse over the wall of the Atheling
plantation. The act annoyed the Squire; he
was proud of his plantation, and did not like tres-
passing through it. Such a little thing often
decides a great thing; and this trifling offence
made it easy for the Squire to say, —

"Good-morning, Piers, I wish you would dis-
mount. I have a few words to speak to you;"
and there was in his voice that shivery half-
tone which is neither one thing nor the other:
and Exham recognised it without applying the
change to himself. He was a little annoyed at
the delay; but he leaped to the ground, put the
bridle over his arm, and stood beside the Squire,
who then said, —

"Piers, I have come to the decision not to
sanction any longer your attentions to Kate —
unless your father also sanctions them. It is
high time your engagement was either publicly
acknowledged or else put an end to."

"You are right, Squire; what do you wish me
to do? I will make Kate my wife at any time
you propose. I desire nothing more earnestly
than this."

"Easy, Piers, easy. You must obtain the
Duke's consent first."

"I could hardly select a worse time to ask
him for it. I am of full age. I am my own

master. I will marry Kate in the face of all opposition."

" I say you will not. My daughter is not for you, if there is any opposition. The Duke and Duchess are at the head of your house; and Kate cannot enter a house in which she would be unwelcome."

" Kate will reside at Exham."

" And be a divider between you and your father and mother. No! In the end she would get the worst of it; and, even if she got the best of it, I am not willing she should begin a life of quarrelling and hatred. You can see the Duke at your convenience, and let me know what he says."

" I will see him to-day," he had taken out his watch and was looking at it as he spoke. " Will you excuse me now, Squire ?" he asked. " I sent Kate a message early this morning promising to call for her about eleven. I am already late."

" You may turn back. I will make an excuse for you. You cannot ride with Kate to-day."

" Squire, I made the offer and the promise. Permit me to honour my word."

" I will honour it for you. There has been enough, and too much, riding and walking, unless you are to ride and walk all your lives together. Good-morning ! "

" Squire, give me one hour ? "

" I will not."

" A few minutes to explain."

" I have told you that I would explain."

"I never knew you unkind before. Have I offended you? Have I done anything which you do not approve? "

"That is not the question. I will see you again — when you have seen your father."

" You are very unkind, very unkind indeed, sir."

"Maybe I am; but when the surgeon's knife is to use, there is no use pottering with drugs and fine speeches. It is the knife between you and Kate — or it is the ring;" and the word reminded him of the lost love gage, and made his face hard and stern. Then he turned from the young man, and had a momentary pleasure in the sound of his furious galloping in the other direction; for he was in a state of great turmoil. He had suddenly done a thing he had been wishing to do for a long time ; and he was not satisfied. In short, passionate ejaculations, he tried to relieve himself of something wrong, and did not succeed. " He deserves it; he was all the time with that Other One, — day by day in the parks, night after night in the House and the opera; he gave her that ring — I 'll swear he did; how else should she have it? My Kate is not going to be second-best — not if I can help it; what do I care for their dukedom? — confound the whole business ! A man with a daughter to watch has a heart full of sorrow — and it is all her mother's fault! "

Setting his steps to such aggravating opinions, he reached the Manor House and went into the parlour. Kate stood at the window in her riding dress. She had lost her usual fine composure, and was nervously tapping the wooden sill with the handle of her whip. On her father's entrance, she turned an anxious face to him, and asked, " Did you see anything of Piers, Father? "

"I did. I have been having a bit of a talk with him."

" Then he is at the door? I am so glad! I thought something was wrong! "

" Stop, Kitty. He is not at the door. He has gone home. I sent him home. Now don't interrupt me. I made up my mind in London that he should not see you again until your engagement was recognised by his father and mother."

" Should not see me again! Father! "

" That is right."

"But I must see him! I must see him! Where is mother? "

" Mother thinks as I do, Kate."

" Oh, what shall I do? What shall I do? "

" Go upstairs, and take off your habit, and think over things. You know quite well that such underhand courting — "

"Piers is not underhand. He is as straightforward as you are, Father."

" There now! Don't cry. I won't have any crying about what is only right. Come here, Kitty. Thou knowest thy father loves every hair of thy head. Will he wrong thee? Will he give thee a moment's pain he can help? Kitty, I heard talk in London that fired me — I saw things that have to be explained."

"Father, you will break my heart!"

"Well, Kitty, I have had a good many heart-aches all winter about my girl. And I have made up my mind, if I die for it, that there shall be no more whispering and wondering about your relationship to Piers Exham. Now don't fret till you know you have a reason. Piers has a deal of power over the Duke. He will win his way — if he wants to win it. Then I will have a business talk with both men, and your engagement and marriage will be square and above-board, and no nodding and winking and shrugging about it. You are Kate Atheling, and I will not have you sought in any by-way. Before God, I will not! Cry, if you must. But I think better of you."

"Oh, Mother! Mother! Mother!"

"Yes! you and your mother have brought all this on, with your 'let things alone, be happy to-day, and to-morrow will take care of itself' ways. If you were a milk-maid, that plan might do; but a girl with your lineage has to look behind and before; she can't live for herself and herself only."

"I wish I was a milk-maid!"

"To be sure. Let me have the lover I want, and my father, and my mother, and my brother, and my home, and all that are behind me, and all

that are to come after, and all honour, and all
gratitude, and all decent affection can go to the
devil!" and with these words, the Squire lifted
his hat, and went passionately out of the room.

Though he had given Kate the hope that Piers
would influence his father, he had no such expectation.   There was a very strained political feeling between the Duke and himself; and, apart
from that, the Squire had failed to win any social
liking from the Richmoors.   He was so independent; he thought so much of the Athelings,
and was so indifferent to the glory of the Richmoors.   He had also strong opinions of all kinds,
and did not scruple to express them; and private
opinions are just the one thing *not* wanted and
not endurable in society.   In fact, the Duke and
Duchess had both been subject to serious re-
lentings for having any alliance, either political
or social, with their opinionated, domineering
neighbour.

And Piers, driven by the anguish of his unexpected calamity, went into his father's presence
without any regard to favourable circumstances.
Previously he had considered them too much;
now he gave them no consideration at all.   The
Duke had premonitory symptoms of an attack of
gout; and the Duchess had just told him that
her brother Lord Francis Gower was going to
Germany, and that she had decided to accompany his party.   "Annabel looks ill," she added;
"the season has been too much for a girl so emo-

tional; and as for myself, I am thoroughly worn out."

"I do not like separating Piers and Annabel," answered the Duke. "They have just become confidential and familiar; and in the country too, where Miss Atheling will have everything in her favour!"

"Annabel is resolved to go abroad. She says she detests England. You had better make the best of the inevitable, Duke. I shall want one thousand pounds."

"I cannot spare a thousand pounds. My expenses have been very great this past winter."

"Still, I shall require a thousand pounds."

The Duchess had just left her husband with this question to consider. He did not want to part with a thousand pounds, and he did not want to part with Annabel. She was the brightest element in his life. She had become dear to him, and the thought of her fortune made his financial difficulties easier to bear. For the encumbrances which the times forced him to lay on his estate need not embarrass Piers; Annabel's money would easily remove them.

He was under the influence of these conflicting emotions, when Piers entered the room, with a brusque hurry quite at variance with his natural placid manner. The Duke started at the clash of the door. It gave him a twinge of pain; it dissipated his reveries; and he asked petulantly, "What brings you here so early, and so noisily, Piers?"

"I am in great trouble, sir. Squire Atheling — "

"Squire Atheling again! I am weary of the man!"

"He has forbidden me to see Miss Atheling."

"He has done quite right. I did not expect so much propriety from him."

"Until you give your consent to our marriage."

"Why, then, you will see her no more, Piers. I will never give it. Never! We need not multiply words. You will marry Annabel."

"Suppose Annabel will not marry me?"

"The supposition is impossible, therefore unnecessary."

"If I cannot marry Miss Atheling, I will remain unmarried."

"That threat is as old as the world; it amounts to nothing."

"On all public and social questions, I am your obedient son and successor. I claim the right to choose my wife."

"A man in your position, Piers, has not this privilege. I had not. If I had followed my youthful desires, I should have married an Italian woman. I married, not to please myself, but for the good of Richmoor; and I am glad to-day that I did so. Your duty to Richmoor is first; to yourself, secondary."

"Have you anything against Miss Atheling?"

"I object to her family — though they are undoubtedly in direct descent from the royal Saxon family of Atheling; I object to her poverty; I object to her taking the place of a young lady who has every desirable qualification for your wife."

"Is there no way to meet these objections, sir?"

"No way whatever." At these words the Duke stood painfully up, and said, with angry emphasis, "I will not have this subject mentioned to me again. It is dead. I forbid you to speak of it." Then he rang the bell for his Secretary, and gave him some orders. Lord Exham leaned against the mantelpiece, lost in sorrowful thought, until the Duke turned to him and said, —

"I am going to ride; will you go with me? There are letters from Wetherell and Lyndhurst to talk over."

"I cannot think of politics at present. I should be no help to you."

"Your mother and Annabel are thinking of going to Germany. I wish you would persuade them to stop at home. Is Annabel sick? I am told she is."

"I do not know, sir."

"You might trouble yourself to inquire."

"Father, I have never at any time disobeyed you. Permit me to marry the woman I love. In all else, I follow where you lead."

"Piers, my dear son, if my wisdom is sufficient for 'all else,' can you not trust it in this matter? Miss Atheling is an impossibility, — mind, I say

an impossibility, — now, and to-morrow, and in
all the future. That is enough about Miss Atheling. Good-afternoon! I feel far from well, and I
will try what a gallop may do for me."

Piers bowed; he could not speak. His heart
beat at his lips; he was choking with emotion.
The very attitude of the Duke filled him with
despair. It permitted of no argument; it would
allow of no hope. He knew the Squire's mood
was just as inexorable as his father's. Mrs.
Atheling had defined the position very well, when
she called the two men, " upper and nether millstones." Kate and he were now between them.
And there was only one way out of the situation
supposable. If Kate was willing, they could
marry without permission. The Rector of Belward would not be difficult to manage; for the
Duke had nothing to do with Belward; it was in
the gift of Mrs. Atheling. On some appointed
morning Kate could meet him before the little
altar. Love has ways and means and messen-
gers; and his face flushed, and a kind of angry
hope came into his heart as this idea entered
it. Just then, he did not consider how far Kate
would fall below his best thoughts if it were
possible to persuade her to such clandestine
disobedience.

The Duke was pleased with himself. He felt
that he had settled the disagreeable question
promptly and kindly; and he was cantering
cheerfully across Belward Bents, when he came

suddenly face to face with Squire Atheling. The surprise was not pleasant; but he instantly resolved to turn it to service.

"Squire," he said, with a forced heartiness, "well met! I thank you for your co-operation. In forbidding Lord Exham your daughter's society, you have done precisely what I wished you to do."

"There is no 'co-operation' in the question, Duke. I considered only Miss Atheling's rights and happiness. And what I have done, was not done for any wish of yours, but to satisfy myself. Lord Exham is your business, not mine."

"I have just told him that a marriage with Miss Atheling is out of all consideration; that both you and I are of this opinion; and, I may add, that my plans for Lord Exham's future would be utterly ruined by a *mésalliance* at this time."

"You will retract the word '*mésalliance*,' Duke. You know Miss Atheling's lineage, and that a duke of the reigning family would make no '*mésalliance*' in marrying her. I say retract the word!" and the Squire involuntarily gave emphasis to the order by the passionate tightening of his hand on his riding-whip.

"I certainly retract any word that gives you offence, Squire. I meant no reflection on Miss Atheling, who is a most charming young lady —"

"There is no more necessity for compliments

than for — the other thing. I have told Miss Atheling to see Lord Exham no more. I will make my order still more positive to her."

" Yet, Squire, lovers will often outwit the wisest fathers."

" My daughter will give me her word, and she would not be an Atheling if she broke it. I shall make her understand that I will never forgive her if she allies herself with the house of Richmoor."

"Come, come, Squire! You need not speak so contemptuously of the house of Richmoor. The noblest women in England would gladly ally themselves with my house."

"I cannot prevent them doing so; but I can keep my own daughter's honour, and I will. Good-afternoon, Duke! I hope this is our last word on a subject so unpleasant."

"I hope so. Squire, there are some important letters from Lyndhurst and Wetherell; can you come to the Castle to-morrow and talk them over with me."

"I cannot, Duke."

Then the Duke bowed haughtily, and gave his horse both rein and whip; and the angry thoughts in his heart were, "What a proud, perverse unmanageable creature! He was as ready to strike as to speak. If I had been equally uncivilised, we should have come to blows as easily as words. I am sorry I have had any dealings with the fellow. Julia warned me — a man ought to

take his wife's advice wherever women are factors
in a question. Confound the whole race of
country squires! — they make all the trouble that
is made."

Squire Atheling had not any more pleasant
thoughts about dukes; but they were an under-
current, his daughter dominated them. He
dreaded his next interview with her, but was not
inclined to put it off, even when he found her, on
his return home, with Mrs. Atheling. She had
been weeping; she hardly dried her tears on his
approach. Her lovely face was flushed and
feverish; she had the look of a rose blown by a
stormy wind. He pushed his chair to her side,
and gently drew her on to his knees, and put his
arm around her, as he said, —

" My little girl, I am sorry! I am sorry! But
it has to be, Kitty. There is no hope, and I will
not fool thee with false promises. I have just
had a talk with Richmoor. He was very rude,
very rude indeed, to thy father." She did not
speak or lift her eyes; and the Squire continued,
" He used a word about a marriage with thee that
I would not permit. I had to bring him to his
senses."

" Oh, Father! "

"Would you have me sit quiet and hear the
Athelings made little of."

" No, Father."

" I thought not."

" After what the Duke has said to me, there

17

can be no thought of marriage between Piers and
thee.   Give him up, now and forever."

"I cannot."

"But thou must."

"It will kill me."

"Not if thou art the good, brave girl I think
thee.   Piers is only one little bit of the happy
life thy good God has given thee.   Thou wilt
still have thy mother, and thy brother, and thy
sweet home, and all the honour and blessings of
thy lot in life — *and thy father, too*, Kitty.   Is
thy father nobody?"

Then she laid her head on his breast and
sobbed bitterly; and the Squire could not speak.
He wept with her.   And sitting a little apart, but
watching them, Mrs. Atheling wept a little also.
Yet, in spite of his emotion, the Squire was inexorable; and he continued, with stern and steady
emphasis, "Thou art not to see him.   Thou art
not to write to him.   Thou art not even to look
at him.   Get him out of thy life, root and branch.
It is the only way.   Come now, give me thy
promise."

"Let me see him once more."

"I will not.   What for?   To pity one another,
and abuse every other person, right or wrong.
The Richmoors don't want thee among them at
any price; and if I was thee I would stay where
I was wanted."

"Piers wants me."

"Now then, if you must have the whole bitter

truth, take it. I don't believe Piers will have any
heartache wanting thee. He was here, there, and
everywhere with Miss Vyner, after thou hadst left
London; and I saw the ring thou loanedst him
on her finger."

Then Kate looked quickly up. Once, when
Annabel had removed her glove, and instantly
replaced it, a vague suspicion of this fact had
given her a shock that she had named to no one.
It seemed so incredible she could not tell her
mother. And now her father's words brought
back that moment of sick suspicion, and confirmed it.

"Are you sure of what you say, Father?"

"I will wage my word and honour on it."

There was a moment's intense silence. Kate
glanced at her mother, who sat with dropped
eyes, unconsciously knitting; but there was not
a shadow of doubt or denial on her face. Then
she looked at her father. His large countenance,
usually so red and beaming, was white and drawn
with feeling, and his troubled, aching soul looked
at her pathetically from the misty depths of his
tearful eyes. Her mother she might have argued
and pleaded with; but the love and anguish sup-
plicating her from that bending face was not to
be denied. She lifted her own to it. She kissed
the pale cheeks and trembling lips, and said,
clearly, —

"I promise what you wish, Father. I will not
speak to Piers, nor write to him, nor even look at

him again — until you say I may," and with the
words she put her hand in his for surety.

He rose to his feet then and put her in his
chair; but he could not speak a word. Trem-
blingly, he lifted his hat and stick and went out
of the room; and Mrs. Atheling threw down her
knitting, and followed him to the door, and
watched him going slowly through the long,
flagged passageway. Her face was troubled
when she returned to Kate. She lifted her knitting and threw it with some temper into her work-
basket, and then flung wide open the casement
and let the fresh air into the room. Kate did
not speak; her whole air and manner was that
of injury and woe-begone extremity.

"Kate," said her mother at last, " Kate, my
dear! This is your first lesson in this world's
sorrow. Don't be a coward under it. Lift up
your heart to Him who is always sufficient."

"Oh, Mother! I think I shall die."

"I would be ashamed to say such words.
Piers was good and lovesome, and I do not
blame you for loving him as long as it was
right to do so. But when your father's word
is against it, you may be very sure it is *not* right.
Father would not give you a moment's pain, if
he could help it."

"It is too cruel! I cannot bear it!"

"Are you asked to bear anything but what
women in all ages, and in all countries, have had
to bear? To give up what you love is always

hard. I have had to give up three fine sons, and your dear little sister Edith. I have had to give up father, and mother, and brothers, and sisters; but I never once thought of dying. Whatever happens, happens with God's will, or with God's permission; so if you can't give up cheerfully to your father's will, do try and say to God, as pleasantly as you can, *Thy* Will be my will."

" I thought you would pity me, Mother."

"I do, Kate, with all my heart. But life has more loves and duties than one. If, in order to have Piers, you had to relinquish every one else, would you do so? No, you would not. Kate, I love you, and I pity you in your great trial; and I will help you to bear it as well as I can. But you must bear it cheerfully. I will not have father killed for Piers Exham. He looked very queerly when he went out. Be a brave girl, and if you are going to keep your promise, do it cheerfully — or it is not worth while."

" How can I be cheerful, Mother?"

" As easy as not, if you have a good, unselfish heart. You will say to yourself, 'What right have I to make every one in the house miserable, because I am miserable?' Troubles must come to all, Kitty, but troubles need not be wicked; and *it is wicked to be a destroyer of happiness.* I think God himself may find it hard to forgive those who selfishly destroy the happiness of others, just because they are not satisfied, or have not the one thing they specially want. When you

are going to be cross and unhappy, say to yourself, 'I will not be cross! I will not be unhappy!
I will not make my good father wretched, and fill
his pleasant home with a tearful drizzle, because
I want to cry about my own loss.'   And, depend
upon it, Kitty, you will find content and happiness in making others happy.   Good comes to
hearts prepared for good; but it cannot come
to hearts full of worry, and fear, and selfish
regrets."

"You are setting me a hard lesson, Mother."

"I know it is hard, Kate.   Life is all a task;
yet we may as well sing, as we fulfil it.   Eh,
dear?"

Kate did not answer.   She lifted her habit over
her arm, and went slowly upstairs.   Sorrow filled
her to the ears and eyes; but her mother heard
her close and then turn the key in her door.

"That is well," she thought.   "Now her good
angel will find her alone with God."

CHAPTER THIRTEENTH

NOT YET

"MOTHERING" is a grand old word for a quality God can teach man as well as woman; and the Squire really "mothered" his daughter in the first days of her great sorrow. He was always at her side. He was constantly needing her help or her company; and Kate was quite sensible of the great love with which he encompassed her. At first she was inexpressibly desolate. She had been suddenly dislodged from that life in the heart of Piers which she had so long enjoyed, and she felt homeless and forsaken. But Kate had a sweet and beautiful soul, nothing in it could turn to bitterness; and so it was not long before she was able to carry her misfortune as she had carried her good fortune, with cheerfulness and moderation.

For her confidence in Piers was unbroken. Not even her father's assertion about the lost ring could affect it. On reflection, she was sure there was a satisfactory explanation; if not, it was a momentary infidelity which she was ready to forgive. And in her determination to be faithful to her lover, Mrs. Atheling encouraged

her. "Time brings us our own, Kitty dear,"
she said; "you have a true title to Piers's love;
so, then, you have a true title to his hand.   I
have not a doubt that you will be his wife."

"I think that, Mother; but why should we be
separated now, and both made to suffer?"

"That is earth's great mystery, my dear, — the
prevalence of pain and suffering; no one is
free from it.   But then, in the midst of this
mystery, is set that Heavenly Love which helps
us to bear everything.   I know, Kitty, I
know!"

"Father is very hard."

"He is not.   When Piers's father and mother
say they will not have you in their house, do you
want to slip into it on the sly, or even in defiance of them?   Wait, and your hour will come."

"There is only one way that it can possibly
come; and that way I dare not for a moment
think of."

"No, indeed!   Who would wish to enter the
house of marriage by the gates of death?   If
such a thought comes to you, send it away with
a prayer for the Duke's life.   God can give you
Piers without killing his father.   He would be
a poor God if He could not.   Whatever happens
in your life that you cannot change, that is the
Will of God; and to will what God wills is sure
to bring you peace, Kitty.   You have your
Prayer-Book; go to the Blessed Collects in it.
You will be sure to find among them just the

prayer you need. They never once failed me,
—never once!"

"If I could have seen him just for an hour,
Mother."

"Far better not. Your last meeting with him
in London was a very happy, joyous one. That
is a good memory to keep. If you met him now,
it would only be to weep and lament; and I'll
tell you what, Kitty, no crying woman leaves a
pleasant impression. I want Piers to remember
you as he saw you last, — clothed in white, with
flowers in your hair and hands, and your face
beaming with love and happiness."

Many such conversations as this one held up
the girl's heart, and enabled her, through a pure
and steadfast faith in her lover, to enter —

> " ———— that finer atmosphere,
> Where footfalls of appointed things,
> Reverberant of days to be,
> Are heard in forecast echoings ;
> Like wave-beats from a viewless sea."

The first week of her trouble was the worst;
but it was made tolerable by a long letter from
Piers on the second day. It came in the
Squire's mail-bag, and he could easily have re-
tained it. But such a course would have been
absolutely contradictious to his whole nature.
He held the thick missive a moment in his
hand, and glanced at the large red seal, lifting
up so prominently the Richmoor arms, and then
said, —

"Here is a letter for you, Kitty.   It is from Piers.   What am I to do with it?"

"Please, Father, give it to me."

"Give it to her, Father," said Mrs. Atheling; and Kate's eager face pleaded still more strongly. Rather reluctantly, he pushed the letter towards Kate, saying, "I would as leave not give it to thee, but I can trust to thy honour."

"You may trust me, Father," she answered. And the Squire was satisfied with his relenting, when she came to him a few hours later, and said, "Thank you for giving me my letter, Father.   It has made my trouble a great deal lighter.   Now, Father, will you do me one more favour?"

"Well, dear, what is it?"

"See Piers for me, and tell him of the promise I made to you.   Say I cannot break it, but that I send, by you, my thanks for his letter, and my love forever more."

"I can't tell him about 'love forever more,' Kitty.   That won't do at all."

"Tell him, then, that all he says to me I say to him.   Dear Father, make that much clear to him."

"John, do what Kitty asks thee.   It isn't much."

"A man can't have his way in this house with two women to coax or bully him out of it. What am I to do?"

"Just what Kitty asks you to do."

"Please, Father!" And the two words were
sent straight to the father's heart with a kiss
and a caress that were irresistible. Three days
afterwards the Squire came home from a ride,
very much depressed. He was cross with the
servant who unbuttoned his gaiters, and he
looked resentfully at Mrs. Atheling as she
entered the room.

"A nice message I was sent," he said to her
as soon as they were alone. "That young man
has given me a heart-ache. He has made me
think right is wrong. He has made me feel
as if I was the wickedest father in Yorkshire.
And I know, in my soul, that I am doing right;
and that there isn't a better father in the three
kingdoms."

"Whatever did he say?"

"He said I was to tell Kate that from the
East to the West, and from the North to the
South, he would love her. That from that
moment to the moment of death, and throughout
all eternity, he would love her. And I stopped
him there and then, and said I would carry no
message that went beyond the grave. And he
said I was to tell her that neither for father nor
mother, nor for the interests of the dukedom,
nor for the command of the King, would he
marry any woman but her. And I was fool
enough to be sorry for him, and to promise I
would give him Kate, with my blessing, when
his father and mother asked me to do so."

"I don't think that was promising very much, John."

"Thou knowest nothing of how I feel, Maude. But he is a good man, and true; I think so, at any rate."

"Tell Kitty what he said."

"Nay, you must tell her if you want her to know. I would rather not speak of Piers at all. Tell her, also, that the Duchess and Miss Vyner are going to Germany, and that Piers goes with them as far as London. I am very glad of this move, for we can ride about, then, without fear of meeting them."

All the comfort to be got from this conversation and intelligence was given at once to Kate; and perhaps Mrs. Atheling unavoidably made it more emphatic than the Squire's manner warranted. She did not overstep the truth, however, for Piers had spoken from his very heart, and with the most passionate love and confidence. Indeed, the Squire's transcript had been but a bald and lame translation of the young man's fervent expressions of devotion and constancy.

Kate understood this, and she was comforted. Invincible Hope was at the bottom of all her sorrow, and she soon began to look on the circumstances as merely transitory. Yet she had moments of great trial. One evening, while walking with her mother a little on the outskirts of Atheling, the Duke's carriage, with its splen-

did outriders, suddenly turned into the little
lane. There was no escape, and they looked at
each other bravely, and stood still upon the turf
bordering the road. Then the Duchess gave an
order to the coachman. There was difficulty in
getting the horses to the precise spot which was
best for conversation; but Mrs. Atheling would
not take a step forward or backward to relieve
it. She stood with her hand on Kate's arm,
Kate's hands being full of the blue-bells which
she had been gathering.

The carriage contained only the Duchess and
Annabel. There had been no overt unpleasant-
ness between the ladies of the two families, and
Mrs. Atheling would not take the initiative,
especially when the question was one referring to
the most delicate circumstances of her daughter's life. She talked with the Duchess of her
German trip, and Kate gave Annabel the flowers,
and hoped she would enjoy her new experience.
In five minutes the interview was over; nothing
but courteous words had been said, and yet Mrs.
Atheling and Kate had, somehow, a sense of
intense humiliation. The Duchess's manner had
been politely patronising, Annabel's languid
and indifferent; and, in some mysterious way,
the servants echoed this covert atmosphere of
disdain. Little things are so momentous; and
the very attitude of the two parties was against
the Athelings. From their superb carriage, as
from a throne, the Duchess and her companion

looked down on the two simply-dressed ladies who had been gathering wild flowers on the roadside.

"How provoking!" was Kate's first utterance. "Mother, I will not walk outside the garden again until they go away; I will not!"

"I am ashamed of you!" answered Mrs. Atheling, angrily. "Will you make yourself a prisoner for these two women? *Tush!* Who are they? Be yourself, and who is better than you?"

"It is easy talking, Mother. You are as much annoyed as I am. How did they manage to snub us so politely?"

"Position is everything, Kate. A woman in a Duke's carriage, with outriders in scarlet, and coachmen and footmen in silver-laced liveries, would snub the Virgin Mary if she met her in a country lane, dressed in pink dimity, and gathering blue-bells. Try and forget the affair."

"Annabel looked ill."

"It was her white dress. A woman with her skin ought to know better than to wear white."

"Oh, Mother! if Piers had been with them, what should I have done?"

"I wish he had been there! You were never more lovely. I saw you for a moment, standing at the side of the carriage; with your brown hair blowing, and your cheeks blushing, and your hands full of flowers, and I thought how beautiful you were; and I wish Piers had been there."

"They go away on Saturday. I shall be glad

when Saturday is over. I do not think I could
bear to see Piers. I should make a little fool of
myself."

"Not you! Not you! But it is just as well
to keep out of danger."

Certainly neither the Squire nor Kate had any
idea of meeting Piers on the following Saturday
night when they rode along Atheling lane
together. Both of them believed Piers to be
far on the way to London. They had been to
the village, and were returning slowly home-
ward in the gloaming. A light like that of
dreamland was lying over all the scene; and the
silence of the far-receding hills was intensified
by the murmur of the streams, and the sleepy
piping of a solitary bird. The subtle, fugitive,
indescribable fragrance of lilies-of-the-valley
was in the air; and a sense of brooding power,
of mystical communion between man and nature,
had made both the Squire and Kate sympathetically silent.

Suddenly there was the sound of horse's feet
coming towards them; and the figure of its rider
loomed large and spectral in the gray, uncertain
light. Kate knew instantly who it was. In a
moment or two they must needs pass each other.
She looked quickly into her father's face, and
he said huskily, "Be brave, Kate, be brave!"

The words had barely been spoken, when
Piers slowly passed them. He removed his
hat, and the Squire did the same; but Kate sat

with dropped eyes, white as marble. From her nerveless hands the reins had fallen; she swayed in her saddle, and the Squire leaned towards her with encouraging touch and words. But she could hear nothing but the hurrying flight of her lover, and the despairing cry which the wind brought sadly back as he rode rapidly up the little lane, —

"*Kate! Kate!. Kate!*"

Fortunately, news of Miss Curzon's and Edgar's arrival at Ashley Hall came to Atheling that very hour; and the Squire and Mrs. Atheling were much excited at their proposal to lunch at Atheling Manor the next day. Kate had to put aside her own feelings, and unite in the family joy of reunion. There was a happy stir of preparation, and the Squire dressed himself with particular care to meet his son and his new daughter. As soon as he heard of their approach, he went to the open door to meet them.

To Edgar he gave his right hand, with a look which cancelled every hard word; and then he lifted little Annie Curzon from her horse, and kissed her on the doorstep with fatherly affection. And between Kate and Annie a warm friendship grew apace; and the girls were continually together, and thus, insensibly, Kate's sorrow was lightened by mutual confidence and affection.

Early in June the Squire and Edgar were to

return to London, for Parliament re-opened on
the fourteenth; and a few days before their
departure Mrs. Atheling asked her husband one
afternoon to take a drive with her. "To be
sure I will, Maude," he answered. "It is n't
twice in a twelvemonth thou makest me such an
offer." She was in her own little phaeton, and
the Squire settled himself comfortably at her
side, and took the reins from her hands. "Which
way are we to go?" he asked.

"We will go first to Gisbourne Gates, and
maybe as far as Belward."

The Squire wondered a little at her direction,
for she knew Gisbourne was rather a sore
subject with him. As they approached the big
iron portals, rusty on all their hinges from long
neglect, he could not avoid saying, —

"It is a shame beyond everything that I have
not yet been able to buy Gisbourne. The place
has been wanting a master for fifteen years; and it
lays between Atheling and Belward as the middle
finger lays between the first and the third. I
thought I might manage it next year; but this
Parliament business has put me a good bit back."

"Many things have put you back, John.
There was Edgar's college expenses, and the
hard times, and what not beside. Look, John!
the gates are open. Let us drive in. It is
twenty years since I saw Gisbourne Towers."

"The gates are open. What does that mean,
Maude?"

"I suppose somebody has bought the place."

"I'm afraid so."

"Never mind, John."

"But I do mind. The kind of neighbour we are to have is a very important thing. They will live right between Atheling and Belward. The Gisbournes were a fine Tory family. Atheling and Gisbourne were always friends. My father and Sir Antony went to the hunt and the hustings together. They were finger and thumb in all county matters. It will be hard to get as good a master of Gisbourne as Sir Antony was."

"John, I have a bit of right good news for thee. Edgar is going to take Sir Antony's place. Will Edgar do for a neighbour?"

"Whatever art thou saying, Maude?"

"The very truth. Miss Curzon has bought Gisbourne. Lord Ashley advised her to do so; and she has brought down a big company of builders and such people, and the grand old house is to be made the finest home in the neighbourhood. She showed me the plans yesterday, and I promised her to bring thee over to Gisbourne this afternoon to meet her architect and Lord Ashley and Edgar. See, they are waiting on the terrace for thee; for they want thy advice and thy ideas."

It was, indeed, a wonderful afternoon. The gentlemen went into consultation with the architect, and a great many of the Squire's suggestions were received with enthusiastic approval.

Mrs. Atheling, Kate, and Annie went through
the long-deserted rooms, and talked of what
should be done to give them modern convenience
and comfort, without detracting from their air of
antique splendour. Then at five o'clock the
whole party met in the faded drawing-room and
had tea, with sundry additions of cold game and
pasties, and discussed, together, the proposed
plans. At sunset the parties separated at Gisbourne Gates, Kate going with Miss Curzon to
Ashley, and the Squire and Mrs. Atheling returning to their own home. The Squire was far
too much excited to be long quiet.

"They were very glad of my advice, Maude,"
he said, as soon as the last good-bye had been
spoken. "Ashley seconded nearly all I proposed. He is a fine fellow. I wish I had known
him long ago."

"Well, John, nobody can give better advice
than you can."

"And you see I know Gisbourne, and what
can be done with it. Bless your soul! I used
to be able to tell every kind of bird that built
in Gisbourne Chase, and where to find their
nests—though I never robbed a nest; I can say
that much for myself. Well, Edgar *has* done
a grand thing for Atheling, and no mistake."

"I told you Edgar—"

"Now, Maude, Edgar and me have washed the
slate between us clean. It is not thy place to
be itemising now. I say Edgar has done well for

Atheling, and I don't care who says different. I
haven't had such a day since my wedding day.
Edgar in Gisbourne! An Atheling in Gisbourne!
My word! Who would have thought of such a
thing? I couldn't hardly have asked it."

"I should think not. There are very few of
us, John, would have the face to *ask* for half of
the good things the good God gives us without
a ' please ' or a ' thank you.' "

"Belward! Gisbourne! Atheling! It will
be all Atheling when I am gone."

"Not it! I do not want Belward to be sunk
in that way. Belward is as old as Atheling."

"In a way, Maude, in a way. It was once
a part of Atheling; so was Gisbourne. As for
sinking the name, thou sunkest thy name in
Atheling; why not sink the land's name, eh,
Maude?"

And until the Squire and Edgar left for London, such conversations were his delight; indeed, he rather regretted his Parliamentary
obligations, and envied his wife and daughter
the delightful interest that had come into their
lives. For they really found it delightful; and
all through the long, sweet, summer days it
never palled, because it was always a fresh wing,
or a fresh gallery, cabinet-work in one parlour,
upholstery work in another, the freshly laid-out
gardens, the cleared chase, the new stables and
kennels. Even the gates were a subject of interesting debate as to whether the fine old ones

should be restored or there should be still finer new ones.

Thus between Atheling, Ashley, and Gisbourne, week after week passed happily. Kate did not forget, did not cease to love and to hope; she just bided her time, waiting, in patience, for Fortune to bring in the ship that longed for the harbour but could not make it. And with so much to fill her hours joyfully, how ungrateful she would have been to fret over the one thing denied her! The return of the Squire and Edgar was very uncertain. Both of them, in their letters, complained bitterly of the obstructive policy which the Tories still unwaveringly carried out. It was not until the twelfth of July that the Bill got into Committee; and there it was harassed and delayed night after night by debates on every one of its clauses. This plan of obstructing it occupied thirty-nine sittings, so that it did not reach the House of Lords until the twenty-second of September. The Squire's letter at this point was short and despondent : —

DEAR WIFE, — The Bill has gone to the Lords. I expect they will send it to the devil. I am fairly tired out ; and, with all my heart, I wish myself at Atheling. It may be Christmas before I get there. Do as well as you can till I come. Tell Kitty, I would give a sovereign for a sight of her.

Your affectionate Husband,

JOHN ATHELING.

About a couple of weeks after this letter, one
evening in October, Mrs. Atheling, Kate, and
Annie were returning to Atheling House from
Gisbourne, where they had been happily busy
all the afternoon. They were easy-hearted, but
rather quiet; each in that mood of careless
stillness which broods on its own joy or sorrow.
The melancholy of the autumn night influenced
them, — calm, pallid, and a little sad, with a dull,
soft murmur among the firs, — so they did not
hurry, and it was nearly dark when they came
in sight of the house. Then Mrs. Atheling
roused herself. "How good a cup of tea will
taste," she said; "and I dare say it is waiting,
for Ann has lighted the room, I see." Laughing and echoing her remark, they reached the
parlour. On opening the door, Mrs. Atheling
uttered a joyful cry.

"Why, John! Why, Edgar!"

"To be sure, Maude," answered the Squire,
leaping up and taking her in his arms. "I
wonder how thou feelest to have thy husband
come home and find thee out of the house, and
not a bit of eating ready for him."

Then Mrs. Atheling pointed to the table, and
said, "I do not think there is any need for com-
plaint, John."

"No; we managed, Edgar and me, by good
words and bad words, to get something for ourselves — " and he waved his hand complacently
over the table, loaded with all kinds of eatables,

— a baron of cold beef, cold Yorkshire pudding, a gypsy pie, Indian preserves, raspberry tarts, clotted cream, roast apples, cheese celery, fine old ale, strong gunpowder tea, and a variety of condiments.

"What do you call this meal, John?"

"I call it a decent kind of a tea, and I want thee to try and learn something from its example." Then he kissed her again, and looked anxiously round for Kitty.

"Come here, my little girl," he cried; and Kitty, who had been feeling a trifle neglected, forgot everything but the warmth and gladness of her father's love and welcome. Edgar had found Annie a seat beside his own, and the Squire managed to get his place between his wife and his daughter. Then the "cup of tea" Mrs. Atheling had longed for became a protracted home festival. But they could not keep politics out of its atmosphere; they were, indeed, so blended with the life of that time that their separation from household matters was impossible, and the Squire was no more anxious to hear about his hunters and his harvest, than Mrs. Atheling was to know the fate of the Reform Bill.

"It has passed at last, I suppose, John," she said, with an air of satisfied certainty.

"Thou supposest very far wrong, then. It has been rejected again."

"Never! Never! Never! Oh, John, John! It is not possible!"

"The Lords did, as I told thee they would, — that is, the Lords and the bishops together."

"The bishops ought to be unfrocked," cried Edgar, with considerable temper. "Only one in all their number voted for Reform."

"I'll never go to church again," said Mrs. Atheling, in her unreasonable anger.

"Tell us about it, Father," urged Kate.

"Well, you see, Mr. Peel and Mr. Croker led our party against the Bill; and Croker *is* clever, there is no doubt of that."

"Not to be compared to Lord Althorp, our leader, — so calm, so courageous, so upright," said Edgar.

"Nobody denies it; but Croker's practical, vigorous views —"

"You mean his ' sanguine despondency,' his delight in describing England as bankrupt and ruined by Reform."

"I mean nothing of the kind, Edgar; but —"

"Did the Bill pass the Commons, Father?" asked Kate.

"It did; although in fifteen days Peel spoke forty-eight times against it, and Croker fifty-seven times, and Wetherell fifty-eight times. But all they could say was just so many lost words."

"Think of such men disputing the right of Manchester, Leeds, and Birmingham to be represented in the House of Commons! What do you say to that, Mother?"

"I only hope father was n't in such a stupid bit of business, Edgar." And the Squire drank a glass of ale, and pretended not to hear.

"But," continued Edgar, "we never lost heart; for all over the country, and in every quarter of London, they were holding meetings urging us not to give way, — not to give way an inch. We were fighting for all England; and, as Lord Althorp said, we were ready to keep Parliament sitting till next December, or even to next December twelvemonth."

"I'll warrant you!" interrupted the Squire. "Well, Edgar, you passed your Bill in a fine uproar of triumph; all London in the street, shouting thanks to Althorp and the others — Edgar Atheling among them." Then the Squire paused and looked at his son, and Mrs. Atheling asked, impatiently, —

"What then, John?"

"Why, then, Lord John Russell and Lord Althorp carried the Bill to the House of Lords. It was a great scene. The Duke told me about it. He said nearly every peer was in his seat; and a large number of peeresses had been admitted at the bar, and every inch of space in the House was crowded. The Lord Chancellor took his seat at the Woolsack; and the Deputy Usher of the Black Rod threw open the doors, crying, 'A Message from the Commons.' Then Lord John Russell and Lord Althorp, at the head of one hundred Members of the House of

Commons, entered, and delivered the Bill to the Lord Chancellor."

"Oh, how I should have liked to have been present!" said Kate.

"Well, some day thou —" and then the Squire suddenly stopped; but the unfinished thought was flashed to every one present, — "some day thou mayst be Duchess of Richmoor, and have the right to be present;" and Kate was pleased, and felt her heart warm to conscious hope.   She caught her mother watching her, and smiled; and Mrs. Atheling, instantly sensitive to the unspoken feeling, avoided comment by her eager inquiry, —

"Whatever did they say, John?"

"They said the usual words; but the Duke told me there was a breathless silence, and that Lord John Russell said them with the most unusual and impressive emphasis: ' My Lords, the House of Commons have passed an Act to Amend the Representation of England and Wales, to which they desire your Lordships' Concurrence.' Lord Grey opened the debate.   I dare say Edgar knows all about it.   I believe Grey is his leader."

"Yes," answered Edgar, "and very proud I am of my leader.   He is in his sixty-eighth year, and he stood there that night to advocate the measure he proposed forty years before, in the House of Commons.   Althorp told me he spoke with a strange calmness and solemnity,

'*for the just claims of the people;*' but as soon
as he sat down Lord Wharncliffe moved that the
Bill be rejected altogether."

"That was like Wharncliffe," said the Squire.
"No half measures for him."

"Wellington followed, and wanted to know,
'How the King's government was to be carried
on by the will of a turbulent democracy?'"

"Wellington would govern with a sword instead of a sceptre. He would try every cause
round a drum-head. I am not with Wellington."

"Lord Dudley followed in an elegant, classi-
cal speech, also against the Bill."

The Squire laughed. "I heard about that
speech. Did not Brougham call it, 'An essay or
exercise of the highest merit, on democracies —
but not on this Bill.'"

"Yes. Brougham can say very polite and very
disagreeable things. He spoke on the fifth and
last night of the debate. Earl Grey said a more
splendid declamation was never made. All
London is now quoting one passage which he
addressed to the Lords: 'Justice deferred,' he
said, 'enhances the price at which you will pur-
chase your own safety; nor can you expect to
gather any other crop than they did who went
before you, if you persevere in their utterly
abominable husbandry of sowing injustice and
reaping rebellion.'"

"Fine words, Edgar, fine words; just like

Brougham, — catch-words, to take the common people."

"They did not, however, alarm or take the Lords. My leader closed the debate, and in a magnificent speech implored the archbishops and bishops not to vote against the Bill, and thus stand before the people of England as the ene-mies of a just and moderate scheme of Reform."

"And yet they voted against it!" said Mrs. Atheling. "I am downright ashamed of them. The very date ought to be put up against them forever."

"It was the seventh of October. All night long, until the dawning of the eighth, the debate was continued; and until three hours after midnight, Palace Yard, and the streets about Westminster, were crowded with anxious watch-ers, though the weather was cold and miserably wet. Towards morning their patience was ex-hausted; and when the carriages of the peers and bishops rolled out in broad daylight there was no one there to greet them with the execrations and hisses they deserved. The whole of our work this session in the Commons has been done in vain. But we shall win next time, even if we compel the King to create as many new Reform peers as will pass the Bill in spite of the old Lords."

"Edgar, you are talking nonsense — if not treason."

"Pardon me, Father. I am only giving you

the ultimatum of Reform. The Bill *must* pass
the Lords next session, or you may call Reform
Revolution. The people are particularly angry
at the bishops. They dare not appear on the
streets; curses follow them, and their carriages
have been repeatedly stoned."

"There is a verse beginning, ' Inasmuch as ye
did it not,' etc., — I wonder if they will ever
dare to repeat it again. They will do the church
a deal of harm."

"Oh, no," said Edgar. "The church does not
stand on the bishops."

"Be easy with the bishops," added the Squire.
"They have to scheme a bit in order to get the
most out of both worlds. They scorn to answer
the people according to their idols. They are
politically right."

"No, sir," said Edgar. "Whatever is morally
wrong cannot be politically right. The church
is well represented by the clergy; they have
generally sympathised with the people. One of
them, indeed, called Smith — Sydney Smith —
made a speech at Taunton, three days after our
defeat, that has gone like wild-fire throughout
the length and breadth of England;" and Edgar
took a paper out of his pocket, and read, with
infinite delight and appreciation, the pungent
wit which made "Mrs. Partington" famous
throughout Christendom: —

" As for the possibility of the House of Lords pre-
venting a reform of Parliament, I hold it to be the

most absurd notion that ever entered into human imagination. I do not mean to be disrespectful, but the attempt of the Lords to stop the progress of Reform reminds me very forcibly of the great storm at Sidmouth, and of the conduct of the excellent Mrs. Partington on that occasion. In the winter of 1824, there set in a great flood upon that town; the waves rushed in upon the houses; and everything was threatened with destruction. In the midst of this sublime and terrible storm, Dame Partington — who lived upon the beach — was seen at the door of her house, with mop and pattens, trundling her mop, squeezing out the sea-water, and vigorously pushing away the Atlantic Ocean. The Atlantic was roused. Mrs. Partington's spirit was up; but I need not tell you, the contest was unequal. The Atlantic Ocean beat Mrs. Partington. She was excellent at a slop or a puddle; but she should not have meddled with a tempest. Gentlemen, be at your ease, be quiet and steady. You will beat Mrs. Partington." [1]

"It was not respectful to liken the Lords of England to an old woman, now was it, Mother?" asked the Squire.

But Mrs. Atheling only laughed the more, and the conversation drifted so completely into politics that Kitty and Annie grew weary of it, and said they wished to go to their rooms. And as they left the parlour together, Edgar suddenly stayed Kitty a moment, and said, "I had nearly forgotten to tell you something. Miss Vyner

[1] Speech at Taunton by Sydney Smith, October 12, 1831.

is to be married, on the second of December, to
Cecil North.   I am going to London in time for
the wedding."

And Kitty said, " I am glad to hear it, Edgar,"
and quickly closed the door.   But she lay long
awake, wondering what influence this event
would have upon Piers and his future, until,
finally, the wonder passed into a little verse
which they had learned together; and with it
singing in her heart, she fell asleep : —

> " Thou art mine ! I am thine !
>   Thou art locked in this heart of mine;
>   Whereof is lost the little key :
>   So there, forever, thou must be ! "

CHAPTER FOURTEENTH

AT THE WORST

In the first joy of their return home, Squire
Atheling and his son had not chosen to alarm
the women of the family; yet the condition of
the country was such as filled with terror every
thoughtful mind. The passionate emotion evoked
by the second rejection of the Reform Bill did
not abate. Tumultuous meetings were held in
every town and village as the news reached them;
houses were draped in black; shops were closed;
and the bells of the churches tolled backward.
In London the populace was quite uncontrollable. Vast crowds filled the streets, cheering the
Reform leaders, and denouncing with furious
execrations the members of either House who
had opposed the Bill. The Duke of Newcastle,
the Marquis of Londonderry, and many other
peers were not saved from the anger of the
people without struggle and danger. Notting-
ham Castle, the seat of the Duke of Newcastle,
was burnt to the ground; and Belvoir Castle, the
seat of the Duke of Rutland, was barely saved.
Bristol saw a series of riots, and during them

suffered greatly from fire, and the Bishop's palace was reduced to ashes.

Everywhere the popular fury settled with special bitterness and hatred upon the bishops ; because, as teachers of the doctrines of Jesus of Nazareth, the "common people" expected sympathy from them. A cry arose, from one end of England to the other, for their expulsion from the Upper Chamber ; and proposals even for the abolition of the House of Lords were constant and very popular. For such extreme measures no speaker was so eloquent and so powerful as Mr. O'Connell. In addressing a great meeting at Charing Cross one day, he pointed in the direction of Whitehall Palace, and reminded his hearers that, " A King had lost his head there. Why," he asked, " did this doom come on him? It was," he cried, " because he refused to listen to his Commons and his people, and obeyed the dictation of a foreign wife." And this allusion to the Queen's bad influence over William the Fourth was taken up by the crowd with vehement cheering.

While Bristol was burning, the cholera appeared in England ; and its terrors, new and awful and apparently beyond human help or skill, added the last element of supernatural fear to the excited and hopeless people. It is hard to realise at this day, and with our knowledge of the disease, the frantic and abject despair which seized all classes. The churches were kept open, supplications ascended night and day from the altars; and on the sixth of November, at one hour, from every place of worship in England, hundreds of thousands knelt to utter aloud a form of prayer which was constantly broken by sobs of anguish: —

"Lord, have pity on thy people! Withdraw thy heavy hand from those who are suffering under thy judgments; and turn away from us that grievous calamity against which our only security is Thy Compassion."

In the presence of this scourge, Mrs. Atheling found it impossible to persuade the Squire to let his family go up with him and Edgar to London. About the cholera, the Squire had the common fatalistic ideas.

"You may escape through God's mercy," he said; "but if you are to die of this fearsome, outlandish sickness, then it is best to face death in your own home."

"But if you should take it in London, and me not near even to bid you 'good-bye,' John! I should die of grief."

"I do hope thou wouldst have more sense, Maude."

"I would follow thee beyond the grave, very quickly, John."

"No, no! Stay where thou art. Thou knowest what Yorkshire is," and though he spoke gruffly, his eyes were dim with unshed tears for the dreadful possibility he thought it right to face.

Kate was specially averse to return to London. It was full of memories she did not wish to revive. Piers was there ; and how could she bear to meet him, and neither speak to nor even look at her lover? There was Annabel's marriage also to consider. If she did not attend it, how many unpleasant inquiries and suppositions there would be? If she did accept the formal invitation sent her, how was she to conduct herself towards Piers in the presence of those who knew them both intimately?

The marriage was to take place shortly before the opening of Parliament ; and, owing to the wretched condition of the country, it was thought best to give it only a private character. The management of the social arrangements were in Piers's hands, and during these last days a very brotherly and confidential affection sprang up in his heart for the brilliant girl who was so soon to leave them forever. One morning he returned to Richmoor House with some valuable jewels for Annabel. He sent a servant to tell her that he was in the small east parlour and desired her company. Then, knowing her usual indifference to time, he sat down and patiently awaited her coming. She responded almost immediately. But her entrance startled and troubled him. She came in hastily, and shut the door with a perceptible nervous tremour. Her face was flushed with anger ; she looked desperate and defiant, and met his curious glance with one of mingled

fear and entreaty and reckless passion. He led
her to a seat, and taking her hands said, —

"My dear Bella, what has grieved you?"

"Oh, Piers! Piers!" she sobbed. "If you have
one bit of pity in your heart, give it to me. I am
the most miserable woman in the world."

"Bella, if you do not love Cecil — if you want
to break off this marriage — "

"Love Cecil? I love him better than my life!
My love for Cecil is the best thing about me.
It is not Cecil."

"Who is it then?"

"I will tell you, though you may hate me for my
words. Piers, I took the ring you lost. I meant
no harm in the first moment; mischief and jealousy were then so mixed, I don't know which of
them led me. I saw you asleep. I slipped the
ring off your finger. I told myself I would give
it to you in the morning, and claim my forfeit.
In the morning, the Duchess was cross; and you
were cross; and the constables were in the house;
and I was afraid. And I put it off and off, and
every day my fear of trouble — and perhaps my
hope of doing mischief with it — grew stronger.
I had then hours of believing that I should like to
be your wife, and I hated and envied Kate Atheling. I hesitated until I lost the desire to explain
things; and then one day my maid Justine flew in
a passion at me, and accused me of stealing the
ring. She said it was in my purse — *and it was.*
She threatened to call in the whole household to

see me found out; and it was the night of the
great dinner; and I bought her off."

"Oh, Bella! Bella! that was very foolish."

"I know. She has tortured and robbed me
ever since. I have wasted away under her
threats. Look at my arms, Piers, and my
hands. I have a constant fever. Last week she
promised me, if I would give her two hundred
pounds, she would go away, and I should never
see or hear of her again. I gave her the money.
Now she says she has made up her mind to go
to India with me. That I cannot endure. She
has kept me on the rack with threats to tell Cecil.
He is the soul of Honour; he would certainly
cease to love me; and if I was his wife, how terrible that would be! What am I to do? What
am I to do? Oh, Piers, help me!"

"Where is the woman now?"

"In my apartments."

"Can I go with you to your parlour?"

"Yes — but, Piers, why?"

"Where is the ring, Bella dear?"

"In her possession. She was afraid I would
give it to you."

"Why did you not tell me all this before?
Come, I will soon settle the affair."

When they reached the room, Annabel sank
almost lifeless on a sofa; and Piers touched a
hand-bell. Justine called from an inner room:

"I will answer at my leisure, Miss."

Piers walked to the dividing door, and threw it

open. "You will answer *now*, at my command. Come here, and come quickly."

"My lord — I did not mean — "

"Stand there, and answer truly the questions I shall ask; or I promise you a few years on the treadmill, if not a worse punishment. Do you know that you are guilty of black-mailing, and of obtaining money on false pretences? — both crimes to be expiated on the gallows."

"My lord, it is a true pretence. Miss Vyner stole your ring. She knows she did."

"She could not steal anything I have; she is welcome to whatever of mine she desires. How much money have you taken from Miss Vyner?"

"I have not taken one half-penny," answered Justine, sulkily. "She gave me the money; she dare not say different. Speak, Miss, you know you gave it to me." But Annabel had recovered something of her old audacity. She felt she was safe, and she was not disposed to mercy. She only smiled scornfully, and re-arranged the satin cushions under her head more comfortably.

"Quick! How much money have you taken?"

Justine refused to answer; and Piers said, "I give you two minutes. Then I shall send for a constable."

"And Miss Vyner's wedding will be put off."

"For your crime? Oh, no! Miss Vyner's wedding is far beyond your interference. She will have nothing to do with this affair. *I* shall prosecute you. You have my ring. Will you give it to me, or to a constable?"

" I did not take the ring."

" It is in your possession. I will send now for an officer." He rose to touch the bell-rope, keeping his eyes on the woman all the time; and she darted forward and arrested his hand.

" I will do what you wish," she said.

" How much money have you taken from Miss Vyner?"

" Eight hundred and ninety pounds."

"Where is it?"

" In my room."

" Go and get it — stay, I will go with you."

In a few minutes Justine returned with her ill-gotten treasure; and then she condescended to explain, and entreat, —

" Oh, my lord," she said, "don't be hard on me. I wanted the money for my poor old mother who is in Marylebone Workhouse. I did, indeed I did! It was to make her old age comfortable. She is sick and very poor, and I wanted it for her."

"We shall see about that. If your story is true, you shall give the money to your poor old sick mother. If it is not true, you shall give my ring and the money to a constable, and sleep in prison this very night."

With impetuous passion he ordered a carriage, and Justine was driven to the Marylebone Work-house. By the time they reached that institution, she was thoroughly humbled and afraid; her fear being confirmed by the subservience of the Master to the rank and commands of Lord Exham. For a moment she had an idea of denying her own statement; but the futility of the lie was too evident to be doubted; and, very reluctantly, she admitted her mother's name to be Margaret Oddy. In a few minutes — during which Lord Exham ordered Justine to count out the money in her bag to the Master — Margaret appeared. She was not an old woman in years, being but little over forty; but starvation, sorrow, and hard work had made her prematurely aged. When she entered the room, she looked around anxiously; but as soon as she saw Justine, she covered her face with her thin hands, and began to weep.

"Is this your daughter?" asked the Master, pointing to Justine.

"I am her mother, sure enough, sir; but she have cast me off long ago. Oh, Justine girl, speak a word to me! You are my girl, for all that's past and gone."

"Justine has come to make you some amends for her previous neglect, Mother," said Lord Exham. "She has brought you eight hundred and ninety pounds for your old age. To-morrow my lawyer will call here, and give you advice concerning its care and its use. Until then, the Master will take it in charge."

"Let me see it! Let me touch it with my

hands! No more hunger! No more cold! No more hard work! It can't be true! It can't be true! Is it true, Justine? Kiss me with the money, girl, for the sake of the happy days we have had together!" With these words she went to her daughter, and tried to take her hands, and draw her to her breast. But Justine would not respond. She stood sullen and silent, with eyes cast on the ground.

"Why, then," said Margaret, with just anger, "why, then, keep the money, Justine. I would rather eat peas and porridge, and sleep on straw, than take a shilling with such ill-will from you, girl." Then, turning to Piers, she added, "Thank you, good gentleman, but I'll stay where I am. Let Justine keep her gold. I don't want such an ill-will gift."

"Mother," answered Piers. "You may take the money from my hands, then. It is yours. Justine's good or ill-will has now nothing to do with it. I give it to you from the noble young lady whom your daughter has wronged so greatly that the gallows would be her just desert. She gives up this money—which she has no right to—as some atonement for her crime. Is not this the truth, Justine?" he asked sternly; and the woman answered, "Yes." Then turning to the Master, he added, "To this fact, and to Justine's admission of it, you are witness."

The Master said, "I am." Then addressing Margaret, he told her to go back to her place, and

think over the good fortune that had so unex-
pectedly come to her; what she wished to do
with her money; and where she wished to make
her future home. And the mother curtsied
feebly and again turned to her child, —

"If I go back to the old cottage in Downham
— the old cottage with the vines, and the bee
skeps, and the long garden, will you come with
me, and we will share all together?"

"No."

"Let her alone, Mother," said Exham. "She
is going to the furthest American colony she can
reach. Only in some such place, will she be safe
from the punishment of her wrong-doing."

"Justine, then, my girl, good-bye!"

No answer.

"Justine, good-bye!"

No answer.

"Why, then, my girl, God be with you, and God
forgive you!"

Then Justine turned to Lord Exham, "I
have done what you demanded. May I now go
my own way?"

"Not just yet. You will return with me."

He gave his card to the Master, and followed
the woman, keeping her constantly under his
hand and eye until they returned to Annabel's
parlour. Annabel was in a dead sleep; but their
entrance awakened her, and it pained Piers to see
the look of fear that came into her face when she
saw her cruel tormentor. She was speedily re-

lieved, however; for the first words she heard, was
an order from Piers, bidding her to be ready to
leave the house in twenty minutes. He took out
his watch as he gave the order, and then added,
" First of all, return to me my ring."

" I did not take your ring, my lord."

" You have it in your possession. Return it at
once."

" Miss Vyner stole it — "

" Give it to me! You know the consequences
of *one* more refusal."

Then Justine took from her purse the long
missing ring. She threw it on the table, and,
with tears of rage, said, —

" May ill-luck and false love go with it, and
follow all who own it!"

" The bad wishes of the wicked fall on themselves, Justine," said Lord Exham, as he lifted the
trinket. " How much money does your mistress
owe you?"

" I have no 'mistress.' Miss Vyner owes me
a quarter's wage, and a quarter's notice, that is
eight pounds.

" Is that correct, Annabel?"

" The woman says so. Pay her what she wants
— only get her out of my sight."

" Oh, Miss, I can tell you — "

" Go. Pack your trunk, and be back here in
fifteen minutes. And, mind what I say, leave
England at once — the sooner the better."

Before the time was past, the woman was out-

side the gates of Richmoor House, and Piers returned to Annabel. "That trouble is all over
and gone forever," he said to her; "now, dear
Bella, lift up your heart to its full measure of love
and joy! Let Cecil see you to-night in your old
beauty. He is fretting about your health; show
him the marvellously bright Annabel that cap-
tured his heart with a glance."

"I will! I will, Piers! This very night you
shall see that Annabel is herself again."

"And in three days you are to be Cecil's
wife!"

"In three days," she echoed joyfully. "Leave
me now, Piers. I want to think over your goodness to me. I shall never forget it."

Smiling, they parted; and then Annabel opened
all the doors of her rooms, and looked carefully
around them, and assured herself that her tyrant
was really gone. "In three days!" she said,
"in three days I am going away from all this
splendour and luxury, — going to dangers of all
kinds; to a wild life in camps and quarters;
perhaps to deprivations in lonely places — and I
am happy! Happy! transcendently happy! Oh,
Love! Wonderful, Invincible, Omnipotent Love!
Cecil's love! It will be sufficient for all things."

Certainly she was permeated with this idea. It
radiated from her countenance; it spoke in her
eyes; it made itself visible in the glory of her
bridal attire. The wedding morning was one of
the darkest and dreariest of London's winter

days. A black pouring rain fell incessantly; the
atmosphere was heavy, and loaded with exhala-
tions; and the cholera terror was on every face.
For at this time it was really "a destruction walking at noon-day" and leaving its ghastly sign of
possession on many a house in the streets along
which the bridal party passed.

It came into the gloomy church like a splendid
dream: officers in gay uniforms, ladies in beautiful gowns and nodding plumes, and at the
altar, — shining like some celestial being, — the
radiant bride in glistening white satin, and spark-
ling gems. And Cecil, in his new military
uniform, tall, handsome, soldierly, happy, made
her a fitting companion. The church was filled
with a dismal vapour; the rain plashed on the
flagged enclosure; the wind whistled round the
ancient tower: there was only gloom, and misery,
and sudden death outside; but over all these
accidents of time and place, the joy of the bride
and the bridegroom was triumphant. And later
in the day, when the Duke and Piers went with
them to the great three-decked Indiaman waiting for their embarkation, they were still won-
drously exalted and blissful. Dressed in fine
dark-blue broadcloth, and wrapped in costly furs,
Annabel watched from the deck the departure of
her friends, and then put her hand in Cecil's with
a smile.

"For weal or woe, Bella, my dear one," he
said.

"For weal or woe, for life or death, Cecil beloved," she answered, having no idea then of
what that promise was to bring her in the future;
though she kept it nobly when the time of its
redemption came.

Three days after this event, Mrs. Atheling
received by special messenger from Lord Exham
a letter, and with it the ring which had caused so
much suspicion and sorrow.   But though the
letter was affectionate and confidential, and full
of tender messages which he "trusted in her to
deliver for him," nothing was said as to the manner of its recovery, or the personality of the one
who had purloined it.

"Your father has been right, no doubt, Kate,"
she said.   "In some weak moment Annabel has
got the ring from him, and on her marriage has
given it back.   That is clear to me."

"Not to me, Mother.   I am sure Piers did
not give Annabel — did not give any one the
ring.   I will tell you what I think.   Annabel
got it while he was asleep, or he inadvertently
dropped it, and she picked it up — and kept it,
hoping to make mischief."

"You may be wrong, Kitty."

"I may — but I *know* I am right."

No Diviner like Love!

On this same day, with the cholera raging all
around, Parliament was re-opened; and Lord
John Russell again brought in the Reform Bill.
There was something pathetic in this persist-

ence of a people, hungry and naked, and over-
shadowed by an unknown pestilence, swift and
malignant as a Fate. It was evident, immediately, that the same course of "obstruction"
which had proved fatal to the two previous Bills
was to be pursued against the third attempt.
Yet the temper of the House of Commons, sul-
lenly, doggedly determined, might even thus
early have warned its opposers. All the unfair-
ness and pertinacity of Peel and his associates
was of no avail against the inflexible steadiness
of Lord Althorp and the cold impassibility of
Lord John Russell.

Week after week passed in debating, while
the press and people waited in alternating fits
of passionate threats and still more alarming
silence, — a silence, Lord Grey declared to be,
"Most ominous of trouble, and of the most vital
importance to the obstructing force." The
Squire was weary to death. He found it impossible to take a dutiful interest in the proceed-
ings. The tactics of the fight did not appeal to
his nature. He thought they were neither fair
nor straightforward; and, unconsciously, his
own opinions had been much leavened by his
late familiar intercourse with Lord Ashley and
his son.

In these days his chief comfort came from the
friendship of Piers Exham. The young man
frequently sought his company; and it became
almost a custom for them to dine together at the

Tory Club.   And at such times words were dropped that neither would have uttered, or even thought of, at the beginning of the contest. Thus one night Piers said, in his musing way, as he fingered his glass, rather than drank the wine in it, —

"I have been wondering, Squire, whether the wish of a whole nation, gradually growing in intensity for sixty years, until it has become, to-day, a command and a threat, is not something more than a wish?"

"I should say it was, Piers," answered the Squire.   "Very likely the wish has grown to — a right."

"Perhaps."

Then both men were silent; and the next topic discussed was the new sickness, and Piers anxiously asked if "it had reached Atheling."

"No, it has not, thank the Almighty!" replied the Squire.   "There has not been a case of it. My family are all well."

Allusions to Kate were seldom more definite than this one; but Piers found inexpressible comfort in the few words.   Such intercourse might not seem conducive to much kind feeling; but it really was.   The frequent silences; the short, pertinent sentences; the familiar, kindly touch of the young man's hand, when it was time to return to the House; the little courteous attentions which it pleased Piers to render, rather than let the Squire be indebted to a ser-

vant for them, — these, and other things quite as
trivial, made a bond between the two men that
every day strengthened.

It was nearly the end of March when the Bill
once more got through the Commons; and hitherto the nation had waited as men wait the
preliminaries of a battle. But they were like
hounds held by a leash when the great question
as to whether the Lords would now give way, or
not, was to be determined. The Squire was an
exceedingly sensitive man; for he was exceedingly affectionate, and he was troubled continually by the hungry, wretched, anxious crowds
through which he often picked his way to Westminster, the more so, as his genial, bluff, thoroughly English appearance seemed to please and
encourage these non-contents. At every step
he was urged to vote on the right side. "God
bless you, Squire!" was a common address.
"Pity the poor! Vote for the right! Go for
Reform, Squire! Before God, Squire, we must
win this time, or die for it!" And the Squire,
distressed, and half-convinced of the justice of
their case, would lift his hat at such words, and
pass a sovereign into the hand of some lean,
white-faced man, and answer, "God defend the
Right, friends!" He could not tell them, as he
had done in his first session, to "go home and
mind their business." He could not say, as he
did then, a downright "No;" could not bid
them, "Reform themselves, and let the Govern-

ment alone," or ask, "If they were bereft of
their senses?" If he answered at all now, it
was in the motto so familiar to them, "God and
my Right;" or, if much urged, "I give my word
to do my best." Or he would bow courteously,
and say, "God grant us all good days without
end." Before the Bill passed the Commons, at
the end of March, it had, at any rate, come to
this, — he was not only averse to vote against
the Bill, he was also averse to tell these waiting sufferers that he intended to vote against it.

On the night of the thirteenth of April, when
the Bill was before the Lords, the Squire was
too excited to go to bed, though prevented from
occupying his seat in the Commons by a smart
attack of rheumatism. He sat in his club, waiting for intelligence, and watching the passing
crowds to try and glean from their behaviour the
progress of events. Piers had promised to bring
him word as soon as the vote was taken. He
did not arrive until eight o'clock the next
morning. The Squire was drinking his coffee,
and making up his mind to return to Atheling,
"whatever happened," when Piers, white and
exhausted, drew his chair to the table.

"The Bill has passed this reading by nine
votes," he said wearily; "and Parliament has
adjourned for the Easter recess; that is, until
the seventh of May. Three weeks of suspense!
I do not know how it is to be endured."

"I am going to Atheling. Edgar will very

likely go to Ashley, **and I** think you had better go with us.   Three weeks of Exham winds will make a new man of you."

At this point Edgar joined them, and, greatly to his father's annoyance, declared both Atheling and Ashley out of the question. "This three weeks," he said, "will decide the fate of England.   I have promised my leader to visit Warwick, Worcester, Stafford, and Birmingham. At the latter place there will be the greatest political meeting ever held in this world."

"And what will Annie say?" asked the Squire.

"Annie thinks I am doing right.   Annie does. not put me before the hundred of thousands to whom the success of Reform will bring happiness."

"It beats all and everything," said the Squire.   "I would n't like my wife to put me back of hundreds and thousands.   Have you been up all night — you and Piers?"

"All night," answered Edgar.   "We were among the three hundred members from the Commons who filled the space around the throne, and stood in a row three deep below the bar.   I was in the second row; but I heard all that passed very well.   Earl Grey did not begin to speak until five o'clock this morning, and he spoke for an hour and a half.   It was an astonishing argument."

"It was a most interesting scene, altogether,"

said Piers. "I shall never forget it. The
crowded house, its still and solemn demeanour,
and the broad daylight coming in at the high
windows while Grey was speaking. Its blue
beams mixed with the red of the flaring candles,
and the two lights made strange and startling
effects on the crimson draperies and the dusky
tapestries on the walls. I felt as if I was in a
vision. I kept thinking of Cromwell and old
forgotten things; and it was like waking out of
a dream when the House began to dissolve. I
was not quite myself until I had drunk a cup of
coffee."

"It was very exciting," said the more practical Edgar; "and the small majority is only to
keep the people quiet. At the next reading the
Bill will be so mutilated as to be practically
rejected, unless we are ready to meet such an
emergency."

Piers rose at these words. He foresaw a discussion he had no mind for; and he said, with a
touching pathos in his voice, as he laid his hand
on the Squire's shoulder, "Give my remembrance to the ladies at Atheling, — my heart's
love, if you will take it."

"I will take all I may, Piers. Good-bye!
You have been a great comfort to me. I am
sure I don't know what I should have done without you; for Edgar, you see, is too busy for
anything."

"Never too busy to be with you, if you need

me, Father. But you are such a host in yourself, and I never imagined you required help of
any kind."

"Only a bit of company now and then. You
were about graver business. It suited Piers and
me to sit idle and say a word or two about
Atheling. Come down to Exham, Piers, *do;* it
will be good for you."

"No, I should be heart-sick for Atheling. I
am better away."

The Squire nodded gravely, and was silent;
and Piers passed quietly out of the room. His
listless serenity, and rather drawling speech,
always irritated the alert Edgar; and he sighed
with relief when he was rid of the restraining
influence of a nature so opposite to his own.

"So you are going to Atheling, Father?" he
said. "How?"

"As quick and quiet as I can. I shall take
the mail-coach to York, or further; and then
trot home on as good a nag as I can hire."

In this way he reached Atheling the third day
afterwards, but without any of the usual *éclat*
and bustle of his arrival. Kate had gone to bed;
Mrs. Atheling was about to lock the big front
door, when he opened it. She let the candlestick in her hand fall when she saw him enter,
crying, —

"John! Dear John! How you did frighten
me! I *am* glad to see you."

"I 'll believe it, Maude, without burning the

house for an illumination. My word! I am
tired. I have trotted a hack horse near forty
miles to-day."

Then she forgot everything but the Squire's
refreshment and comfort; and the house was
roused, and Kitty came downstairs again, and
for an hour there was at least the semblance of
rejoicing. But Mrs. Atheling was not deceived.
She saw her lord was depressed and anxious;
and she was sure the Reform Bill had finally
passed; and after a little while she ventured to
say so.

"No, it has not passed," answered the Squire;
"it has got to its worst bit, that's all. After
Easter the Lords will muster in all their power,
and either throw it out, or change and cripple it
so much that it will be harmless."

"Now, then, John, what do you think, *really?*"

"I think, really, that we land-owners are all
of us between the devil and the deep sea. If the
Bill passes, away go the Corn Laws; and then
how are we to make our money out of the land?
If it does not pass, we are in for a civil war and
a Commonwealth, and no Cromwell to lead and
guide it. It is a bad look-out."

"But it might be worse. We have n't had
any cholera here. We must trust in God,
John."

"It is easy to trust in God when you don't see
the doings of the devil. You would n't be so
cheerful, Maude, if you had lived in the sight

of his handiwork, as I have for months. I
think surely God has given England into his
power, as he did the good man of Uz."

"Well, then, it was only for a season, and a
seven-fold blessing after it. It is wonderful how
well your men have behaved; they have n't
taken a bit of advantage of your absence. That
is another good thing."

"I am glad to hear that. I will see them,
man by man, before I go back to London."

The villagers, however, sent a deputation as
soon as they heard of the Squire's arrival, asking
him to come down to Atheling Green, and tell
them something about Reform. And he was
pleased at the request, and went down, and
found they had made a temporary platform out
of two horse-blocks for him; and there he stood,
his fine, imposing, sturdy figure thrown clearly
into relief by the sunny spring atmosphere.
And it was good to listen to his strong, sympathetic voice, for it had the ring of truth in all its
inflections, as he said, —

"Men! Englishmen! Citizens of no mean
country! you have asked me to explain to you
what this Reform business means. You know
well I will tell you no lies. It will give lots of
working-men votes that never hoped for a vote;
and so it is like enough working-men will be
able to send to Parliament members who will
fight for their interests. Maybe that is in your
favour. It will open all our ports to foreign

wheat and corn.   You will get American wheat, and Russian wheat, and French wheat — "

"We won't eat French wheat," said Adam Sedbergh.

"And then, wheat will be so cheap that it will not pay English land-owners to sow it.   Will that help you any?"

"We would rather grow our own wheat."

"To be sure.   Reform will, happen, give you shorter hours of work."

"That would be good, Master," said the black-smith.

"It will depend on what you do with the extra hours of leisure."

"We can play skittles, and cricket, and have a bit of wrestling."

"Or sit in the public house, and drink more beer.   I don't think your wives will like that. Besides, if you work less time won't you get less wage?   Do you think I am going to pay for twelve hours' work and get ten?   Would you? Will the mill-owners run factories for the fun of running them?   Would you?   And they say they hardly pay with twelve hours' work.   Men, I tell you truly, I know no more than the babe unborn what Reform will bring us.   It may be better times; it may be ruin.   But I can say one thing, sure and certain, you will get more trouble than you bargain for if you take to rioting about it.   Your grandfathers and your fathers fought this question; and they left it to

you to quarrel over.   Very well, as long as you
keep your quarrel in the Parliament Houses, I
want you to have fair play.   But if ever you
should forget that there is the great Common
Law behind all of us, rich and poor, and think
to right yourselves with fire and blood, then I
— your true friend — would be the first to answer
you with cannon, and turn my scythes and shares
into swords against you.   Wait patiently a bit
longer.   In a few more weeks I do verily believe
you will have Reform, and then I hope, in my
soul, you will be pleased with your bargain.   I
don't think, as far as I am concerned, Reform
will change me or my ways one particle."

"We don't want you changed, Squire; you are
good enough as you are."

"I'm glad you think so, very glad.   Now
here is Atheling and Belward meadows and
corn-fields.   We can raise our wheat and cattle
and wool, and carry on our farms — you and I
together, for I could not do without you; and
if I do right by you is there any reason to want
better than right?   And if I do not do right,
then shout 'Reform,' and come and tell me
what you want, and we will pass our own Reform
Bill.   Will that suit you?"

And they answered him with cheers, and he
sent them into the Atheling Arms for a good
dinner, and then rode slowly home.   But a great
sadness came over him, and he said to himself:

"It is not capital; it is not labour; it is not

land: it is a bit of human kindness and human relations that lie at the root of all Reform. Maude says true enough, that we don't know the people, and don't feel for them, and don't care for them.   A word of reason, a word of truth and trust and of mutual good-will, and how pleased them poor fellows were!   Reform has nothing on earth to do with Toryism or Whigism.   God bless my soul! what kind of a head must the man have that could think so?   *I begin to see — I begin to see!*"

CHAPTER FIFTEENTH

LADY OF EXHAM HALL AT LAST

THE three weeks' recess was full of grave anxiety; and the Squire had many fears they were to be the last weeks of peace and home before civil war called him to fulfil the promise he had made to his working-men. The Birmingham Political Union declared that if there was any further delay after Easter, two hundred thousand men would go forth from their shops and forges, and encamp in the London squares, till they knew the reason why the Reform Bill was not passed. The Scots Greys, who were quartered at Birmingham, had been employed the previous Sabbath in grinding their swords; and it was asserted that the Duke of Wellington stood pledged to the Government to quiet the country in ten days. These facts sufficiently indicated to the Squire the temper of the people; and he set himself, as far as he could, to take all the sweetness out of his home life possible. The memory of it might have to comfort him for many days.

With his daughter always by his side, he rode up and down the lands he loved; uncon-

sciously giving directions that might be service-
able if he had to go to a stormier field than the
House of Commons. To Mrs. Atheling he
hardly suggested the possibility; for if he did,
she always answered cheerfully, "Nonsense,
John! The Bill *will* pass; and if it does not
pass, Englishmen have more sense than they had
in the days of Cromwell. They are n't going to
kill one another for an Act of Parliament."

But to Kate, as they rode and walked, he
could worry and grumble comfortably. She was
always ready to sympathise with his fears, and
to encourage and suggest any possible hope of
peace and better days. To see her bright face
answering his every thought filled the father's
heart with a joy that was complete.

"Bless thy dear soul!" he would frequently
say to her. "God's best gift to a man is a
daughter like thee. Sons are well enough to
carry on the name and the land, and bring
honour to the family; but the man God loves
is n't left without a daughter to sweeten his days
and keep his heart fresh and tender. Kitty!
Kitty, how I do love thee!" And Kitty knew
how to answer such true and noble affection;
for, —

> "Down the gulf of his condoled necessities,
> She cast her best: she flung herself."

Oh, sweet domestic love! Surely *it is* the spiritual world, the abiding kingdom of heaven, not
far from any one of us.

With a heavy heart the Squire went back to London. Mrs. Atheling took his gloom for a good sign. "Your father is always what the Scotch call 'fay' before trouble," she said to Kate. "The day your sister Edith died his ways made me angry. You would have thought some great joy had come to Atheling. He said he was sure Edith was going to live; and I knew she was going to die. I am glad he has gone to London sighing and shaking his head; it is a deal better sign than if he had gone laughing and shaking his bridle. He will meet Edgar in London, and Edgar won't let him look forward to trouble."

But the Squire found Edgar was not in London when he arrived there; and Piers was as silent and as gloomy a companion as a worrying man could desire. He came to dine with his friend, and he listened to all his doleful prognostications; but his interest was forced and languid. For he also had lost the convictions that made the contest possible to him, and there was at the bottom of all his reasoning that little doubt as to the justice of his cause which likewise infected the Squire's more pronounced opinions.

They were sitting one evening, after dinner, almost silent, the Squire smoking, Piers apparently reading the *Times*, when Edgar, with an almost boyish demonstrativeness, entered the room. He drew a chair between them, and sat

down, saying, "I have just returned from the
great Newhall Hill meeting. Father, think of
two hundred thousand men gathered there for
one united purpose."

"I hope I have a few better thoughts to keep
me busy, Edgar."

Piers looked up with interest. "It must have
been an exciting hour or two," he said.

"I hardly knew whether I was in the body or
out of the body," answered Edgar. "For a
little while, at least, I was not conscious of the
flesh. I had a taste of how the work of eternity
may be done with the soul."

"The *Times* admits the two hundred thousand," said Piers, "and also that it was a remark-
ably orderly meeting. Who opened it? Was it
Mr. O'Connell?"

"The meeting was opened by the singing of
a hymn. There were nine stanzas in it, and
every one was sung with the most enthusiastic
feeling. I remember only the opening lines:

> "'Over mountain, over plain,
>   Echoing wide from sea to sea,
>   Peals—and shall not peal in vain—
>   The trumpet call of Liberty!'

But can you imagine what a majestic volume of
sonorous melody came from those two hundred
thousand hearts? It was heard for miles. The
majority of the singers believed, with all their
souls, that it was heard in heaven."

"Well, I never before heard of singing a hymn to open a political meeting," said the Squire. "It does not seem natural."

"But, Father, you are used to political meetings opened by prayer, for the House has its chaplain. The Rev. Hugh Hutton prayed after the hymn."

"I never heard of the Rev. Hugh Hutton."

"I dare say not, Father. He is an Unitarian minister; for it is only the Unitarians that will pray with, or pray for, Radicals. I should not quite say that. There is a Roman Catholic priest who is a member of the Birmingham Union, — a splendid-looking man, a fine orator, and full of the noblest public spirit; but a Birmingham meeting would never think of asking him to pray. They would not believe a Catholic could get a blessing down from heaven if he tried."[1]

"What of O'Connell?" said the Squire; "he interests me most."

"O'Connell outdid himself. About four hundred women in one body had been allowed to stand near the platform, and the moment his eyes rested on them his quick instinct decided the opening sentence of his address. He bowed to them, and said, 'Surrounded as I am by the fair, the good, and the gentle.' They cheered at these words; and then the men behind them

[1] This intolerance, general and common in the England of that day, is now happily much mitigated.

cheered, and the crowds behind cheered, because the crowds before cheered; and then he launched into such an arraignment of the English Government as human words never before compassed. And in it he was guilty of one delightful bull. It was in this way. Among other grave charges, he referred to the fact that births had decreased in Dublin five thousand every year for the last four years, and then passionately exclaimed, 'I charge the British Government with the murder of those twenty thousand infants!' and really, for a few moments, the audience did not see the delightful absurdity."

"Twenty thousand infants who were never born," laughed the Squire. "That is worthy of O'Connell. It is worthy of Ireland."

"And did he really manage that immense crowd?" asked Piers. "I see the *Times* gives him this credit."

"Sir Bulwer Lytton in a few lines has painted him for all generations at this meeting. Listen!" and Edgar took out of his pocket a slip of paper, and read them:—

> "'Once to my sight the giant thus was given—
> Walled by wide air, and roofed by boundless heaven;
> Methought, no clarion could have sent its sound
> Even to the centre of the hosts around.
> And as I thought, rose the sonorous swell
> As from some church tower swings the silver bell.
> Aloft and clear, from airy tide to tide,
> It glided easy as a bird may glide,
> To the last verge of that vast audience.'"

"After O'Connell, who would try to manage such a crowd?" asked Piers.

"They behaved splendidly whoever spoke; and finally Mr. Salt stood forward, and, uncovering his head, bid them all uncover, and raise their right hands to heaven while they repeated, after him, the comprehensive obligation which had been given in printed form to all of them:

"*'With unbroken faith, through every peril, through every privation, we here devote ourselves, and our children, to our country's cause!'*

And while those two hundred thousand men were taking that oath together, I find the House of Lords was going into Committee on the Reform Bill. This time it *must* pass."

"It will *not* pass," said Piers, "without the most extreme measures are resorted to."

"You mean that the King will be compelled to create as many new peers as will carry it through the House of Lords."

"Yes; but can the King be 'compelled'?"

"He will find that out."

"Now, Edgar, that is as far as I am going to listen."

Then Piers put down his paper, and said, "The House was in session, and would the Squire go down to it?" And the Squire said, "No. If there is to be any 'compelling' of His Majesty, I will keep out of it."

The stress of this compulsion came the very

next day. Lord Lyndhurst began the usual
policy by proposing important clauses of the
Bill should be postponed; and the Cabinet at
once decided to ask the King to create more
peers.   Sydney Smith had written to Lady
Grey that he was, "For forty, in order to make
sure;" but the number was not stipulated. The
King promptly refused.   The Reform Ministry
tendered their resignation, and it was accepted.
For a whole week the nation was left to its fears,
its anger, and its despair.   It was, however, ·
almost insanely active.   In Manchester twenty-
five thousand people, in the space of three hours,
signed a petition to the King, telling him in it
that "the whole North of England was in a state
of indignation impossible to be described."
Meanwhile, the Duke of Wellington had failed
to form a Cabinet, and Peel had refused; and the
King was compelled to recall Lord Grey to
power, and to consent to any measures necessary
to pass the Reform Bill.   It was evident, even
to royalty, that it had at length become — The
Bill or The Crown.   For His Majesty was now
aware that he was denounced from one end of
England to the other; and several painful experiences convinced him that his carriage could
not appear in London without being surrounded
by an indignant, hooting, shrieking crowd.

Yet it was in a very wrathful mood he sent for
Grey and Brougham, so wrathful that he kept
them standing during the whole audience, al-

though this attitude was contrary to usage. "My people are gone mad," he said, "and must be humoured like mad people. They will have Reform. Very well. I give you my royal assent to create a sufficient number of new peers to carry Reform through the House of Lords. It is an insult to my loyal and sensible peers; but they will excuse the circumstances that force me to such a measure." His manner was extremely sullen, and became indignantly so when Lord Brougham requested this permission to be given them in the King's handwriting. The request was, however, necessary, and was reluctantly granted.

With the King's concession, the great struggle virtually ended. For the creation of new peers was not necessary. A private message from the King to the House of Lords effected what the long-continued protestations and entreaties of the whole nation had failed to effect. Led by the Duke of Wellington, those Lords who were determined *not* to vote for Reform left the House until the Bill was passed; and thus a decided majority for its success was assured. They felt it to be better for their order to retire to their castles, than to suffer the "swamping of the House of Lords" by a force of new peers pledged to Reform, and sure to control all their future deliberations. Consequently, in about two weeks, the famous Bill was triumphantly carried by a majority of eighty-four; and three days afterwards it received the royal assent.

The long struggle was over; and the tremen-

dous strain on the feelings of the nation relieved
itself by an universal and unbounded rejoicing.
All night long, the church bells answered one another from city to city, and from hamlet to hamlet. It was said to be impossible to escape, from one
end of the country to the other, the *tin-tan-tabula*
of their jubilation. Illuminations must have made
the Island at night a blaze of light; the people
went about singing and congratulating each
other; and for a few hours the tie of humanity
was a tie of brotherhood, even when men and
women were perfect strangers.

The Duke of Richmoor retired with the majority of his peers, and shut himself up in his Yorkshire Castle, a victim to the most absurd but
yet the most sincere despondency. The Squire
applied for the Chiltern Hundreds, and returned
to Atheling as soon as possible. Edgar remained
in the House until its dissolution in August. As
for Piers, he had taken the turn of affairs with a
composure that had produced decided differences
between the Duke and himself; and he lingered
in London until he heard of the Squire's departure for the North. Then he sought him with a
definite purpose. "Squire," he said, "may I go
back to Exham in your company?"

" I 'll be glad if you do, Piers," was the answer.

The young man laid his hand on the Squire's
hand, and looked at him steadily and entreatingly.
"Squire, I am going away from England. Let
me see Kate before I go."

"You are asking me to break my word, Piers."

"The law of kindness may sometimes be greater than the law of truth; the greatest of these is charity — is love. I love her so! I love her so that I am only half alive without her. I do entreat you to have pity on me — on us both! She loves me!" and Piers pleaded until the Squire's eyes were full of tears. He could not resist words so hot from a true and loving heart; and he finally said, —

" It may be that my word, and my pride in my word, are of less consequence than the trouble of two suffering human hearts; Piers, right or wrong, you may see Kitty. I am not sure I am doing right, but I will risk the uncertainty — this time."

However, if the Squire had any qualms of conscience on the subject, they were driven away by Kitty's gratitude and delight. He arrived at Atheling about the noon hour, and Kitty was the first to see and to welcome him. She had been gathering cherries, and was coming through the garden with her basket full of the crimson drupes, when he entered the gates. She set the fruit on the ground, and ran to meet him, and took him proudly in to her mother, and fussed over his many little comforts to his heart's content and delight.

Nothing was said about Piers until after dinner, which was hurried forward at the Squire's re-

quest; but afterwards, when he sat at the open
casement smoking, he called Kate to him. He
took her on his knee and whispered, " Kate, there
is somebody coming this afternoon."

" Yes," she said, " we have sent word to Annie.
She will be here."

" I was not thinking of Annie. I was thinking
of thee, my little maid. There is somebody coming to see *thee*."

" You can't mean Piers? Oh, Father, do you
mean Piers? "

" I do."

Then she laid her cheek against his cheek.
She kissed him over and over, answering in low,
soft speech, " Oh, my good Father! Oh, my dear
Father! Oh, Father, how I love you! "

" Well, Kitty," he answered, " thou dost not
throw thy love away. I love thee, God knows
it. Now run upstairs and don thy prettiest
frock."

" White or blue, Father? "

" Well, Kitty," he answered, with a thoughtful
smile, " I should say white, and a red rose or
two to match thy cheeks, and a few forget-me-
nots to match thy eyes. Bless my heart, Kitty!
thou art lovely enough any way. Stay with me."

" No, Father, I will go away and come again
still lovelier; " and she sped like a bird upstairs.
" It may be all wrong," muttered the Squire;
" but if it is, then I must say, wrong can make
itself very agreeable."

"*Piers is coming!*" That was the song in Kitty's heart, the refrain to which her hands and feet kept busy until she stood before her glass lovelier than words can paint, her exquisite form robed in white lawn, her cheeks as fresh and blooming as the roses at her girdle, her eyes as blue as the forget-me-nots in her hair, her whole heart in every movement, glance, and word, thrilling with the delight of expectation, and shining with the joy of loving.

So Piers found her in the garden watching for his approach. And on this happy afternoon, Nature was in a charming mood; she had made the garden a Paradise for their meeting. The birds sang softly in the green trees above them; the flowers perfumed the warm air they breathed; and an atmosphere of inexpressible serenity encompassed them. After such long absence, oh, how heavenly was this interview without fear, or secrecy, or self-reproach, or suspicion of wrong-doing! How heavenly was the long, sweet afternoon, and the social pleasure of the tea hour, and the soft starlight night under the drooping gold of the laburnums and the fragrant clusters of the damask roses! Even parting under such circumstances was robbed of its sting; it was only "such sweet sorrow." It was glorified by its trust and hope, and was without the shadow of tears.

Kitty came to her father when it was over; and her eyes were shining, and there was a little sob in her heart; but she said only happy words.

With her arms around his neck she whispered,
"Thank you, dear!" And he answered, "Thou
art gladly welcome! Right or wrong, thou art
welcome, Kitty. My dear little Kitty! He will
come back; I know he will. A girl that puts
honour and duty before love, crowns them with
love in the end — always so, dear. That *is sure*.
When will he be back?"

"When the Duke and Duchess want him more
than they want their own way. He says disputing will do harm, and not good; but that if a
difference is left to the heart, the heart in the
long run will get the best of the argument. I am
sure he is right. Father, he is going to send you
and mother long letters, and so I shall know
where he is; and with the joy of this meeting to
keep in my memory, I am not going to fret and
be miserable."

"That is right. That is the way to take a
disappointment. Good things are worth waiting
for, eh, Kitty?"

"And we shall have so much to interest us,
Father. There is Edgar's marriage coming; and
it would not do to have two weddings in one
year, would it? Father, you like Piers? I am
sure you do."

"I would not have let him put a foot in Atheling to-day if I had not liked him. He has been
very good company for me in London, very
good company indeed — thoughtful and respectful. Yes, I like Piers."

"Because — now listen, Father — because, much as I love Piers, I would not be his wife for all England if you and mother did not like him."

"Bless my heart, Kitty! Is not that saying a deal?"

"No. It would be no more than justice. If you should force on me a husband whom I despised or disliked, would I not think it very wicked and cruel? Then would it not be just as wicked and cruel if I should force on you a son-in-law whom you despised and disliked? There is not one law of kindness for the parents, and another law, less kind, for the daughter, is there?"

"Thou art quite right, Kitty. The laws of the Home and the Family are *equal* laws. God bless thee for a good child."

And, oh, how sweet were Kitty's slumbers that night! It is out of earth's delightful things we form our visions of the world to come; and Kate understood, because of her own pure, true, hopeful love, how "God is love," and how, therefore, He would deny her any good thing.

So the summer went its way, peacefully and happily. In the last days of August, Edgar was married with great pomp and splendour; and afterwards the gates of Gisbourne stood wide-open, and there were many signs and promises of wonderful improvements and innovations. For the young man was a born leader and organiser. He loved to control, and soon devised means to secure what was so necessary to his happiness. The Curzons had made their money in manufactures; and Annie approved of such use of money. So very soon, at the upper end of Gisbourne, a great mill, and a fine new village of cottages for its hands, arose as if by magic, — a village that was to example and carry out all the ideas of Reform.

"Edgar is making a lot of trouble ready for himself," said the Squire to his wife; "but Edgar can't live without a fight on hand. I'll warrant that he gets more fighting than he bargains for; a few hundreds of those Lancashire and Yorkshire operatives are n't as easy to manage as he seems to think. They have 'reformed' their lawgivers; and they are bound to 'reform' their masters next."

The Squire had said little about this new influx into his peaceful neighbourhood, but it had grieved his very soul; and his wife wondered at his reticence, and one day she told him so.

"Well, Maude," he answered, "when Edgar was one of my household, I had the right to say this and that about his words and ways; but Edgar is now Squire, and married man, and Member of Parliament. He is a Reformer too, and bound to carry out his ideas; and, I dare say, his wife keeps the bit in his mouth hard enough, without me pulling on it too. I have taken notice, Maude, that these sweet little women are often very masterful."

" I am sure his grandfather Belward would never have suffered that mill chimney in his sight for any money."

" Perhaps he could not have helped it."

" Thou knowest different. My father always made everything go as he wanted it. The Belwards know no other road but their own way."

"I should think thou needest not tell me that. I have been learning it for a quarter of a century."

" Now, John! When I changed my name, I changed my way also. I have been Atheling, and gone Atheling, ever since I was thy wife."

" Pretty nearly, Maude. But Edgar's little, innocent-faced, gentle wife will lead Edgar, Curzon way. She has done it already. Fancy an Atheling, land lords for a thousand years, turning into a loom lord. Maude, it hurts me; but then, it is a bit of Reform, I suppose."

For all this interior dissatisfaction, the Squire and his son were good friends and neighbours; and, in a kind of a way, the father approved the changes made around him. They came gradually, and he did not have to swallow the whole dose at once. Besides he had his daughter. And Kitty never put him behind Gisbourne or any other cause. They were constant companions. They threw their lines in the trout streams together through the summer mornings; and in the winter, she was with him in every hunting field. About the house, he heard her light foot and her happy voice; and in the evenings, she read the papers to him, and helped forward his grumble at Peel, or his anger at Cobbett.

At not very long intervals there came letters to the Squire, or to Mrs. Atheling, which made sunshine in the house for many days afterwards, — letters from Boston, New York, Baltimore, Washington, New Orleans, and finally from an outlandish place called Texas. Here Piers seemed to have found the life he had been unconsciously longing for. "The people were fighting," he said, "for Liberty: a handful of Americans against the whole power of Mexico; fighting, not in words — he was weary to death of words — but with the clang of iron on iron, and the clash of steel against steel, as in the old world battles." And he filled pages with glowing encomiums of General Houston, and Colonels Bowie and Crockett, and their wonderful courage and deeds. "And, oh, what a Paradise the land was! What sunshine! What moonshine! What wealth of every good thing necessary for human existence!"

When such letters as these arrived, it was holiday at Atheling; it was holiday in every heart there; and they were read, and re-read, and discussed, till their far-away, wild life became part and parcel of the calm, homely existence of this insular English manor. So the years went by; and Kate grew to a glorious womanhood. All the promise of her beauteous girlhood was amply redeemed. She was the pride of her county,

and the joy of all the hearts that knew her.   And
if she had hours of restlessness and doubt, or
any fears for Piers's safety, no one was made
unhappy by them.   She never spoke of Piers but
with hope, and with the certainty of his return.
She declared she was " glad that he should have
the experience of such a glorious warfare, one
in which he had made noble friends, and done
valiant deeds.   Her lover was growing in such
a struggle to his full stature."   And, undoubtedly,
the habit of talking hopefully induces the habit of
feeling hopefully ; so there were no signs of the
love-lorn maiden about Kate Atheling, nor any fears
for her final happiness in Atheling Manor House.

The fears and doubts and wretchedness were
all in the gloomy castle of Richmoor, where the
Duke and Duchess lived only to bewail the dangers of the country, and their deprivation of their
son's society, — a calamity they attributed also
to Reform.   Else, why would Piers have gone
straight to a wild land where outlawed men
were also fighting against legitimate authority.

One evening, nearly four years after Piers had
left England, the Duke was crossing Belward
Bents, and he met the Squire and his daughter,
leisurely riding together in the summer gloaming.
He touched his hat, and said, " Good-evening,
Miss Atheling !   Good-evening, Squire ! "   And
the Squire responded cheerfully, and Kate gave
him a ravishing smile, — for he was the father of
Piers, accordingly she already loved him.   There

was nothing further said, but each was affected by the interview; the Duke especially so. When he reached his castle he found the Duchess walking softly up and down the dim drawing-room, and she was weeping. His heart ached for her. He said tenderly, as he took her hand, —

"Is it Piers, Julia?"

"I am dying to see him," she answered, "to hear him speak, to have him come in and out as he used to do. I want to feel the clasp of his hand, and the touch of his lips. Oh, Richard, Richard, bring back my boy! A word from you will do it."

"My dear Julia, I have just met Squire Atheling and his daughter. The girl has grown to a wonder of beauty. She is marvellous; I simply never saw such a face. Last week I watched her in the hunting field at Ashley. She rode like an Amazon; she was peerless among all the beauties there. I begin to understand that Piers, having loved her, could love no other woman; and I think we might learn to love her for Piers's sake. What do you say, my dear? The house is terribly lonely. I miss my son in business matters continually; and if he does not marry, the children of my brother Henry come after him. He is in constant danger; he is in a land where he must go armed day and night. Think of our son living in a place like that! And his last letters have had such a tone of home-sickness in them. Shall I see Squire Atheling, and ask him for his daughter?"

" Let him come and see you."

" He will never do it."

"Then see him, Richard. Anything, anything, that will give Piers back to me."

The next day the Duke was at Atheling, and what took place at that interview, the Squire never quite divulged, even to his wife. " It was very humbling to him," he said, " and I am not the man to brag about it." To Kate nothing whatever was said. " Who knows just where Piers is? and who can tell what might happen before he learns of the change that has taken place?" asked the Squire. " Why should we toss Kitty's mind hither and thither till Piers is here to quiet it? "

In fact the Squire's idea was far truer than he had any conception of. Piers was actually in London when the Duke's fatherly letter sent to recall his self-banished son left for Texas. Indeed he was on his way to Richmoor the very day that the letter was written. He came to it one afternoon just before dinner. The Duchess was dressed and waiting for the Duke and the daily ceremony of the hour. She stood at the window, looking into the dripping garden, but really seeing nothing, not even the plashed roses before her eyes. Her thoughts were in a country far off; and she was wondering how long it would take Piers to answer their loving letter. The door opened softly. She supposed it was the Duke, and said, fretfully, " This climate is detestable, Duke. It has rained for a week."

" Mother ! Mother! Oh, my dear Mother !"

Then, with a cry of joy that rung through the
lofty room, she turned, and was immediately folded
in the arms she longed for.   And before her rapture had time to express itself, the Duke came in
and shared it.   They were not an emotional family ; and high culture had relegated any expression
of feeling far below the tide of their daily life ; but,
for once, Nature had her way with the usually un-
demonstrative woman.   She wept, and laughed,
and talked, and exclaimed as no one had ever seen
or heard her since the days of her early girlhood.

In the happy privacy of the evening hours,
Piers told them over again the wild, exciting
story he had been living ; and the Duke acknowledged that to have aided in any measure such
an heroic struggle was an event to dignify life.
"But now, Piers," he said, " now you will remain
in your own home.   If you still wish to marry
Miss Atheling, your mother and I are pleased
that you should do so.   We will express this
pleasure as soon as you desire us.   I wrote you
to this effect; but you cannot have received my
letter, since it only left for Texas yesterday."

" I am glad I have not received it," answered
Piers.   " I came home at the call of my mother.
It is true.   I was sitting one night thinking of
many things.   It was long past midnight, but
the moonlight was so clear I had been reading
by it, and the mocking birds were thrilling the
air, far and wide, with melody.   But far clearer, far

sweeter, far more pervading, I heard my mother's
voice calling me.   And I immediately answered,
'I am coming, Mother!' Here I am. What must
I do, now and forever, to please you?"

And she said, "Stay near me. Marry Miss Atheling, if you wish. I will love her for your sake."

And Piers kissed his answer on her lips, and then
put his hand in his father's hand.   It was but a simple act; but it promised all that fatherly affection
could ask, and all that filial affection could give.

Who that has seen in England a sunny morning after a long rain-storm can ever forget the
ineffable sweetness and freshness of the woods
and hills and fields?   The world seemed as if it
was just made over when Piers left Richmoor for
Atheling.   A thousand vagrant perfumes from
the spruce and fir woods, from the moors and
fields and gardens, wandered over the earth.
A gentle west wind was blowing; the sense of
rejoicing was in every living thing.   The Squire
and Kate had been early abroad.   They had had
a long gallop, and were coming slowly through
Atheling lane, talking of Piers, though both of
them believed Piers to be thousands of miles
away.   They were just at the spot where he had
passed them that miserable night when his cry
of "*Kate! Kate! Kate!*" had nearly broken the
girl's heart for awhile.   She never saw the place
without remembering her lover, and sending her
thoughts to find him out, wherever he might be.
And thus, at this place, there was always a little

silence; and the Squire comprehended, and re-
spected the circumstance.

This morning the silence, usually so perfect,
was broken by the sound of an approaching
horseman; but neither the Squire nor Kate
turned. They simply withdrew to their side of
the road, and went leisurely forward.

"*Kate! Kate! Kate!*"

The same words, but how different! They
were full of impatient joy, of triumphant hope
and love. Both father and daughter faced round
in the moment, and then they saw Piers coming
like the wind towards them. It was a miracle.
It was such a moment as could not come twice
in any life-time. It was such a meeting as defies
the power of words; because our diviner part
has emotions that we have not yet got the
speech and language to declare.

Imagine the joy in Atheling Manor House that
night! The Squire had to go apart for a little
while; and tears of delight were in the good
mother's eyes as she took out her beautiful
Derby china for the welcoming feast. As for
Kate and Piers, they were at last in earth's
Paradise. Their lives had suddenly come to
flower; and there was no canker in any of the
blossoms. They had waited their full hour.
And if the angels in heaven rejoice over a sinner
repenting, how much more must they rejoice in
our happiness, and sympathise in our innocent
love! Surely the guardian angels of Piers and

Kate were satisfied. Their dear charges had shown a noble restraint, and were now reaping the joy of it. Do angels talk in heaven of what happens among the sons and daughters of men whom they are sent to minister unto, to guide, and to guard? If so, they must have talked of these lovers, so dutiful and so true, and rejoiced in the joy of their renewed espousals.

Their marriage quickly followed. In a few weeks Piers had made Exham Hall a palace of splendour and beauty for his bride, and Kate's wedding garments were all ready. And far and wide there was a most unusual interest taken in these lovers, so that all the great county families desired and sought for invitations to the marriage ceremony, and the little church of Atheling could hardly contain the guests. Even to this day it is remembered that nearly one hundred gentlemen of the North Riding escorted the bride from Atheling to Exham.

But at last every social duty had been fulfilled, and they sat alone in the gloaming, with their great love, and their great joy. And as they spoke of the days when this love first began, Kate reminded Piers of the swing in the laurel walk, and her girlish rhyming, —

> " It may so happen, it may so fall,
>   That I shall be Lady of Exham Hall."

And Piers drew her beautiful head closer to his own, and added, —

> "Weary wishing, and waiting past,
>   *Lady of Exham Hall* at last ! "

CHAPTER SIXTEENTH

AFTER TWENTY GOLDEN YEARS

AFTER twenty years have passed away, it is safe to ask if events have been all that they promised to be; and one morning in August of 1857, it was twenty years since Kate Atheling became Lady Exham. She was sitting at a table writing letters to her two eldest sons, who were with their tutor in the then little known Hebrides. Lord Exham was busy with his mail. They were in a splendid room, opening upon a lawn, soft and green beyond description; and the August sunshine and the August lilies filled it with warmth and fragrance. Lady Exham was even more beautiful than on her wedding day. Time had matured without as yet touching her wonderful loveliness, and motherhood had crowned it with a tender and bewitching nobility. She had on a gown of lawn and lace, white as the flowers that hung in clusters from the Worcester vase at her side. Now and then Piers lifted his head and watched her for a moment; and then, with the faint, happy smile of a heart full and at ease, he opened another letter or paper. Suddenly he became a little excited. " Why, Kate," he said, "here is my speech on the blessings which Reform has brought to England. I did not expect such a thing."

"Read it to me, Piers."

"It is entirely too long; although I only reviewed some of the notable works that followed Reform."

"Such as — "

"Well, the abolition of both black and white slavery; the breaking up of the gigantic monopoly of the East India Company, and the throwing open of our ports to the merchants of the world; the inauguration of a system of national education; the reform of our cruel criminal code; the abolition of the press gang, and of chimney sweeping by little children, and such brutalities; the postal reform; and the spread of such good, cheap literature as the *Penny Magazine* and *Chambers's Magazine*. My dear Kate, it would require a book to tell all that the Reform Bill has done for England. Think of the misery of that last two years' struggle, and look at our happy country to-day."

"Prosperous, but not happy, Piers. How can we be happy when, all over the land, mothers are weeping because their children are not. If this awful Sepoy rebellion was only over; then!"

"Yes," answered Piers; "if it was only over! Surely there never was a war so full of strange, unnatural cruelties. I wonder where Cecil and Annabel are."

"Wherever they are, I am sure both of them will be in the way of honour and duty."

There was a pause, and then Piers asked, "To whom are you writing, dear Kate?"

"To Dick and John. They do not want to return to their studies this winter; they wish to travel in Italy."

"Nonsense! They must go through college before they travel. Tell them so."

The Duke had entered as Piers was speaking, and he listened to his remark. Then, even as he stooped to kiss Kate, he contradicted it. "I don't think so, Piers," he said decisively. "Let the boys go. Give them their own way a little. I do not like to see such spirited youths snubbed for a trifle."

"But this is not a trifle, Father."

"Yes, it is."

"You insisted on my following the usual plan of college first, and travel afterwards."

"That was before the days of Reform. The boys are my grandsons. I think I ought to decide on a question of this kind. What do you say, my dear?" and he turned his kindly face, with its crown of snowy hair, to Kate.

"It is to be as you say, Father," she answered. "Is there any Indian news?"

"Alas! Alas!" he answered, becoming suddenly very sorrowful, "there is calamitous news, —the fort in which Colonel North was shut up, has fallen; and Cecil and Annabel are dead."

"Oh, not massacred! Do not tell us *that!*" cried Kate, covering her ears with her hands.

"Not quite as bad. A Sepoy who was Cecil's orderly, and much attached to him, has been permitted to bring us the terrible news, with some valuable gems and papers which Annabel confided to him. He told me that Cecil held out wonderfully; but it was impossible to send him help. Their food and ammunition were gone; and the troops, who were mainly Sepoys, were ready to open the gates to the first band of rebels that approached. One morning, just at daybreak, Cecil knew the hour had come. Annabel was asleep; but he awakened her. She had been expecting the call for many days; and, when Cecil spoke, she knew it was death. But she rose smiling, and answered, 'I am ready, Love.' He held her close to his breast, and they comforted and strengthened one another until the tramp of the brutes entering the court was heard. Then Annabel closed her eyes, and Cecil sent a merciful bullet through the brave heart that had shared with him, for twenty-five years, every trial and danger. Her last words were, 'Come quickly, Cecil,' and he followed her in an instant. The man says he hid their bodies, and they were not mutilated. But the fort was blown up and burned; and, in this case, the fiery solution was the best."

"And her children?" whispered Kate.

"The boys are at Rugby. The little girl died some weeks ago."

The Duke was much affected. He had loved
Annabel truly, and her tragic death powerfully
moved him. "The Duchess," he said, "had
wept herself ill; and he had promised her to
return quickly." But as he went away, he turned
to charge Piers and Kate not to disappoint his
grandsons. "They are such good boys," he
added; "and it is not a great matter to let them
go to Italy, if they want to — only send Stanhope
with them."

No further objection was then made. Kate
had learned that it is folly to oppose things yet
far away, and which are subject to a thousand
unforeseen influences. When the time for decision
came, Dick and John might have changed their
wishes. So she only smiled a present assent, and
then let her thoughts fly to the lonely fort where
Cecil and Annabel had suffered and conquered
the last great enemy. For a few minutes, Piers
was occupied in the same manner; and when he
spoke, it was in the soft, reminiscent voice which
memory — especially sad memory — uses.

"It is strange, Kate," he said, "but I remember
Annabel predicting this end for herself. We were
sitting in the white-and-gold parlour in the
London House, where I had found her playing
with the cat in a very merry mood. Suddenly
she imagined the cat had scratched her, and she
spread out her little brown hand, and looked for
the wound. There was none visible; but she
pointed to a certain spot at the base of her finger,

and said, 'Look, Piers. There is the sign of my
doom, — my death-token. I shall perish in fire
and blood.' Then she laughed and quickly
changed the subject, and I did not think it worth
pursuing. Yet it was in her mind, for a few
minutes afterwards, she opened her hand again,
held it to the light, and added, 'An old Hindoo
priest told me this. He said our death-warrant
was written on our palms, and we brought it into
life with us.'"

"You should have contradicted that, Piers."

"I did. I told her, our death-warrant was in
the Hand of Him with whom alone are the issues
of life and death."

"She was haunted by the prophecy," said Kate.
"She often spoke of it. Oh, Piers, how merciful
is the veil that hides our days to come!"

"I feel wretched. Let us go to Atheling; it
will do us good."

"It is very warm yet, Piers."

"Never mind, I want to see the children.
The house is too still. They have been at
Atheling for three days."

"We promised them a week. Harold will
expect the week; and Edith and Maude will
rebel at any shorter time."

"At any rate let us go and see them."

"Shall we ride there?"

"Let us rather take a carriage. One of the
three may possibly be willing to come back with
us."

Near the gates of Atheling they met the Squire
and his grandson Harold. They had been fishing. "The dew was on the grass when we went
away; and Harold has been into the water after
the trout. We are both a bit wet," said the
Squire; "but our baskets are full." And then
Harold leaped into the carriage beside his father
and mother, and proudly exhibited his speckled
beauties.

Mrs. Atheling had heard their approach, and
she was at the open door to meet them. Very
little change had taken place in her. Her face
was a trifle older, but it was finer and tenderer;
and her smile was as sweet and ready, and her
manner as gracious — though perhaps a shade
quieter than in the days when we first met her.
Her granddaughter Edith, a girl of eight years,
stood at her side; and Maude, a charming babe
of four, clung to her black-silk apron, and half-
hid her pretty face in its sombre folds. To her
mother, Kate was still Kate; and to Kate, mother
was still mother. They went into the house together, little Maude making a link between them,
and Edith holding her mother's hand. But, in the
slight confusion following their arrival, the children
all disappeared.

"They were helping Bradley to make tarts,"
said Mrs. Atheling, "when I called them, and
they have gone back to their pastry and jam.
Let them alone. Dear me! I remember how
proud I was when I first cut pastry round the

patty pans with my thumb," and Mrs. Atheling looked at Kate, who smiled and nodded at her own similar memory.

They were soon seated in the large parlour, where all the windows were open, and a faint little breeze stirring the cherry leaves round them. Then the Squire began to talk of the Indian news; and Piers told, with a pitiful pathos, the last tragic act in Cecil's and Annabel's love and life. And when he had finished the narration, greatly to every one's amazement, the Squire rose to his feet, and, lifting his eyes heavenward, said solemnly, —

"I give hearty thanks for their death, so noble and so worthy of their faith and their race. I give hearty thanks because God, knowing their hearts and their love, committed unto them the dismissing of their own souls from the wanton cruelty of incarnate devils. I give hearty thanks for Love triumphant over Death, and for that faith in our immortality which could command an immediate re-union, 'Come quickly, Cecil!'

"There is nothing to cry about," he added, as he resumed his seat. "Death must come to all of us. It came mercifully to these two. It did not separate them; they went together. Somewhere in God's Universe they are now, without doubt, doing His Will together. Let us give thanks for them."

After a little while, Kate and her mother went away. They had many things to talk over about

which masculine opinions were not necessary, nor
even desirable. And the Squire and Piers had,
in a certain way, a similar confidence. Indeed
the Squire told Piers many things he would not
have told any one else, — little wrongs and wor-
ries not worth complaining about to his wife, and
perhaps about which he was not very certain of
her sympathy. But with Piers, these crept into
his conversation, and were talked away, or at
least considerably lessened, by his son-in-law's
patient interest.

This morning their conversation had an unconscious tone of gratified prophecy in it. "Edgar
is in a lot of trouble," he said; "but then he seems
to enjoy it. His hands gathered in the mill-yard
yesterday and gave him what they call, 'a bit of
their mind.' And their 'mind' is n't what you
and I would call a civil one. Luke Staley, a big
dyer from Oldham, got beyond bearing, and
told Edgar, if he did n't do thus and so, he would
be made to. And Edgar can be very provoking.
He did n't tell me what he said; but I have no
doubt it was a few of the strongest words he
could pick out. And Luke Staley, not having
quite such a big private stock as Edgar, doubled
his fist, to make the shortage good, almost in
Edgar's face; and there would have, maybe,
been a few blows, if Edgar had not taken very
strong measures at once, — that is, Piers, he
knocked the fellow down as flat as a pancake.
And then all was so still that, Edgar said, the

very leaves rustling seemed noisy; and he told
them in his masterful way, they could have five
minutes to get back to their looms. And if they
were not back in five minutes, he promised them
he would dump the fires and lock the gates, and
they could go about their business."

"And they went to their looms, of course?"

"To be sure they did. More than that, Luke
Staley picked himself up, and went civilly to
Edgar and said, ' That was a good knock-down.
I'm beat this time, Master;' and he offered his
hand, blue and black with dyes, and Edgar took
it. My word! how his grandfather Belward
would have enjoyed that scene. I am sorry he
is not alive this day. He missed a deal by dying
before Reform. Edgar and he together could
keep a thousand men at their looms — and set
the price, too."

"What did the men want? "

"A bit of Reform, of course, — more wage and
less work. I am not much put out of the way
now, Piers, with the mill. I get a lot of pleasure
out of it, one road or another. Did I ever tell
you about the Excursion Edgar gave them last
week? "

"I have not heard anything about it."

"Well, you see, Edgar sent all his hands and
their wives and sweethearts to the seaside, and
gave them a good dinner; and they had a band
of music to play for them, and a little steamer to
give them a sail; and they came home at mid-

night, singing and in high good humour. Edgar
thought he had pleased them. Not a bit of it!
Two nights after they held a meeting in that
Mechanics Hall Mrs. Atheling built for them.
What for? To talk over the jaunt, and try and
find out, ' *What Master Atheling was up to.*' You
see they were sure he had a selfish motive of
some kind."

"I don't believe he had a single selfish motive;
he is not a selfish man," said Piers.

"I would n't swear to his motives, Piers. Between you and me, he wants to go to Parliament
again."

"He ought to be there; it is his native heath,
in a manner."

"Well, as I said, one way or another, I get a
lot of pleasure out of these men. There is a
truce on now between them and Edgar; but, in
the main, it is a lively truce."

"Edgar seems to enjoy the conditions, also,
Father."

"Well, he ought to have a bit of something
that pleases him. He has a deal of contrary
things to fight. There is his eldest son."

"Augustus?"

"Yes, Augustus."

"What has Augustus done?"

"He will paint pictures and make little figures,
and waste his time about such things as no
Atheling in this world ever bothered his head
about, — unless he wanted his likeness painted.

The lad does wonders with his colours and
brushes, and I'll allow that. He brought me a
bit of canvas with that corner by the fir woods
on it, and you would have thought you could
pull the grass and drink the water. But I did
not think it right to praise him much. I said,
'Very good, Augustus, but what will you make
by this?'"

"Well?"

"Well, Piers, the lad talked about his ideals,
and said Art was its own reward, and a lot of
rubbishy nonsense. But I never expected much
from a boy called Augustus. That was his
mother's whim; no Atheling was ever called
such a name before. He wants to go to Italy,
and his father wants him in the mill. Edgar is
finding a few things out now he didn't believe
in when he was twenty years old. The point of
view is everything, Piers. Edgar looks at things
as a father looks at them now; then, he had an
idea that fathers knew next to nothing. Augustus is no worse than he was. Maybe, he will
come to looms yet; he is just like the Curzons,
and they were loom lovers. Now Cecil, his
second boy, has far better notions. He likes a
rod, and a horse, and a gun; and he thinks a
gamekeeper has the best position in the world."

"Mrs. Atheling sets us all an example. She is
always doing something for the people."

"They don't thank her for it. She brings
lecturers, and expects them to go and hear them;

and the men would rather be in the cricket field.
She has classes of all kinds for the women and
girls; and they don't want her interfering in their
ways and their houses. I'll tell you what it is,
Piers, you cannot write Reform upon flesh and
blood as easy as you can write it upon paper.
It will take a few generations to erase the old
marks, and put the new marks on."

" Still Reform has been a great blessing. You
know that, Father."

"Publicly, I know it, Piers. Privately, I keep
my own ideas. But there is Kate calling us, and
I see the carriage is waiting. Thank God, Reform has nothing to do with homes. Wives and
children are always the same. We don't want
them changed, even for the better."

" You do not mean that? "

"Yes, I do," said the Squire, positively. " My
wife's faults are very dear to me. Do you think
I would like to miss her bits of tempers, and her
unreasonableness? Even when she tries to get
the better of me, I like it. I wouldn't have her
perfect, not if I could."

Then Piers called for his son; but Harold could
not be found. The Squire laughed. " He has
run away," he said. " The boy wants a holiday.
I'll take good care of him. He isn't doing nothing; he is learning to catch a trout. Many a
very clever man can't catch a trout." Then Piers
asked his little daughters to come home with
him; and Edith hid herself behind the ample

skirts of her grandfather's coat, and Maude lifted her arms to her grandmother, and snuggled herself into her bosom.

"Come, Piers, we shall have to go home alone," Kate said.

"You have Katherine at home," said the Squire.

And then Kate laughed. "Why, Father," she said, "you speak as if Katherine was more than we ought to expect. Surely we may have one of our six children. The Duke thinks he has whole and sole right in Dick and John; and you have Harold and Edith and Maude."

"And you have Katherine," reiterated the Squire.

When they got back to Exham Hall, the little Lady Katherine was in the drawing-room to meet them. She was the eldest daughter of the house, a fair girl of fifteen with her father's refined face and rather melancholy manner. Piers delighted in her; and there was a sympathy between them that needed no words. She had a singular love for music, though from what ancestor it had come no one could tell; and it was her usual custom after dinner to open the door a little between the drawing-room and music-room, and play her various studies, while her father and mother mused, and talked, and listened.

This evening Piers lit his cigar, and Kate and he walked in the garden. It was warm, and still, and full of moonshine; and the music rose and

fell to their soft reminiscent talk of the many interests that had filled their lives for the past
twenty golden years. And when they were
wearied a little, they came back to the drawing-
room and were quiet. For Katherine was striking
the first notes of a little melody that always
charmed them; and as they listened, her girlish
voice lifted the song, and the tender words
floated in to them, and sunk into their hearts, and
became a prayer of thanksgiving.

> " We have lived and loved together,
> Through many changing years;
> We have shared each other's gladness,
> And wept each other's tears."

And while Kate's face illuminated the words,
Piers leaned forward, and took both her hands in
his, and whispered with far tenderer, truer love
than in the old days of his first wooing.

And if any thought of The Other One entered
his mind at this hour, it came with a thanksgiving
for a life nobly redeemed by a pure, unselfish
love, and a death which was at once sacrificial
and sacramental.